A Love So Strong: A Jenkins Family Reunion

Jenkins Family Series, Volume 6

Sharon C Cooper

Published by Sharon C Cooper, 2023.

A Love So Strong

By

Sharon C. Cooper

ISBN: 978-1-946172-39-6

Paperback

Amaris Publishing LLC

Disclaimer

This story is a work of fiction. Names, characters, and incidents are either products of the author's imagination or are used fictitiously. Any resemblance to actual events, locales, organizations or persons, living or dead, is entirely coincidental.

Acknowledgments

Huge shout out to my amazing husband for his constant support and patience. I love you, Al!

A special thanks to my dear friend Brenda S. for being the world's greatest cheerleader and for always being willing to brainstorm and read rough, rough drafts! Lol. You make this writing journey fun! (((HUGS)))

Carolyn J. you are amazing! Thanks for always coming through for me and having my back. I so appreciate you! And did I mention that you're amazing?

Dear Reader

In the last few years, many of you have asked if there will be updates on the "Jenkins girls". Well, I listened. Here's your chance to catch up with Toni, Jada, Christina, Martina, and Peyton, as well as the loves of their lives. Of course, Gram and Grampa make appearances, and as usual, they are armed with life advice for their granddaughters.

For those of you who are new to the Jenkins family series, A LOVE SO STRONG can be read as a standalone. However, you might enjoy it even more if you read the first five books in the series.

Still the Best Woman for the Job (Toni & Craig)

All You'll Ever Need (Jada & Zack)

Tempting the Artist (Christina & Luke)

Negotiating for Love (Martina & Paul)

Seducing the Boss Lady (Peyton & Michael)

Enjoy!

Love, Sharon

Chapter One

"How do you feel about having sex in a supply closet?"

Craig Logan stared down at his wife, trying to determine if she was serious. Toni Jenkins-Logan was the most beautiful, spontaneous, aggravating woman he'd ever met, and he loved her more than life itself. But there were days, like today, when he wondered if she was losing her mind.

They were standing in the middle of her office, and excitement oozed from her as she grinned up at him. His gaze skittered over her smooth skin that was the color of toasted caramel and her kissable lips that always called to him. Of course, he wanted to touch her, kiss her, and make love to her.

But he wouldn't. Not now.

His attention gravitated to the mischievous glint in her pretty brown eyes that normally had him bending to her will.

Not today.

Not when he had rescheduled a meeting to get to her. And not when he knew why she wanted to have sex with him on the spur of the moment...in the middle of a workday. In a damn supply closet.

In her defense, they'd had sex in stranger places, but it was the timing of this request that rubbed him the wrong way.

"You left me an urgent message, telling me to get to J&S as soon as possible, and *this* is the emergency?" Craig seethed, struggling to keep his voice down since they were at her workplace. "You want to jump my bones in a supply closet? Apparently, the last few nights of wild sex weren't enough for you."

Toni's grin dropped. She huffed out a breath and brushed long tendrils of hair out of her face that had fallen from her messy ponytail. "I thought it would be fun. Most men would love for their wives to call them for an afternoon rendezvous. Clearly, I was mistaken."

Craig moved closer to her, which forced her to crane her head back to look up at him. At six feet tall, he had her by at least seven inches, but what she lacked in height, she made up for in stubbornness. He wanted nothing more than to have sex with her anytime, anywhere, but not like this. Not when he knew she was only using him for one purpose—to get pregnant...again.

He stared into her eyes and reined in his anger while trying to choose his next words carefully. He didn't know what else he could say to her that he hadn't said a million times already. Any other time, he'd give her anything she wanted, and he had, but this...he couldn't do this. He couldn't keep playing this little game of hers.

"Baby, I love you," he said, cupping her face between his hands. He needed her to understand what he was saying because he couldn't keep up this madness that she'd brought into their marriage. "Do you hear me? Do you understand what I'm saying? I. Love. You. I know what you're up to, but this craziness has to stop. You're my heart, and you already know there's nothing I wouldn't do for you, but having another baby? My answer is still the same. You and Junior are enough for me, and so are Bailey and Kimani," he said of their biological son and their two foster children.

"And I love you guys too," Toni said, tears welling in her eyes. "I can't help it if I want a big family. One adoption already fell through, and we still don't know if Bailey and Kimani's adoption will ever happen. I—I want us to be proactive," she said optimistically despite the tears hanging on her long eyelashes, and the brightness in her eyes from a moment ago returned. "All we have to do is keep—"

"No. I told you after that last miscarriage—I'm not going through that shit again. I almost lost you, Toni!" Craig growled, unable to keep the anguish out of his tone. "You just don't get it, do you? You don't understand how much that gutted me. The first couple of miscarriages were devastating, but knowing you could've died that last time..." He shook his head and stepped back as he struggled to express the fear and heartbreak he'd felt back then. "You don't give a damn about how I was affected. You don't care."

She grabbed his hands to stop him from moving back farther. "I do care, and I do love you," she hurried to say. "I love you more than anything, and I know you said that you don't—"

"I would love to have another baby with you, Toni, but not at the expense of your life. That's why we're trying to go the adoption route, and we even became foster parents. All so that you can get what you want. But it's still not enough. Nothing will ever be enough for you."

Toni released him and huffed out a sigh before moving away from him. She didn't speak and looked everywhere but at him.

"Yeah, I thought so," Craig said bitterly.

There was no use trying to get through to her. One thing he had learned early in their relationship was that all the Jenkins women were stubborn. He happened to marry the most stubborn one of them all. Though he was fairly sure the other husbands would disagree with that.

Craig shook his head and pulled his sunglasses from the front collar of his button-down shirt. God knows he loved his wife, but he was standing firm on this. There was nothing she could say or do that would change his mind.

"Let me know when you want to sex me up because you love me. Not because you're using me to get pregnant again."

Without another word, Craig slipped on his shades and stormed out of her office. With each step he took, his anger started to subside, but they couldn't keep going like this. They couldn't keep having the same old conversation over and over again.

What the hell was it going to take to get through to her?

**

Hours later, Toni wrangled her two foster children into the back door of her grandparents' estate.

"All right, you guys. Let's get downstairs before Grampa starts the movie without you."

Toni lifted the youngest one, Kimani, into her arms and held on to his sister Bailey's hand as she escorted them down the stairs to the basement. Toni had hoped that, after leaving daycare, they'd be tired. No such luck. If anything, they had even more energy than usual.

"I want to go with Daddy Craig," Bailey said. "He—he wants me to go with him a—and Junior," she said with confidence as they slowly made their way down the stairs. "Can I go? I won't *aks* a lot of questions. I *pwomise*," she said.

Toni smiled, finding it cute how the little girl's *r*'s sounded like a *w*, and the idea of her not asking questions was ludicrous. Bailey was a social butterfly who talked constantly. She was three going on fifteen and one of the smartest kids Toni had ever met. She was also curious and soaked up information like a sponge. For her, asking questions was comparable to breathing.

Kimani, Bailey's two-year-old brother, was the opposite. He was more reserved until he warmed up to a person. Most of the time, he wanted Toni to carry him around, while Bailey insisted on exploring her surroundings on her own.

They had come to live with Toni and Craig six months ago after their mother, an alcoholic who struggled to stay sober, was in a car accident. The collision could've killed her and the kids, but they all survived. After their mother was arrested and charged with a DUI and child endangerment, the kids had been put in the system. That's when Toni received the call asking if they could take them in.

The smell of popcorn wafted up the stairs along with kids' music spilling out of the theater room.

"Well, well, well. Who do we have here?" Steven Jenkins, the patriarch of the family, appeared at the bottom of the stairs, smiling.

Even in his eighties, he was still a big, tall man with a powerful presence. His hair was mostly gray now, but mentally, he was as sharp as ever. He was aging well. His dark skin showed very few wrinkles and reminded Toni of the saying *Black don't crack*. But his posture wasn't as upright as it used to be, and he was relying more on the handcrafted, mahogany walking cane that he kept nearby. Still, he was in amazing physical shape for his age.

Bailey gasped. "Grampa!" she screamed and tried to double-time it down the stairs to get to him. "You're here," she said with enthusiasm, as if she hadn't known they were planning to watch a movie with him.

Toni chuckled, remembering herself at Bailey's age. Her grandfather had been her favorite person in the world, and still held the title...well, next to Craig. That was the same with Bailey from the first time she met them. Her eyes had lit up when Craig picked her up, and it was the same with Grampa, but then again, Bailey made a friend wherever she went.

"I was starting to think you had changed your mind about coming by," Grampa said to Toni as he kissed her cheek.

The familiar woodsy scent of his cologne that he'd worn all her life surrounded her, and a sense of calm seeped into Toni's body. He'd always had the ability to bring peace with his presence, and she wanted to soak it up.

He picked up Bailey, smothering her little brown-skin face with kisses. "She reminds me of you when you were little."

"Really?" Toni said. "Did I talk as much as she does?"

He chuckled, and the deep rumble made him sound like Santa Claus. He set Bailey on her feet, and they watched as she took off running toward the theater room. "No, you didn't talk as much as her, but your enthusiasm was like hers. Hey, li'l man. You came to watch a movie with your old grandfather?"

Kimani nodded and reached for Grampa. Seconds after he was in his arms, he wiggled to get down, then went in search of Bailey.

Grampa leveled Toni with a look. "Is everything all right?" he asked.

He was studying her in that knowing way, like he did when they were kids. Like when he knew they were hiding something or had gotten themselves in a bind and needed his help.

"I was surprised when you called to say that you and the little ones were stopping by," he said.

He was probably surprised because they'd been there the day before for Sunday brunch. Every week, the family came together to eat, laugh, and catch up with each other. It had always been a large production. Especially now that the family was growing, and several generations of Jenkins attended. And since everyone usually showed up, most of the family rarely stopped by on Monday.

"Everything is fine." Toni tried adding a little lightness in her voice that she didn't feel. "Craig took Junior to karate lessons," she said of her and Craig's biological son. "I figured the little ones and I could hang out with you guys for a while."

Her grandfather didn't respond, just looked at her as if expecting her to say more.

"Grampa!" Bailey called from the theater room.

Toni grinned. "You might want to hurry in there before she starts pushing buttons on your theater equipment."

He grimaced and Toni laughed. Only certain people in the family were allowed to touch the sensitive controls. Especially after one of her younger cousins had turned the equipment off incorrectly, and something was thrown out of whack. It took a couple of days to have the system repaired.

"You're right. The last thing I need is for her to destroy something in there." He started to walk away, but stopped, and turned. "You know you can still talk to me, right?"

Toni smiled at him, and her heart thumped a little faster with all the love she felt for him. How many times over the years had she gone to him for advice? He was her go-to person. "I know, Grampa, and I love you for that. But everything is fine."

He nodded and left her standing at the foot of the stairs.

Toni sighed and headed back up the stairs as the conversation that she'd had with Craig earlier filtered into her mind.

"I love you. Do you hear me?" he had said with so much conviction that Toni felt it to the depths of her soul. His gorgeous hazel eyes had sparked with each word. *"Do you understand what I'm saying? I. Love. You. You're my heart, and you and Junior are enough for me."*

Toni sighed as the words played over and over in her mind. She couldn't imagine her life without Craig, but she could tell he was starting to lose patience with her. He and their kids should've been enough for her too, and they were, for the most part.

But she couldn't help it. She wanted more children. She was an only child but had a ton of cousins who were closer than most siblings. Toni wanted a large family of her own. One miscarriage after another proved that maybe going the traditional route wasn't a good idea, but she didn't want to give up.

Unfortunately, the last miscarriage had almost taken her life, and it scared her as much as it scared her husband. Craig was the strongest, bravest man she knew. As a former cop and then detective, he'd had to be, but that day had shaken him to the core. After that, he'd said enough. He hadn't wanted another child if there was a chance that he might lose her in the process.

Toni knew how much he loved her, but months after that miscarriage, she'd told him she wanted to try again. Craig threatened to leave her. That had been almost a year ago.

Toni loved and adored her son and her foster kids, but Craig... He was her everything.

I can't lose him.

Chapter Two

After leaving the kids in the basement, Toni strolled into her grandparents' humongous, state-of-the-art kitchen. The space was a cook's paradise and had been designed by her cousin Liam.

It wasn't unusual to find her grandmother, Katherine Jenkins, in there pulling out leftovers. She loved feeding people, and no doubt, the moment she heard them in the house she thought of food.

"Hey, sweetheart. I was surprised when your grandfather told me that you and the kids were stopping by," Toni's grandmother said. "I take it they are already downstairs. Steven took plenty of snacks down there with him. Are you hungry?"

"Yes, the kids are downstairs," Toni said and rinsed her hands in the kitchen sink, then moved to the counter loaded with food. "They're probably already stuffing their faces. And I could eat, but I'm not hungry enough for all the dishes you're pulling out. Did you and Grampa eat already?"

"Yes, we ate earlier. If I'd known you were coming over, I would've waited so we could eat together."

"After you texted me this morning, saying that you had an idea you wanted to run by me, I figured I'd come in person."

"Oh, yes. I want us to have a family reunion on the Fourth of July."

Toni's brows shot up, and the spatula in her hand hovered over the lasagna. "Umm...which Fourth of July?"

"This year," her grandmother said nonchalantly.

"Gram, you do realize that it's April, and July 4th is less than three months away, right?"

"I know that, honey. If we start working on the plans now, we should be able to pull everything together by the first week of July," she said, as if it was the simplest thing in the world to do. And by *we*, she meant Toni and her cousins, Jada, Christina, Martina, and Peyton.

Katherine, the matriarch of the Jenkins family, didn't ask for much, but this request was pushing it. This was a huge ask, especially since she and some of her cousins worked for the family business, Jenkins & Sons Construction, and they were swamped. Even if they hired every task out for the reunion, it still wasn't enough time to create an event that would meet their grandmother's standards.

Toni's grandparents had seven children, and there was a ton of grandchildren, as well as great-grands. Their immediate family was enormous, and the weekly Sunday brunch was practically out of control with people. Toni couldn't even imagine how wild and loud the house would be if the extended family showed up for a reunion. That could mean over two hundred people in attendance, and those were just the ones Toni could think of off the top of her head.

As she sat at the kitchen table and dug into the leftover lasagna, savoring the cheesy goodness, she listened to her grandmother's ideas for the event. She wanted more than just a weekend of activities and even envisioned a formal night. If they could pull it together in time, it would be a reunion to remember.

"Your ideas are great, but that doesn't give us much time to plan," Toni reiterated. Her grandmother seemed excited about hosting the reunion, and Toni didn't want to just shoot the idea down. No, there would be plenty of others in the family to do that. Especially those who would be pulled in to help her vision become a reality.

Martina Jenkins-Kendricks, also known as MJ, was the first person to come to mind.

Toni's loud-mouth cousin, who didn't have a filter, would be the first to complain. She might've loved family, but she'd be quick to point out that she loved her immediate family. Not necessarily the extended family who she barely knew.

"I'll reach out to the girls to see if we can get together and start planning," Toni said, knowing this family reunion was going to happen whether she wanted to be a part of it or not. "Just know that we'll probably have to ease MJ into the idea."

"Thanks, sweetheart. Keep me posted, and you can put me on the cooking crew," her grandmother said, placing two small plates on the table with a slice of chocolate cake on each.

Toni finished off her lasagna and then dug into the dessert. "Of course, you'll be on the cooking crew," she said and moaned when the cake melted on her tongue. Most of the family knew how to cook, but no one cooked like her grandmother.

"So, what's your real reason for being here on a Monday night? I know it's not because of my message about the reunion," her grandmother said knowingly. "Did something happen with the adoption?"

Toni sighed loudly. "The father of the kids gave up his rights, but not the mother. Her charges ended up being misdemeanors, and she only spent three months in jail along with being fined." Toni couldn't hide the frustration in her tone. "They also revoked her driver's license, and she's on probation, but none of that is enough for me. She should still be in jail for what she did. Supposedly, she's been trying to get herself together, but I don't think so."

"Why?"

"Because she missed two hearings with the judge, and they have set yet another date. It's coming up soon, but I have a feeling she's not going to show up. She hasn't even kept any of the supervised visitations with us. I don't know why the judge can't revoke her parental rights, especially with her drinking problem."

"Can't the courts do something?" Grams asked.

Toni shrugged. "Our lawyer is using her car accident to express to the judge that she's an endangerment to herself and the kids. But the woman's lawyer is saying that now that the mom doesn't have a driver's license, there won't be any more DUIs. And supposedly she's been in treatment for her drinking problem and hasn't had a drink since the accident. I'm not buying it. She shouldn't be allowed to get the kids back. She doesn't deserve them."

Toni loved Bailey and Kimani like she'd birthed them herself. It wasn't fair that someone should have those precious little ones and not take their well-being seriously.

"What is Craig saying about all this?" her grandmother asked.

Knowing her grandmother, she probably knew there was tension in their marriage when it came to having more children. Craig also wanted a big family, but not at the expense of Toni's health. And when their first adoption fell through, Toni had fallen apart. Craig was afraid that was going to happen again.

"He's..." Toni startled when she heard a door slam, and she started to stand up, thinking one of the kids might've come upstairs.

"What the hell is this nonsense about a family reunion on the Fourth of July?" Martina yelled as she stormed through the house and eventually made it to the kitchen. "Who has time to pull shit like that together?"

"So much for easing her into the idea," Toni mumbled.

Chapter Three

Gram stood from the table and shuffled over to the drawer that held the large spoons. She jerked it open, and without a word, she pulled out a wooden spoon and pointed it at Martina as she approached her.

"What did I tell you about your mouth?" she snapped.

Toni could feel her grandmother's anger from across the room, and apparently, Martina felt it too. She took several steps back and lifted her hands.

"Okay, Gram, I'm sorry, all right? I didn't—"

"I don't know how many times I have to say it, but I will *not* have you cursing in my house! Now get out until you know how to act like a lady," she said, waving the spoon at Martina. "I mean it. Get. Out!"

"Come on, Gram. You don't mean that. I'm your favorite granddaughter, and I know how much you adore me."

Toni didn't know how Martina could say that with a straight face. She was the troublemaker in the family and drove their grandmother nuts. Yet, there were times when she did seem like the favorite and could get away with anything. Probably because Martina had spent so much time at their house when she was growing up. Their grandmother practically raised her, and their bond was tight despite Martina being a pain in the butt.

"I know you don't want me to leave," Martina said with all seriousness, and she had the nerve to bat puppy-dog eyes at her. "Besides, I didn't know you were down here. It's almost seven o'clock at night. At your age, shouldn't you be upstairs asleep?"

Toni glanced away to keep from laughing, but she must have made a sound because when she looked back at them, their gazes were trained on her. Unable to hold back, she burst out laughing.

"I'm...I'm sorry, but Gram, come on. You gotta admit that was funny, but I'm surprised you didn't whack her with your spoon since she's so full of crap."

"Hey!" Martina yelled. "Stay out of it. This is between me and my grandmother. I came over to let her know that I'll do whatever I can to help with the reunion."

Toni's mouth dropped open. "How is it that you can lie with a straight face? A minute ago, you said—"

"She wouldn't lie to me," their grandmother interrupted, and her lips lifted into a smile. She lovingly patted Martina's cheek. "I knew she would jump in and help. Give me a hug, honey."

They hugged as if nothing had happened, and Martina grinned at Toni over their grandmother's shoulder. All Toni could do was shake her head, and she went back to eating her cake. The two of them were a trip.

"I'm sure you're hungry," Gram said and moved over to the sink.

Martina was the biggest eater in the family. There was no doubt that she planned to eat.

"Grab a plate. I'm glad you girls are on board with the reunion idea," Gram said as she leaned against the counter. "I also sent the other girls a text, but I didn't give them details."

Hmm...so only Martina got the heads up about the reunion. Interesting.

"You all can work together to make this reunion happen. In the meantime, I'm going back upstairs to relax," their grandmother said. "Put the food away when you're done and have a good night. Oh, but before I forget..." She pulled an address book from one of the drawers and held it up, not seeming to care that one of the pages floated to the floor. "I want to invite everyone in this notebook."

"Um...Gram. Exactly how many people are in that book?" Toni asked.

"I don't know. Just make sure they all get an invitation."

The moment their grandmother left the room, Martina pounced. "This is some bullshit. There is no way we can pull this off in a couple of months."

Toni stared at her cousin. "Whatever, you kiss up. You're so full of crap."

"Yeah, maybe, but it worked. I didn't get hit with a spoon, nor did I get kicked out. It took years of practice to learn how to get away with stuff with her."

"I guess that works both ways since she got you to come around to her way of thinking when it comes to her family reunion idea."

Martina rolled her eyes and sighed. "Yeah, well, she's Gram. Of course, I'll do anything she wants me to do. I just like giving her a hard time. So, if we're going to make this reunion happen, we need to start now." She pulled her cell phone from the back pocket of her jeans and sighed. "Gram is slick. She's always roping us into things. She's like the queen of manipulating, and she acts like we were put on this earth to serve her. Like we all don't have fifty-million other things we need to be doing."

"Just call PJ while you're grumbling," Toni said of one of their oldest cousins, Peyton Jenkins-Cutter.

Peyton used to run the family business—Jenkins & Sons Construction. She had taken the business from a mom-and-pop shop to a multi-million-dollar organization. After she got married the second time, she left the company, and their cousin Nick took over. Now, Peyton lived in Brooklyn with her husband and their two kids.

"Yeah, we're calling her. She's the most organized of all of us," Martina said.

Toni agreed. When their grandfather decided to retire, none of his kids wanted to take over the family business. So, Peyton had stepped up, and with her work ethic and leadership ability, the rest of the cousins followed. Toni, along with the others, went through apprenticeships and joined the construction trades. They eventually started playing key roles in the company.

"Let's do a conference call. I'll call Peyton and JJ, and you call CJ," she said of their cousins Jada and Christina.

Toni didn't feel like having a conference call, and though she rarely agreed with Martina, she agreed they needed to get started ASAP.

"Hey, Cuz," Christina said when she answered the phone. Her bubbly voice filled the kitchen.

"Hey, you're on speaker," Toni said and explained to her that Martina suggested they talk for a few minutes via conference call.

Once everyone was on the line, Martina opened the conversation by saying, "Gram wants us to plan a damn family reunion."

Toni shook her head and smiled.

"Oh good!" Christina chimed in. "It's been years since we've had a Jenkins family reunion."

"I'm glad she's planning ahead, but still, next summer will be here before we know it," Peyton said.

"Not next summer," Martina snapped. "Gram wants this to happen on the Fourth of July."

Silence filled the room before Jada said, "The Fourth?"

"No way," Peyton said quickly. "That's not enough time unless she means she wants a reunion with just her side of the family."

Their grandmother's side of the family wasn't as large as the Jenkins' side, and Toni and the others weren't as close to those relatives.

"Nope. She wants a Jenkins family reunion," Toni said.

"Okay, now that's insane." Jada *tsked*, sounding distracted. There was rustling of some sort in the background. "I don't have time to help. I have the fashion show coming up, and...heck, to be honest, I don't want to work on a reunion."

"Yeah, we don't either," Martina said.

"You guys are being selfish," Christina chimed in. "Gram doesn't ask for much. The least we can do is give her this. Besides, she's not getting any younger. She probably wants to see everyone before she dies."

"What the hell, CJ?" Martina roared. "Don't be putting that mess out into the universe. Gram is going to outlive us all. So quit talking about her dying."

"Fine, but we need to face facts that Gram and Grampa aren't getting any younger. Why not have a reunion? It'll be nice to create more memories with them and the extended family," Christina explained.

Seconds ticked by without anyone speaking.

Peyton sighed loudly. "Okay, I'll come up with a plan of action," she said. "Then we can get together and discuss the next steps. In the meantime, I already know that me and Toni will be responsible for pulling together a guest list with Gram's help. Toni, you'll be taking care of logistics there, like hotel accommodations. MJ will be on the food committee. CJ, right now, I'm thinking that you will be over activities. Jada, no one can decorate like you. So, one of your projects will be overseeing any decorations we might need. After I plot out a solid plan, run it by you guys, then we'll pull in the rest of the family and assign duties."

"Sounds good." They all agreed.

"I love the idea of a family reunion. It's been a long time," Christina squealed.

She was like a ray of sunshine on any given day, and a huge family gathering was right up her alley. She loved people. The more the merrier.

"It'll be phenomenal. There's so much we can do. We can have a scavenger hunt, fly kites, order some sand, and have a sandcastle-building contest, and we can even do a homemade cookie exchange!" Christina said. Her excitement burst through the phone line. "Oh, and we might be able to rent some go-karts! It's been like forever since we've done stuff like that. We can also—"

"Girl, you watch too many Hallmark movies. I like the shows as much as the next person, but you know how this family is. None of us will be hanging outside playing with beanbags unless you're talking about having beanbag fights. And as greedy as we all are, those cookies will be gone before there's any type of exchanging," Martina said, exasperated as she poked holes in Christina's ideas. "And maybe I'm mistaken, but ain't yo ass still pregnant? What do you think the Thug Lawyer would say about you climbing into a go-kart?" she asked, using the nickname that she'd given CJ's husband, Luke.

Luke used to be one of the most sought-after defense attorneys in New York, but years ago, he moved to Cincinnati. He'd said he needed a change. Yet, Toni was pretty sure there was something else, besides Christina, that had him leaving the Big Apple. He was a sweetheart of a man, super intelligent, and had a swagger about him that was almost thug-like.

"He'll raise all types of hell if his six-month-pregnant wife was found karting down some insane hill," Jada added. "He already doesn't want you working since some paint smells make you sick."

That was a big deal since Christina was a painter by trade, as well as a world-famous artist. For the last few months, instead of painting full-time for Jenkins & Sons Construction, she was working part-time supervising and doing office work.

"As a matter of fact, you're too pregnant to be of much help to us," Martina continued and, as expected, sparked an argument between her and Christina.

"It would be wonderful if we could trammel your lips because your benightedness on what pregnant women can and can't do is showing."

"All hell. There she goes again, using words no one knows the meaning of," Martina spat. "I thought you were done with that whole *word-a-day* crap. For all we know, you're probably not even using the damn words correctly!"

While the others laughed, Toni's chest tightened at the pregnant comments. She was glad they weren't meeting in person. She hated to admit that it was tough for her to be around pregnant people, even her cousin CJ, who she adored.

Christina was the epitome of a flower child and practically floated through life. She was one of those women who lit up a room whenever she entered, and now that she was expecting, she seemed to glow even brighter.

Toni could admit to being jealous that her cousin was having a baby in a few months. There'd been a time when Christina had admitted to not wanting children, and here she was pregnant without even trying.

Stop it, Toni chastised herself.

Instead of being salty about someone else's good fortune, she needed to be thinking about a way to talk Craig into trying for a baby again if the adoption didn't go through this time. He rarely said no to her, so she was pretty sure she could get him to come around to her way of thinking. But she had to figure out how.

I'll think of something. I always do.

Chapter Four

Craig strolled into Kendricks Seafood and Steak House and made a beeline to the bar. Jazz pumped through the overhead speakers and the chatter from people taking in happy hour flowed to his ears.

Some of the tension that he'd been carrying around for the last couple of days, ever since his blowup with Toni, started easing from his body. He hated when they argued, which seemed to be happening more often than not. Nothing would stop him from loving her, but Toni's obsession with having more kids was taking its toll. And his guilty conscience wasn't helping.

The place was as crowded as he'd expected for a Friday night, and he was glad when two people sitting next to each other vacated their bar stools. He grabbed the one at the end and lifted his hand to snag the bartender's attention. When she saw him, her ruby-red lips kicked up at the corners, and she headed his way.

She set a napkin on the bar in front of him. "Hey, handsome. What can I get you?" Her high-pitched voice matched her valley-girl appearance. The reddish-blonde ponytail sitting on the top of her head and pale skin with rosy cheeks had her looking too young to work in the bar.

There had been a time when Craig was a detective with Cincinnati PD that he would've questioned the owner about her age. But he knew the owner, his cousin-in-law, was serious about his business. No way would he have an underage person working behind the bar.

"Whatever you have on tap will be fine," Craig said.

A few minutes later, he had a beer in hand. He'd been waiting all day to take that first swig, and it was as rewarding as he'd hoped. Too bad it wasn't enough to give him answers to his problems. One in particular.

Craig sighed as thoughts of Toni floated around his mind. She might've meant the world to him, but he was seriously thinking they needed a break from each other.

He shook his head at that last thought.

No, he didn't need a break from her. They needed a break from the constant talk of kids, adoption, and now the Jenkins family reunion.

Actually, what he needed was a miracle. One that included no more delays with the adoption and no drama. But marrying into a huge family, specifically the Jenkins family, you were guaranteed some drama every few weeks.

"I need you to formalize the support group for men married to Jenkins women. And I need you to do it like yesterday."

Craig chuckled and glanced to his left to where Paul Kendricks, Martina's husband and the owner of Kendricks Seafood and Steak House, was standing. There was a running joke with all the husbands who had married into the family. They needed some type of support to deal with their wives. Anyone who wasn't married into the family would think they were exaggerating about the Jenkins women being a handful.

"Oh, boy. What has MJ done now? Actually, you know what? I'm sure I don't want to know. Just dealing with her cousin is enough for me right now."

Paul laughed. "All right, I'll keep it to myself, but we're going to have to stop talking about the support group and go ahead and get it started."

All the guys might complain on occasion, but like Craig, they adored their wives. There was just something about a Jenkins woman that lured you in and you were defenseless to let go.

Paul leaned against the bar. "Do you have some time to hang out?"

Craig lifted an eyebrow. "Yeah, why?"

"Let's grab a table." Paul nodded toward the main dining room behind them. The place had filled up in just the few minutes that Craig had been there. "Dinner is on me if you're up for it," Paul added.

"A free meal at the city's finest restaurant?" Craig stood and dropped a few bills on the bar before grabbing his beer. "You don't have to ask me twice. Lead the way." He followed his friend to a booth in a quiet corner of the restaurant that had a *reserved* sign on it.

The moment they sat down, the server showed up almost immediately to take their order. There was definitely an advantage to hanging out with the owner. The service was always good, but not always as fast, especially on a busy Friday evening.

Small talk flowed between them, and again, Craig was glad he had stopped by. He saw Paul and the rest of the family practically every Sunday during brunch, but it was nice to have a one-on-one. Even if they were only discussing sports, the weather, and on occasion, politics.

Paul, a former U.S. senator, came from an affluent family and a long line of politicians. Yet, he was down to earth and easy to talk with. He had become one of Craig's confidants, especially since his brothers lived out of state.

"What else has been going on?" Paul asked as they dug into their food. They both had ordered a steak with two side dishes. "You looked like you were deep in thought when I walked up to you."

Craig cut a small piece of the tender ribeye and stuck it into his mouth. Deep down, he didn't want to talk about Toni. His heart ached each time she hinted around about them growing their family, and he wanted that for her. But he still couldn't get over that last miscarriage and when she hemorrhaged from a damaged blood vessel.

Just thinking about that day had Craig's heart pounding a little faster. He set his fork down and ran a hand down his face.

"I still haven't told Toni that I got a vasectomy," he said quietly as the guilt that had been his constant companion for the past month lodged in his chest.

Craig was sure that was part of the reason why the arguments were more frequent. Normally, he tried to hear Toni out and keep the peace when she expressed what she wanted, but not lately. His frustration had been getting the best of him.

When seconds ticked by without Paul speaking, Craig glanced up. His friend looked at him with his brows raised.

Craig shook his head and sighed. He knew he was wrong in not telling his wife before he'd made the decision. But at the time, it was something he'd had to do. She wouldn't listen to reason when he told her that he didn't want them to try for another baby. So, he took matters into his own hands.

"Why haven't you told her?"

"Why do you think? You know the Jenkins women are crazy. I'm not trying to get her to go upside my head with a frying pan. Or worse."

"What could be worse than that?"

"Her messing with the house plumbing and adding itching powder to the water or something."

Paul's eyes widened, then he burst out laughing.

"It's not that funny," Craig said dryly.

"It is when you know she's capable of doing just that."

Craig shivered at the thought. As a master plumber by trade, she had the skills to do it, but as a Jenkins woman, she had the balls to do it. He wouldn't put anything past his woman. She and her cousin were more of the *don't get mad, get even* type of women. It didn't matter that they were adults and parents with kids. That only made them more creative.

He didn't bother telling Paul that his bigger fear was that she'd divorce him. "I have to tell her. She thinks I've been sullen because she's obsessing over adopting the kids. That's part of it, but the biggest problem is the guilt that's been eating at me."

Paul shook his head. "It's been a month. Do you think Toni doesn't know? Though I haven't said a word, you know my wife is like a bloodhound when it comes to getting into people's business."

"Nah, if Toni knew, she would've confronted me," Craig said.

He had the procedure done in Columbus and had stayed with one of his buddies for a week. Toni thought that he and the guys were going on a golfing trip, which they had, sort of. Craig had played golf the first day, but the next day had been his procedure, and he used the rest of the days to recover. Even when he returned, he'd used the excuse of a pulled groin muscle to keep from having sex for another week even though he wasn't in pain.

"I'm going to tell her...soon," Craig insisted, knowing he couldn't keep this secret much longer.

Despite the tension between him and Toni, they had a solid marriage that he treasured. He didn't want to do anything to jeopardize it, and secrets could do that.

"Listen, this probably goes without saying," he said to Paul, "but can we keep this conversation between us? You know as well as I do how close our wives are. I don't want Toni finding out about my procedure from anyone but me."

"My lips are sealed, and trust me, I know how my wife is. Her lack of filter is the bane of our relationship. As far as I'm concerned, you and I never had this conversation. Still, you should tell Toni sooner than later."

"Yeah, I agree. Let's hope she doesn't kick my ass to the curb when I do."

Chapter Five

Craig held Toni close, and her slim but curvy body molded against him while they slow danced to "Sweet Love" by Anita Baker. His wife had always been a perfect fit in his arms, and he cherished moments like this. A night out without the kids had been a long time coming, and he wouldn't mind turning the night into a week.

He lowered his head and pressed his nose against her scented neck as they rocked in perfect sync. He loved dancing with her, especially at one of their favorite hangouts. They were at Teddy's Bar & Grill, a bar that they'd been frequenting for years. Except lately, with the demands of their careers, nights out together had become a luxury. They both loved dancing, and when he'd decided they needed a date night, the activity was at the top of the list.

They were surrounded by other couples on the dance floor, but it was easy to block out everyone as Toni sang along with the next song. The melody poured through the speakers, but all Craig heard was Toni. He closed his eyes and reveled in Toni's beautiful voice that sounded much like an angel as her sexy body rubbed up against his.

Between her lusciousness, her fresh scent of roses and vanilla, and her singing, his body throbbed with need. But he had to tamp down the desire to make love to her right there on the dance floor.

Actually, he needed to change his train of thought. Nothing physical could happen tonight until he told her his truth.

Craig opened his eyes and swallowed hard at the thought. He'd been on edge ever since the other night when he talked to Paul. Granted, Craig had planned to tell Toni his news over the weekend, but it never seemed to be the right time. They'd been busy with the kids' activities—swim lessons, basketball, and gymnastics. Or at least those were the excuses he used. He wasn't sure how the conversation would go, but he couldn't keep this secret any longer.

He placed a kiss against Toni's temple as the song ended. "What do you say we get out of here?"

"Sounds good to me," she said, smiling up at him, and his heart kicked against his chest.

God, he loved this woman, and it scared the hell out of him that he could lose her because of keeping secrets.

He held her small hand in his and guided her off the dance floor. After they said their goodbyes to a few people they knew at the bar, they headed home. The ride wasn't long enough to taper his concerns about how the conversation would go. He played several scenarios in his head, and none of them had a happy ending.

It didn't take long for them to arrive home, but of course, when they did, everyone was still awake. While he paid the sitter, Toni got the kids settled into their bedrooms. Forty-five minutes later, the house was quiet.

Instead of going to their bedroom, Craig headed to the kitchen to pour them a drink and waited for Toni. Suddenly, he felt as if there were a two-ton boulder sitting on his shoulders. He couldn't chicken out and not tell her about the procedure, but that's exactly what he was tempted to do.

Craig sipped his whiskey. He already knew it wasn't going to go well. She had backed off in talking about them making a baby, and she hadn't mentioned the upcoming adoption hearing. As a matter of fact, she was acting like the woman he had first met when she came to his house to fix his plumbing issue. He'd fallen in love with her soon after.

Craig smiled at the memory. When Toni stood on his doorstep, he hadn't believed the petite woman was a plumber. Not only had she shown him otherwise, but she'd also proven that she was one of the best in the city.

"What are you smiling at?"

Craig glanced up at the sound of Toni's voice. Her hair was piled on top of her head, and she had changed into one of his Cincinnati PD T-shirts. He loved when she wore his shirts, especially when she wore nothing underneath them.

The material was thin enough for him to see the outline of her full breasts, and her nipples stood at attention. Her shapely legs were bare, and all he wanted in that moment was to have them wrapped around his waist.

She must have taken a quick shower because her rose-and-vanilla fragrant body wash was even more potent than earlier. The scent filled the space and practically drew him to her.

"Craig?"

Toni called his name, and his attention snapped to her freshly scrubbed face. She was one of those women who wore make-up though she didn't need to. Her blemish-free skin was soft and smooth to the touch, and her gorgeous face needed nothing else to highlight her beauty.

"What's wrong?" she asked frowning, then approached him. She slid her arms around his waist and lifted up on tiptoes and gave him a quick peck on the lips.

"Oh, nothing. I was just admiring my sexy wife," he said and then covered her mouth with his. The kiss started gentle, but as his hands moved over her body, his lips devoured hers. She returned his kiss with just as much passion, and Craig's need for her multiplied.

He gripped the back of her bare thighs and lifted her onto the counter. Now that she was up higher, he deepened their connection. Desire pulsed through him with every lap of their tongues, and he couldn't get enough of her. He wanted more.

But when one of them moaned, Craig suddenly remembered that they needed to talk. He couldn't make love to her again until he told her what he should've told her weeks ago.

He reluctantly eased his mouth from hers but touched her forehead with his. "We need to talk."

"Okay, but I was thinking that we could do a little something else." Her hands slid up his torso, and then she started unbuttoning his dress shirt. "And don't worry, I'm not trying to use your body to make a baby," she said with a smile. "I'm actually interested in using it to have a couple of orgasms just for the fun of it."

Craig couldn't help but laugh. "Mmm, I love it when you talk dirty." He gave her a quick peck on the lips before lifting her and setting her back on her feet. "I want nothing more than to take you to bed, but we need to talk."

He stepped back, then moved to the other side of the center island. He needed some space between them. One: because she looked so tempting standing before him. And two: he couldn't say what he needed to say with her being so close.

"Sounds serious," she said and sipped the drink that he had poured for them. "Is everything okay?"

Craig sighed and the heavy weight he'd been feeling moments ago returned.

"Come and sit with me," he said and pulled out one of the kitchen chairs.

Toni narrowed her eyes as she carried the drink to the table. "This is a sitting conversation? I already don't like it."

Craig tried to smile at the statement, but what they had to discuss was going to be bad before it turned good.

"There's something I have to tell you."

"What's so important that it can't wait until after we make love?" Toni asked. *There's something I should've told you awhile ago*, he wanted to say, but didn't. Normally, he didn't have a problem expressing himself, but how could he tell her this? How could he tell her that he took away her chance to have a baby? The one thing she wanted more than anything.

Craig's chest tightened, and a heaviness that was almost suffocating loomed over him. He couldn't tell her. He couldn't break her heart like that.

Toni stood and sat on his lap. "Now you're scaring me. What is it? You look like you're going to be sick."

"About a month ago, I got a vasectomy," he blurted, then braced himself for the tongue-lashing he knew was coming.

Toni stared at him as if seeing him for the first time. Craig tightened his hold around her waist.

"I'm sorry, baby, but I didn't know what else to do. You weren't hearing me. You didn't seem to care that you almost died the last time you were pregnant. I couldn't go through that again."

Toni's breathing grew labored, and she trembled in his hold. It was as if she was struggling to maintain her control.

"Let go of me," she said, her voice eerily quiet as she tried to stand. Craig didn't let her go. "Get. Your. Hands. Off. Of. Me!" she said with so much venom, Craig released her immediately.

She moved across the room at lightning speed. Hurt and anger marred her beautiful face as tears filled her eyes.

"How could you?" she breathed and swiped a rogue tear off her cheek, but others followed.

Craig stood but stayed near the table. "Babe, I didn't mean to hurt you, but you have to understand. I love you more than anything else in this world, and there's nothing I wouldn't do for you, but..."

"Don't you dare say that you love me!" she growled.

Craig huffed out a breath. He wanted so badly to cross the room and pull her into his arms, but he knew that wasn't a good idea. He wasn't sure if there was anything he could say to make this right. He had to make her understand his frame of mind at the time.

"I kept telling you that I didn't want us to try for another baby, and you know why," he said. "Yet, you kept talking about us having another child, even after we agreed to try adoption. You weren't listening to me. It didn't seem to matter that almost losing you last year scared me to death. You didn't care."

"So, you decided to take the decision out of my hands," she said as a statement more than a question.

"It wasn't like that, Toni. I had to make sure we didn't have any more children. At least not in the traditional way. Like you, I'd love a big family, but not at the risk of losing you."

"Well, it's too bad that you've lost me anyway. There's no way in hell I'm staying with a man I can't trust."

Craig reared back as if he'd been punched. "You can't mean that. Baby, we can get through this. I *love* you. Yes, I should've talked to you before having the procedure, but why can't you understand that—"

"What I understand is that the man I vowed to spend the rest of my life with betrayed me," she said in that eerily quiet voice again as she paced back and forth on the other side of the center island. "What I know is that the man who vowed to give me *anything* I want, fixed it so that we can never have another child together."

"Toni...please..."

"We usually talk about everything, but that's the one thing you never brought up to me." She balled her hands into fists as her breathing increased. "You never said a damn thing!" she screamed and with lightning speed grabbed the small pot on the stove and slung it across the counter.

Craig didn't get out of the way quick enough. The stainless-steel pot slammed against the side of his face, and a searing pain shot through his temple and forehead. He dropped to his knees and grabbed his head.

"Dammit, Toni! What the hell is wrong with you?" he roared. He no longer cared if he woke the kids. This woman had clearly lost her damn mind.

"Get out!" she screamed. "Get out of my house!"

As he slowly stood, realizing that the cut over his eyebrow was bleeding, he didn't bother telling her that it was their house. Instead, he was too focused on ducking when a mug zoomed past his head and shattered against a nearby wall. Next came large serving spoons.

"Enough!" he barked, holding his hands out in front of him. "You're acting crazy. What if the kids come down here? Is this what you want them to see, you throwing shit?"

He didn't take a breath until she set the plate that was in her hands down on the counter. Then she huffed out a breath and didn't bother wiping the tears from her cheeks.

"Okay," Craig said, sighing in relief. "Let's talk about this and—"

"Now you're the one not listening. There's nothing to talk about," she ground out. "What's done is done. As for me acting like a crazy woman, how did you expect me to act? You've made a fool of me!" She folded her bottom lip between her teeth, and there was so much hurt in her eyes. "You had me going around talking about us possibly trying for another baby. When all along you took that option off the table."

That guilt that had been ever-present was thick enough to choke Craig.

I messed up. I royally messed up.

"You never said a word about what you were going to do, and it scares me to know that you had to lie to me at some point to even go through the procedure."

When Craig started to speak, she lifted her hand to stop him, and her face twisted into a scowl.

"I don't want to hear your excuses. I no longer care about anything you have to say. I honestly thought I'd be able to convince you to have another baby with me." She shook her head. "I'm so stupid. Well, you'll never have to worry about me asking you for anything else. I want you out of this house."

"I'm not going anywhere until we...until we fix this," Craig said, his voice pleading as he held a napkin against his head. "Toni, I'm sorry. Maybe I didn't go about this the right way, but you weren't listening to me."

"And I'm still not. You either get out or...actually, you know what? You can stay. I'll go, and I'll take the kids with me since you don't want—"

"Don't you dare say that I don't want my kids! I love them as much as you do, and how dare you say otherwise." He burned with anger, and it felt as if he was going to explode if he didn't calm down. After a few breaths, he said, "I get that you're pissed, but don't you *ever* say I don't want my kids. I love them! All of them," he choked out, struggling to catch his breath as fury swirled inside him.

He closed his eyes, trying to pull himself together before he said something else that he might not be able to take back. When he finally opened his eyes and looked at Toni, her shoulders sagged, and more tears flowed.

This was all on him. He hurt the one woman he had vowed to always protect and cherish.

She covered her mouth with her hands and cried outright. "Please. Just go," she struggled to say. "Go."

Craig's heart crumbled, and he struggled to hold his own emotions in check. "I'll go," he said. "But this is not over. *We* are not over. I love you too much to ever let you go. You're *mine*!" he said with conviction as he headed out of the kitchen. "You'll always be mine."

Chapter Six

"I want you to call that customer and tell her that you'll be out to handle the job yourself. I want it done today!" Toni slammed her fist on top of her desk, jostling a few items.

"Toni, it wasn't my crew's fault that the job isn't done. There were two mornings that the customer wasn't there, and—"

"I don't want to hear any excuses!" she yelled. "Just get the damn job done."

Jake stormed out of the office and slammed the door behind him, and Toni jumped. She saw that coming, but it still caught her off guard.

Sighing, she dropped into her desk chair and held her head between her hands. As a master plumber, she'd worked in the field for years. Now she oversaw the plumbing department and enjoyed her job. But lately, she'd been alienating those who reported to her.

Two days. It had been two days since Craig had broken her heart, and she was still flailing. Her head was pounding, her stomach was upset, and she couldn't stop thinking about how her husband had made a total fool of her.

How could he let her believe that they could get pregnant again? More than that, how could he make such an important decision that affected both of them without first discussing it with her?

I'm such an idiot.

He lied by omission.

So caught up in what she wanted, Toni had missed the signs. Craig rarely spent more than a day or two away from the family. Yet, a month or so ago, he'd gone on a golfing trip with his buddies. Something he never did. She hadn't thought much of it. As a matter of fact, she loved that he was getting together with his friends. No one could ever accuse him of not being present for her and the kids, and she knew he had needed a break.

Yep, I'm an idiot.

Worse than all that, she missed her husband. She missed him more than she was willing to admit, and that pissed her off more.

She hadn't seen Craig since that night, but he wasn't slacking on his responsibility. He showed up every day to take Junior to school and to his after-school activities. Toni made it a point to not be anywhere downstairs when he arrived at the house.

She wasn't ready to see him or talk to him.

But the kids knew something was wrong. Kimani had been clingier, and Bailey was acting out, while Junior had been quieter. They all were feeling the effects of the separation, and Toni wasn't sure how to fix it.

That first day, Junior had asked why his dad wasn't sleeping at their house. Toni had told him to ask Craig. She hadn't been sure how Craig would respond, but the next morning, Junior had made a comment about Craig working on a project with *Uncle Luke.* Technically, Luke wasn't his uncle, but the kids referred to Toni's cousins as uncle or aunt.

Toni was glad that Craig had come up with a cover story, though he probably did have a project with Luke. Her husband used to be a detective with Cincinnati PD. Now he provided consulting and private investigating for a few lawyers, as well as training for security firms.

Toni had felt a little guilty when Junior also told her that his dad had been in some kind of accident. He had a cut over his eyebrow that needed four stitches. That had her feeling worse. She could've seriously hurt him with that heavy-duty pot.

Toni covered her face with her hands. She might've been miserable, but she still couldn't get over the betrayal. She lifted her head when her office door flew open.

"Dammit, Toni! What the hell?" her cousin Nick roared and waved a sheet of paper in front of her. His fair complexion had a reddish tint, and it was safe to say he was beyond pissed. "Yesterday, you were supposed to order a thousand feet of one-inch copper piping for the Benedict project, but you tripled the amount."

Toni lunged out of her seat and snatched the paper from him. Her chest tightened at seeing the colossal mistake. "Crap. I didn't—"

"Lucky for you, Shelly caught the mistake this morning and called," he said of the manager of the plumbing wholesaler. "I don't know what the hell is going on with you, but that could've set us back tens of thousands of dollars. And don't even get me started on you snapping at Ernest earlier today."

Toni dropped back in her seat behind the desk and shook her head. "I'm sorry about the order, but I won't apologize for going off on Ernest," she said of one of the plumbing foremen. "He was supposed to have some paperwork to me two days ago, and I still don't have it."

"Well, if you would've given him a chance to explain, you would've known that I had the paperwork. You were out of the office the other day, and I told him that I'd give it to you. I forgot to tell you, but I uploaded the information into the system last night."

Toni huffed out a loud sigh and felt like a total jerk. "Oh. I didn't know." But she would've known had she let the guy get a word in—which she hadn't. "Sorry."

"You need to take some time off and get yourself together. You're going to mess around and make everyone quit, and we can't afford to lose any employees right now. It's hard enough to keep up as it is."

Nick didn't stick around for a response. He turned on his heels and marched out of the office as fast as he'd entered.

She might take him up on his suggestion, but for now, she had work to do. For the next hour, she took care of paperwork, but was interrupted when Martina entered. A second later, Jada strolled in looking as if she had just stepped off the cover of Vogue.

Jada "JJ" Jenkins-Anderson wore a pink tweed suit that was probably one of her creations. She had paired it with a set of pearls and a lace camisole beneath the jacket. The short skirt stopped above her knees, which helped to accentuate the white, high-heeled boots that covered her legs.

The woman was always dressed to impress, even if she was going grocery shopping. That only made Toni and Martina, who typically walked around in T-shirts and jeans, look like slobs.

All of them had gone through an apprenticeship, but Jada was the only one who had left her skills behind. She'd been a sheet metal worker for years but hated it from day one. Even as a kid, she hadn't liked getting dirty, and after marrying a wealthy, former NFL running back, she quit. Now she was a fashion designer, something that she'd been born to do.

"I'm surprised you're still here," MJ said and sat in one of the guest chairs while Jada leaned against the desk. "Nick is ready to fire your ass, and from the complaints that I've been hearing about, I can't much blame him."

"He can't fire me," Toni said with conviction. It was a family business, and in the Jenkins family, that meant everything. If he even tried to fire her, she'd go straight to their grandfather.

"For the record, your attitude ain't cute. So, what's your problem?" Martina asked. "You still stressing over having another baby?"

"MJ!" Jada said in a warning tone, then cast sad eyes Toni's way. She was the only one Toni had told what was going on with her and Craig.

Martina was just being a busybody, and Toni wasn't in the mood. "MJ, get out of my office. I'm not dealing with you today."

She didn't move. Instead, she smirked at Toni. "Oh, so that is it. You're still tripping over not having another kid." She shook her head. "There are thousands of children out in the world who would love to be adopted. Why can't you do that instead of driving everyone around here crazy?"

Toni lunged across the desk. "I said get out!"

Martina bolted out of her seat, and Jada grabbed the back of Toni's T-shirt before she could clear the desk.

"Toni, stop it!" Jada ground out, barely able to hold her back. "If I break a nail, MJ is going to be the least of your problems."

"Let me go, JJ," Toni growled, still struggling against her cousin. "Somebody needs to teach her big mouth a lesson because I'm sick of her!"

"And they think I'm the crazy one," Martina taunted. "Girl, you got issues, and I suggest you deal with them before you return to work."

"Martina, just go," Jada said.

"I'll go, but *I'll be back*," she said in a horrible impersonation of Arnold Schwarzenegger in the Terminator movie.

The moment the door closed behind her, Toni whimpered and dropped into her seat. "She gets on my damn nerves."

"I know and you know she can't help herself," Jada said. "She came into this world like that, and she'll probably be that way until we're too old to care."

Toni sighed and was almost too embarrassed to look at her cousin. Nick was right. Maybe she should take some time off. If Martina, who was always trying to start something, could set her off, it was time to regroup.

"What are you doing here?" Toni finally asked Jada.

Her cousin rarely stopped by now that she was a big-time fashion designer. She had a partnership with a New York designer who helped set her up with a small shop in Cincinnati a few miles away. Jada and her team had offices in that building, but she didn't show up at J&S too often.

"I've been working on my part of the reunion," she said and dug through her large designer bag that was big enough to hold a laptop, which she pulled out. "Did you see the email where PJ tasked me to work with Liam and design the invitations?" she said of their cousin Peyton and Liam. Liam was the architect in the family.

"I figured since you and her were responsible for sending out the invites, y'all should've been the ones to design them."

"You and Liam have a better eye for that stuff," Toni said and skimmed the designs that they'd come up with.

"Yeah, you're right," Jada said and scrolled down the page for Toni to see all four designs next to each other. "I guess we can't be like normal folks and just email everyone in the family with the reunion details. We have to mail out fancy invitations."

Toni smiled. They'd never done things like other families. No sense in starting now.

"Which one are you leaning towards?" she asked.

"This one." Jada pointed to the most elegant one that had a navy background with a burst of fireworks on the right side, elaborate silver stars, and lettering that seemed to pop off the screen.

"Of course, you'd pick that one. It's fine with me. Actually, I'm cool with either one," Toni said and sat back in her seat. She needed to catch up on emails that Peyton had sent them all over the last few days.

Toni rubbed her eyes, suddenly feeling tired.

"You need to forgive your husband, and let him come back home," Jada said without preamble, and Toni looked at her. "You love him, and I know he loves you. It's time you two talked so that you guys can get back on track and get ready for the adoption trial. You don't want anything else to delay the process, especially a separation."

Mention of the adoption almost made Toni cry. She loved Bailey and Kimani. The last thing she wanted was for the adoption to fall through.

Jada put her laptop away and moved closer, then bent down to hug Toni. "If I didn't know that you two were still madly in love, I wouldn't be encouraging you to fix this. But I do know. You're miserable without him."

"He betrayed me. I'll never be able to trust Craig again," Toni said. "Besides—"

"Toni don't get mad with what I'm about to say," Jada said carefully and put a little distance between them. "Though Craig was wrong for having the procedure done without telling you, I understand why he did."

Toni gasped and her hand flew to her chest. "How can you say that?"

"Hear me out. You have been obsessed with birthing another child. I don't think you realize how much you've talked about it. Honestly, I was going to suggest you seek psychiatric help. It's been *that* bad."

Toni reluctantly listened as her cousin gave examples of just how obsessed she'd been regarding the subject. Sadly, she remembered the instances, and those were just the ones Jada knew about.

I didn't know what else to do. You weren't hearing me. Craig's words came back to her.

Toni sighed and covered her face with her hands.

What have I done?

She dropped her hands and looked at her cousin. "Why didn't you say something to me sooner?"

Jada's mouth dropped open. "Are you serious right now? We all have said enough for you to get a clue that you were obsessing over having a kid. Need I bring MJ back here to remind you of some of those times?"

"No," Toni said quickly. "That's not necessary."

The more Toni thought about it, the more she knew her cousin was right. It was her pride that was keeping her from picking up the phone to call Craig. Just like it had been her stubbornness to not concede defeat after the last miscarriage.

"Do you think you and Zack will have any more children?" Toni asked, unsure why that mattered at the moment.

Jada *tsked*, and the frown on her perfectly made-up face was comical. "Girl, look at me." She stood up straighter and waved her hands down her petite body. "I ain't trying to ruin all this...again. When I was pregnant with Zack Jr., I gained like a thousand pounds. I love my baby boy more than anything, but I couldn't see my feet for most of my pregnancy." She looked down and turned her feet to the side. "And my shoe game is *way* too fierce not to be able to see what I'm wearing."

Toni shook her head, then laughed outright harder than she'd laughed in days. Her cousin might've matured over the years, but she was still as superficial and vain as ever.

Toni stood and hugged her. "Thanks for the pep talk. I needed it."

"So, what are you going to do about Craig?" Jada asked when they released each other.

"I'm not sure, but I have to do something."

And she had to do something soon before he thought she had given up on their marriage.

Chapter Seven

I miss my wife, Craig thought as he and Junior headed to the house.

On Wednesdays, he usually picked up his son from the after-school program, then they'd hang out and do guy stuff. After that, they grabbed dinner for everyone and headed home, especially since Toni worked late on Wednesdays. She'd pick up the little ones from the daycare that Jenkins & Sons had added in their office building, and they all would arrive home around the same time.

Tonight, Craig wanted to stay, and he wanted to see his wife. He just wanted to know that she was all right. Junior's one-word responses when Craig asked about her were helpful, but it wasn't like seeing her for himself.

It had been days since their fight, and she had done a good job at making herself scarce whenever he came around. She was still pissed, and he couldn't blame her.

She had every right to be.

He had screwed up.

What loving husband went behind his wife's back to have a vasectomy? That wasn't normally his style. He and Toni usually talked about everything. Yet, he hadn't said a word to her about the procedure, and that mistake was on him.

Now he needed to fix this mess.

He had planned to stay away for a week to let her calm down, but he missed her too much. He missed being with his family.

"Daddy," Junior said from the back seat.

Craig stopped at a traffic light and glanced back at him. "Yeah, son."

"Can you eat with us today? Don't you want some pizza?"

Craig smiled at the seriousness on his kid's face. "I'd love some pizza because it smells super good."

"It does. I want to eat it now, but I know you'll say no."

Craig laughed and started driving again. "You're right. I don't want sauce and cheese to get all over the place back there. We'll be home soon so you can eat."

"I—I want you to eat with us too."

Craig released a sigh. "Yeah, I want that too, li'l man, but..." Hell, he wasn't sure how to respond and ended up saying the two words that he'd hated as a kid. "We'll see."

A few minutes later, Craig pulled into their driveway and grabbed the pizza boxes. As they walked to the front door, he thought about what he'd say to Toni because he wasn't leaving until they talked. They needed to have a conversation, and it couldn't wait any longer.

He let them into the house, and Craig heard Bailey and Kimani running around upstairs. No doubt Toni was hiding up there until he left. She was going to be surprised to find him downstairs whenever she decided to make an appearance.

Junior headed to the den while Craig took the pizzas to the kitchen. He had just set the boxes on the counter when Toni screamed. Not a "You scared me" shriek, but an "I'm hurt" scream that cut right through his heart.

Craig bolted for the stairs, taking them two at a time. "Toni!" he yelled, trying to determine where she was. "Toni!"

He didn't hear her, but Bailey was crying and saying that she was sorry, and then Kimani started crying.

Craig jogged down the hall. He didn't slow even when he heard his son running up the stairs behind him. He entered Junior's room to get to the Jack & Jill bathroom that sat between the kids' rooms. He pulled up short when he reached the entrance to the bathroom. Toni was pacing back and forth, holding her hand in an awkward position. While the two little ones were standing near the door to their bedroom. Kimani had his little arms around Bailey's waist. They were crying and staring at Toni.

"What happened?" Craig said.

The kids' gazes snapped to him, and they both stopped crying at the same time. And Toni glanced at him with tears in her eyes. She opened her mouth to speak, but nothing came out. She was breathing hard, and pain marred her face.

"Mommy, are you hurt?" Junior asked from his position next to Craig.

Craig's heart broke seeing her in so much pain.

"Finger...slammed," she finally said, clearly struggling to keep her composure. "In the door."

"I—I sorry." Bailey started crying again, which only made Kimani cry. "I sorry I hurt Mommy Toni," she said in a tiny voice that shook.

Craig snatched a washcloth from the bathroom shelf. "Okay, guys. Let's calm down. We need to help Mommy, but first, we have to stop crying. Okay?" Craig said while he quickly wet the towel.

"Mommy's okay," Toni said in a strained voice, but the little girl started crying harder.

Craig hated tears, especially when they belonged to those he loved, and he was crazy about Bailey. "Come here, sweetie." He bent down and pulled her tiny body into his arms. He kissed her baby-soft cheek and used his free hand to wipe her tears. "Mommy is going to be fine. You and Kimani go with Junior, and Daddy will put a Band-aid on Mommy's finger. Okay?"

Still not looking convinced, Bailey glanced at Toni, then nodded. "Okay," she said and moved away from Craig and wrapped her arms around Toni's leg.

"I sorry."

"It—it's all right, honey," Toni said tightly but wasn't able to hug her back.

Craig tugged gently on the little girl's ponytail and smiled at her. "Go on downstairs."

"'Kay," Bailey said, still sniffling.

He turned to Junior. "You guys go on down and start eating. I'll help Mommy, and we'll be down in a minute." The kid looked at him as if he wanted to argue. "Go on, son. Mommy's going to be fine. Take your brother and sister. I know you guys are probably hungry. Get the trays out of the pantry, and you can all eat in the den."

That's all it took for them to hurry out of the bathroom. They didn't often get the privilege of eating in front of the television, and no way would they pass up the opportunity.

Toni started back pacing and holding her hand.

"Let me see it, baby," he said, and she stopped moving while biting down on her bottom lip and trying not to cry.

Craig carefully reached for her hand, hoping that it wasn't broken considering the way she was holding it out.

He gently slid his hand under hers. Damn, she had smashed her forefinger good. The tip around the nail bed was already starting to swell, and there was a small cut leading from the nail. It was dripping blood.

He cringed inside because he knew how much pain she was in. Smashing a finger in a door was literally breathtaking. He'd done it a time or two.

"It—it," Toni swallowed hard, "hurts so...bad," she struggled to say as he examined the offended finger.

"I know it does," he said, softly, still holding his hand under hers. "Can you move the finger and ball your hand into a fist?"

She shook her head. "Not...not yet. It hurts so bad."

Without jostling her hand, Craig wrapped his free arm around her shoulders and kissed the top of her head. It wasn't until after he'd done it that he remembered that she was mad at him. She didn't say anything, but she was still wound tight in pain.

"Let's go to our bedroom so I can get you cleaned up."

43

She nodded, and he guided her down the hall. When they reached their bathroom, he grabbed first aid supplies from the cabinet and set everything on the vanity. As he cleaned her wound, the fingernail was turning dark blue. It looked bad, but thankfully nothing seemed broken.

Craig glanced down at her while she slowly moved her fingers. Her freshly showered scent wafted to his nose, and he wanted to pull her back into his arms again. If only she'd let him hold her. Comfort her. He wanted things back the way they were between them, but he had to tread carefully. Telling her how much he loved and needed her wouldn't work, at least not yet from what he could tell.

"How's your finger feel?" he asked, noticing that she was still wincing with each move. He grabbed the bottle of ibuprofen out of the medicine cabinet and gave her a couple of pills.

"It hurts like hell, but at least I can breathe now," she said with a small chuckle and shook her head. She took the pills dry and sighed. "Thank you for being here. I was momentarily paralyzed by the pain, and that freaked the kids out. I'm glad you were able to calm them down."

"Yeah, me too." He wanted to add that if she'd stop being mad at him, he'd be there all the time, but he didn't. At least she wasn't scowling at him and throwing things at his head.

As if reading his mind, she glanced at the cut above his eyebrow that was closed with several stitches.

"Oh, Craig." Toni reached up to touch his wound but stopped when she saw him flinch, which had been an involuntary response on his part. Like her finger, his cut was still tender and hurt to the touch.

She lowered her hand and rested it on his chest. "I'm so sorry about...everything. I was planning to be downstairs today when you arrived because I wanted to apologize. The things I said the other night were out of line, and I'm so sorry for..." She nodded towards his forehead. "I didn't mean to hurt you. Like usual, I reacted before thinking."

"Toni, this is all on me," Craig said, cupping her face between his hands. "I should've talked to you before doing anything. Sweetheart, I am so sorry. You know I would never intentionally hurt you."

She swallowed visibly and nodded. "I know." She wrapped one arm around his waist and laid her head against his chest. "I've missed you so much. I hate when we fight," she said quietly.

Early in their relationship, they'd had their share of disagreements. One that stood out the most was after another time when she'd reacted before thinking. She'd been angry with him and had ended up going out with a guy she didn't know. The night had gone downhill quickly, especially after she ended up getting arrested during a drug raid. It was a mess, but they'd come out of the situation alive and more in love.

Toni lifted her head and stared up at him. "I love you. I love you more than anything in this world, and I know we still have to talk. And I promise to listen for a change," she said with a small smile. "But not tonight, okay? Let's have a nice night with the kids, and then we can figure things out between us tomorrow. Deal?"

Instead of responding, Craig leaned down and covered her mouth with his. He kissed her with every bit of love he felt for her. She was his everything, and he tried to show that in their kiss. The last few days had been torture, but if it made their relationship even stronger, it would be worth it.

He was in agreement about them saving a deep conversation until tomorrow morning, but tonight, what he wanted to do was make love to her. He wanted to show her in more ways than one that they belonged together. That nothing could keep them apart. That—

"Daddy! Bailey's not listening to me!" Junior yelled up the stairs.

Craig moaned against his wife's lips and slowly lifted his head. He stared into Toni's beautiful dark eyes, and his heart flipped inside his chest.

"I love you so much, baby," he said, unable to keep emotion out of his tone. He planned to spend the rest of his life showing her that she and their kids were enough for him. If she wanted ten more kids, he'd figure out how to give her that, but not at the risk of her life. Right now, though, he was glad that they were back together.

"Daddy!"

Craig gave Toni another quick peck and eased away from her. He stepped out of the bathroom and into their bedroom and went to the door.

"I'll be down in a second, and Bailey, listen to your brother." Craig heard her tiny voice when she said something before he headed back into the room.

"Well, I guess that's my cue. I should go and check on them," he said to Toni who was now standing at the foot of their king-size bed. "Are you sure the finger is okay?"

"It's throbbing, but the meds have already kicked in. I'll head down in a few minutes. That way Bailey can see that I'm fine."

"All right. I'll be downstairs and—"

"Can you come home...for good?" she blurted. "I don't want to assume that our making-up means that you're back, but this house isn't the same without you in it. We all missed you...a lot."

Craig smiled and pulled her into his arms. "I want nothing more than to come home. We're a unit, and we don't operate well apart. We belong together...all of us."

He was going to do whatever he had to do to make sure Bailey and Kimani's adoption went through. It would break Toni's heart...hell, it would break his heart too if it didn't.

"I agree," Toni said and slipped her arm around his waist. Together they walked out of the room, and for the first time in days, Craig knew they were going to make it.

Chapter Eight

"Alone at last," Craig said when he closed the door after Toni's parents wrangled the kids out of the house.

Toni grinned and watched him watch her. He was leaning against the front door, looking at her as if trying to decide if he should pounce.

He was such a big, handsome man. At over six feet tall with wide shoulders and a broad chest, he still kept in good physical shape even though he was no longer in law enforcement. It didn't matter how many years they'd been together. Toni was just as attracted to him as she'd been the first time they'd met.

She thought about the conversation that she and Craig had three days ago, the night that her finger had gotten slammed in the door. They hadn't planned to discuss their issues then, but once the kids fell asleep, they talked.

She finally understood the turmoil that he had experienced over the past year of dealing with her. He'd been right. She hadn't been listening. Sure, she heard him express his fears about her trying to have another baby, but Toni thought she could change his mind. Instead, she'd pushed him to do something that he wouldn't have normally done without talking with her first.

Lesson learned. Always listen to what your spouse is saying whether you want to hear it or not.

Toni had been so caught up in her own wants, nothing anyone said mattered. Not even her man. The man she loved more than life. For that, she would be forever sorry for treating him like his concerns didn't matter.

They both had been wrong in the situation. Craig kept apologizing for doing something so selfish without first discussing it, while she felt awful that she had pushed him to take such measures.

What if something had gone wrong during the procedure and he'd died? He insisted that it was a procedure that had been done millions of times. But they both knew that things could go wrong with the simplest of surgeries. Toni would've been devastated if something had happened to him.

But now they were on the same page. Three kids were enough, assuming the adoption went through. If it didn't, they'd figure it out.

For the first time in a long time, Toni was feeling encouraged. As long as she and Craig were united, they could get through anything.

"Nice t-shirt," he said. "Is it new?"

Toni grinned and glanced down at the bright yellow shirt as if she didn't know what was written on it. *Who knew I'd grow up to be a sex goddess and a plumber?* Was written in black, bold lettering. She had a drawer full of similar shirts, and this was her new favorite one.

"Thanks. I'm glad you like it," she said, slowly lifting it over her head and tossing it to the travertine floor of the foyer.

The move left her in black shorts and a yellow lace bra that was cuter than it was functional. Then again, maybe the garment was more functional than she thought. Especially if the heat in her husband's gorgeous eyes was any indication.

Craig pushed away from the front door, and desire soared through Toni's body as he stalked toward her like a tiger on the prowl. His gaze was unwavering, and every cell within her was electrified by the intensity in his hazel eyes.

This man.

This incredibly sexy man could still turn her on with just a look, and she smiled. They were home alone, and she planned to take full advantage. She pushed her shorts down her legs, kicked them off, and chuckled when Craig growled.

"For a person who wanted a house full of kids, I have to say that I'm glad it's just you and me right now," she said and squealed when he effortlessly lifted her into his arms.

"Yeah, me too," he said gruffly as she wrapped her legs around his waist. "And I'm glad that you're only wearing your underwear. Easy access."

Her arms went around his neck as he cradled her close.

God, she loved this man. She stared down into his gorgeous eyes, and her heart was so full it felt as if it would burst. Craig was such a sweetheart. Despite the crap that she'd put him through over the years, he never gave up on her.

She touched her forehead to his. "I can't imagine my life without you. I know I haven't acted like it lately, but I love you so much."

"And I love you more. I hope it's not too presumptuous of me to think you might want the same thing I want right now," Craig said as he headed for the stairs.

"Oh, we definitely want the same thing." Her hands rested at the back of his head, and she brought his face closer and nibbled on his lower lip, then his top one. He groaned as she peppered kisses along his neck, then sucked.

Craig flinched, then stumbled and tightened his hold on her. "Damn, baby. You can't be distracting me like that while I'm walking."

Toni didn't stop. She couldn't. She was too turned on. Besides, he smelled so good and enticing.

As he climbed the stairs, she sucked on his neck and bit him without thinking. Craig gasped and stumbled forward causing her to almost slip from his grasp.

She winced, grateful that he was quick to recover, but she still hit her back against the carpeted stair and yelped.

"Ah hell. Are you okay?" Craig released her and dropped down on the step beside her. "I am so sorry, baby," he said as he massaged the small of her back. "Lean forward and let me see."

"I'm fine. It didn't hurt, and I'm anxious to get this little rendezvous started," she said and straddled his lap.

"Babe, are you sure you're—"

Toni crushed her mouth against his, swallowing any words he planned to say. Her arms went around his neck, and she rotated her hips and ground her sex over his dick. No doubt that let him know how she was feeling. *Horny.*

She wanted him. She didn't care if it was quick and hard as long as he was buried inside her in the next few minutes.

They only separated long enough to get Craig out of his t-shirt, then they were back to pawing at each other. Their tongues tangled, and the kiss was hard and frantic.

Toni was burning up with need as she ground against him, wanting...no, needing to get closer. She was starting to see the disadvantage of making out on the stairs.

Craig moaned loudly against her lips and the sound pierced the air. His hands tightened on her waist, and he pulled her closer. She could feel his thick erection pressing against her, but it wasn't enough.

She wanted more.

"I need to be inside you," Craig mumbled against her lips as if reading her mind.

He ripped his mouth from hers and moved beneath her, forcing Toni to scoot back some. She thought he was about to stand up. Instead, he reached his hand between them and loosened the drawstring on his gray jogging pants.

Toni smiled. They'd had sex all over the house, but never on the steps.

First time for everything.

They moved at the same time. Craig reached behind her to unhook her bra, and she slid her hand inside his gray jogging pants. Now, Toni was the one moaning when she wrapped her fingers around his long, thick shaft.

She stroked him. Her hand slid up and down his length, squeezing, teasing, and eliciting a growl from him. She'd had a nice rhythm going until he sucked one of her nipples into his mouth.

All rational thought flew from her mind, and her eyes slid closed as he licked, teased, and swirled his tongue around the hardened bud. He paid the same attention to her other breast until she couldn't take it any longer.

"Now, baby. I need you now," she whispered. She was wearing a thong and was getting ready to shimmy out of the lace material.

Craig stopped her with a hand on her hip. "I'll work around it," he said gruffly and repositioned her on top of him.

Nudging her thong aside, he slid into her heat, and their moans of pleasure filled the quietness of the house. Toni's internal muscles tightened around his thick shaft and they started moving together.

He felt so damn good inside her. It was safe to say that this was going to be a quickie. It didn't matter. They had all night.

As Craig picked up speed, Toni ignored the way her knees scraped against the carpet. Nor did she care that she had to hold on for dear life because of the way Craig was pistoning in and out of her.

An intense tide of passion built inside her at the way he went deeper with every thrust. Toni marveled at his strength at how he could hold on to her while balancing them on the step. She always loved being on top, and right now, she felt all of him as his dick bumped against the back of her core.

"Aww, baby..." he groaned and picked up speed as his fingers dug into her hips.

Panting, Toni rode him hard, her body moving as if it had a mind of its own. "Craig...I'm coming!" she screamed just as an orgasm gripped her, hurtling her beyond the point of no return.

Craig was right behind her, growling his release.

They collapsed against each other. Their upper bodies were slick with sweat as their chests heaved. Toni rested her head on his shoulder while aftershocks shook her.

"Whew...that was fun," she said, feeling as if she had run a marathon.

Craig, still breathing hard, chuckled. "Yeah, it was, and we're just getting started."

Toni lifted her head and grinned. "Good, 'cause we still have some making up to do. Maybe this time we'll make it to the bedroom."

Craig laughed and lifted her into his arms. "I think I can handle that."

As he carried her up the stairs, Toni wrapped her arms around her man's neck. Despite their challenges over the years, their love had always been strong enough to get through anything.

And she was beyond grateful.

Chapter Nine

"Hey, girly. You made it," Jada Jenkins-Anderson said when she opened the front door for Toni. "I figured you and your hunk of a husband would be trying to make up for lost time."

Toni grinned. She had told Jada that she and Craig had kissed and made up.

"You know us so well. He let me up for air for a couple of hours so I could hang with you and the girls."

Jada rolled her eyes. "Oh, how kind of him. You'll have to let me know how everything is going, but first, let's get this meeting over with. I need to get MJ out of my house before she starts getting on my nerves."

Toni laughed and followed her inside. "I don't care how many times I come here, I'm still awed by this entrance.

Jada loved her and Zack's home. She had always liked nice things, even as a child growing up. Her parents weren't wealthy, but they, along with the rest of the Jenkins clan, catered to her *princess* ways.

As she and Toni walked through the home, Jada tried to see the place from her cousin's eyes. There was a show-stopping crystal chandelier hanging over the stairs that glittered like stars sparkling in a dark sky. The whole house was grand, and Jada had decorated it with warm colors of blue, beige, and brown that made the large space feel homey.

When they strolled through the kitchen, Jada grabbed a charcuterie board loaded with meats, cheeses, crackers, fruit, and even dark chocolate.

"We're meeting in the sunroom," she said of one of her favorite spots in the house. It had everything to do with the wall-to-wall windows overlooking the perfectly manicured backyard. The eastern red cedar trees lining the perimeter of the property provided privacy though the house was a good distance from neighbors. The kidney-shaped in-ground pool, custom deck, and gazebo helped make the space park-like and perfect for summer cookouts.

"It's about time you got here," Martina said to Toni, barely taking a breath as she stuffed her face with nacho chips and salsa. "Hopefully, you're not still in your funk because we're not in the mood."

"Martina, hasn't anyone ever taught you not to talk with your mouth full?" Christina asked as she pulled Toni into a hug. "Are you feeling better?"

"Much. Thank you," Toni said, giving their cousin an extra squeeze.

She said something else to Christina that Jada couldn't hear, but she assumed it had something to do with her behavior towards CJ the last few months. The two of them were as close as sisters, but it hadn't gone unnoticed that Toni had put distance between them. Everyone knew why and Christina, being Christina, wasn't one to hold grudges. She loved Toni throughout the tension between them, and she always would.

Jada didn't possess that type of grace toward people. It wasn't something she was proud of. It was just fact. You get on her bad side, and you were on her shit list forever.

"God, I miss you guys." Peyton's voice filled the space.

They had videoed her in, and her beautiful face came into view on the laptop screen that sat on the table in front of the sofa.

"We miss you, too," Jada said and sat in front of the computer. "How are you?"

"I'm fine, but I miss Cincinnati. I think I want to come home," Peyton said in a tiny voice, which was so unlike her. She was the cousin who had it all together, the leader of the pack who usually kept them all in line.

"You'll be here in a couple of months for the reunion. You know how fast time flies. July will be here before you know it."

"No, I mean I *miss* home, and I want to move back," Peyton explained.

The room went silent as they all stared at the screen. Back in the day, Peyton couldn't wait to get away from all of them and Cincinnati. The Jenkins were known to be a lot, and she had also needed a break from the pressure of running the family business.

But what changed? Why was she suddenly homesick?

Seconds ticked by before anyone spoke.

"Sis, I thought you loved New York," Christina said. The sisters had gotten even closer after Peyton moved away. "What happened?"

"I still love it, but lately, I've been missing home, and a visit is not going to be enough. And I know Martina is going to make me regret sharing this with all of you, but it's been on my mind a lot."

"What does Michael say about this?" Jada asked.

"Are you serious about moving back?"

"What the hell do you mean that I'm going to make you sorry about saying anything?"

The cousins all spoke at once, and more questions were thrown at Peyton one after another.

"I'm not the blabber mouth in the family. That would be Jada who can't keep a secret," Martina insisted.

Jada gasped and scowled at Martina.

Arguing ensued, and it wasn't until Peyton yelled, "Enough!" that everyone stopped talking. "I'm sorry I said anything. This was something that's been on my mind. The feeling might pass. I don't know, but please keep this conversation to yourself." She looked pointedly at Jada and Martina until they agreed. Then she said, "Now, let's discuss the reunion."

An hour later, everyone had more tasks, and Peyton had even come up with tasks for the women who'd married into the family over the last few years. Sumeera and Liberty, who were married to the twins, Nick and Nate, were going to work with Toni on housing logistics and getting the invitations printed and mailed out. Rayne, Jerry's wife, and Charlie, Liam's wife would help Christina with entertainment for the four-day event.

Of course, Peyton also had plans to pull in their male cousins, as well as all the uncles and aunts who lived in Cincinnati. There would be something for everyone to do, which was one of the positives of having a lot of family in town. Peyton's ability to get everyone together and lay out a plan was second to none. Not only was their grandmother going to get her family reunion, but it was going to be a fun and spectacular event.

***

"*So*, you and hubby are back on track," Jada said as more of a statement than a question as she and Toni tidied the kitchen after everyone left.

Toni smiled, and there was a glow about her. "Things are going well, and I have you to thank. I appreciate you calling me out on my BS the other day. I needed the straight talk to get my act together."

Jada put the last dish in the dishwasher and wiped down the counter. "That's what we do, give each other that kick in the butt when needed."

Toni nodded. "Yeah, we do. Hey, I saw your sketch pad on the kitchen table. Are you ready for the fashion show?"

"I am and oh, let me show you some of the designs that will be featured." She strolled across the room to her sketchbook. "Before I forget, will you still be able to watch Little Zack next weekend?" she asked of her son who was a year younger than Toni's son Junior.

"Definitely," Toni said and sat in one of the kitchen chairs.

For the next few minutes, Jada showed her the new designs that would be featured in the Miami fashion show next weekend. She was excited and a little nervous about the show. It was like that with each one mainly because of the type of people who'd be in the audience.

People from around the world would be there, including actresses and rich and famous socialites.

Jada was proud of the outfits that would be modeled and couldn't wait to see everyone's reaction.

"Girl, you're talented with a pencil and paper and have always had a good eye for fashion," Toni said, flipping through the pages. "But these drawings are better than anything I've seen you come up with."

Jada grinned. She knew she was good and didn't need the praise, but she'd be lying if she said it didn't make her feel good. As a child, she knew she wanted to do something in fashion. Yet, she'd joined the family business and became a sheet metal worker. It wasn't until a few years ago that she went back to school for fashion design.

"What do I have to do to get this one made for me before the reunion?" Toni asked, pointing at the off-white sequin dress that stopped mid-thigh. "It's gorgeous with the plunging neckline and long bell sleeves. It would be perfect for the reunion's formal night. I want something that will blow Craig's mind."

"Girl, that man is crazy about you even if you wear a potato sack."

Toni grinned, and a blush tinted her cheeks.

"I'll get one made, and it'll be a birthday gift for you," Jada said.

Toni leaped up and almost knocked Jada out of her seat with a fierce hug. "Thank you! Thank you! That's why you're my favorite cousin."

Jada laughed and swatted her away. "Yeah, yeah, whatever. I'm sure you say that to the others too."

"Okay, enough about me," Toni said, reclaiming her seat. "How's it going with Zack, especially since he's working full-time with ESPN? I can't believe you're doing so well with him spending most of his weeks in Connecticut."

"Girl don't get me started. I miss that man so much. I'm almost tempted to pack me and Little Zack up and go to him. The distance is tough on all of us. He's only agreed to a six-month contract for now, but he likes the job. I have a feeling he's going to want to go all in, especially when football season rolls back around."

"Man, that's a tough one," Toni said.

"It is, and we're going to have to figure something out because I don't like us living in two different cities."

"Well, take it from me. Don't let too much distance get between you two. You don't want some woman to sneak in and fill the gap because it can happen."

Jada *tsked*. "I wish some skank would try to get with Zack. She would soon learn that I don't share, especially where my husband is concerned."

Chapter Ten

Jada tried to get her heart to beat normally as a flurry of activity floated around her. There were times when she loved the energy backstage of a fashion show, but right now, her nerves were on edge. The show was starting soon, and there was still so much to do. But she could barely take two steps without running into a model, makeup artist, or a rack of clothes.

It was madness.

"How about this?" Jada's intern jogged over carrying a gorgeous multicolor scarf. "You said you wanted to switch out the red belt for the gold, but I thought you might like this better."

Jada studied the printed scarf that included every color of the rainbow. She held it up next to one of the outfits that her model would wear and then smiled. "Liz, girl, I think you might be on to something. It goes perfectly with the top and will easily fit around Tanya's waist."

"Oh good!" Liz said, beaming.

Jada hung the scarf next to the outfit and removed the gold belt that she originally planned to use. Liz had a good eye for fashion. She was extremely talented, and Jada had no doubt that she would go far in the industry.

For the next few minutes, they double-checked a small poster board that hung on the rack of clothes. Also on the rack were the accessories, including jewelry, handbags, belts, and shoes.

Jada compared all the items to the poster which held photos of the complete looks that the models would wear.

"Jada, you're needed over here," another intern called out.

For the next hour, she bounced around the room, getting everything ready for her portion of the show.

"We're going to have to take in the waist since you're a little smaller than Samantha," Jada said to one of her models.

She gathered the material on each side of the woman's waist, trying to determine how much needed to be taken in. She only had a few minutes for the alteration and used pins to make the quick fix.

This was her first fashion show of the year, and she was excited, but she couldn't wait until it was over. Though she loved Miami, she hated traveling when Zack was in Connecticut because that meant they were both away from home and had to leave their son with family. But this was an opportunity that Jada hadn't been able to pass up.

She had gone back to college a few years ago, and even before she finished her degree in fashion design, one opportunity after another landed on her doorstep. The best one being her partnering with a well-known designer. Thanks to him, not only did she have access to his seamstresses in Columbus, Ohio, but he also carried her line of casual business and formal wear in one of his New York stores.

But the part of the business agreement that she had a love-hate relationship with were the fashion shows. Jada had agreed to participate in at least two per year, but she'd had no idea how much work was involved and how exhausting they could be. Still, she was thrilled that her designs garnered a ton of attention.

"Jada, you have a delivery," Bryan, one of the wardrobe assistants said. "Looks like that gorgeous husband strikes again."

When Jada looked up, she couldn't stop the smile that spread across her face. Bryan carried a large bouquet of orange calla Lilies and red and yellow roses. Yep, they were definitely from her husband, and though she loved the flowers, she couldn't wait to read the card.

"Thank you," Jada said, accepting the bouquet. She turned the heavy, crystal vase from side to side looking for the small envelope that was usually stuck somewhere in the flowers. "Hmm, there's no card?" She glanced at Bryan. "Did you see..." Her words trailed off when she realized he was holding it.

"Is this what you're looking for?" He waved the white envelope back and forth.

"Give me that." Jada snatched it from his hand. "Since you're playing around, hold these for a second. Or better yet, can you set them down over there near Liz?"

"Yes ma'am." He tried to peek over her shoulder to read the card, but she moved it from his view. "You're the only woman I know who gets more excited by the card than the flowers. What type of love notes does that hunk write?"

"Wouldn't you like to know?" she teased.

Jada hadn't seen Zack in what seemed like forever. She treasured his sweet text messages, phone calls, and any other means of communication when they were apart. That's what helped her to not miss him as much.

Bryan walked away with the flowers, and Jada read the card.

To my talented, sexy-ass wife. Have an amazing show. Oh, by the way, I'm in the audience.

Jada's breath caught and her head jerked up.

Oh my God. He's here?

"Jada, you're up in ten," the show's organizer yelled.

Jada cursed under her breath. She wanted to see Zack with her own eyes, but it looked like she'd have to wait. She stuffed the card into the pocket of her short, multi-color, swing skirt.

"Okay, Cassie," she said to her first model. "Sorry about that. Let me finish up with you and then we'll be all set."

She went back to pinning. "Cassie and Monica, you two will go out first, and Francis and Bianca will be a part of the second act."

Ten minutes later, her models lined up with the others, preparing to shine on stage. She counted them off and sent them out. This was the part that never got old. This was when she got to show off her latest designs to folks who were more than ready to buy what she was selling.

When Jada sent out the last model, she peeked around the heavy red curtain in hopes of spotting Zack. The place was packed with people dressed to impress. As her gaze darted back and forth, she saw a few familiar faces in the crowd but not her husband.

She was a little disappointed, but knowing he was there somewhere sent a burst of excitement shooting through her. She'd see him soon.

When the show ended, Jada congratulated her models on a job well done. Too bad she couldn't leave yet. She and her interns started packing up their area.

"Jada," Bryan called from across the room. "You're needed at the door."

"Be right there."

She snapped the lid closed on a container that she'd been filling with accessories, then glanced in a nearby full-length mirror. The last show she had participated in, she'd been summoned to meet with an A-list actress. The woman had been in the audience and wanted to commission her to design and make several outfits. It had been one of her biggest projects and sales to date.

Jada gave herself a once-over in the mirror. Her make-up was flawless, and she tugged down the hot pink wrap blouse with the pleated sleeves. It was one of her recent creations and went perfectly with her skirt and knee-high boots.

Satisfied with her appearance, Jada approached the intern. "Liz, can you help them out of the clothes?"

"Sure thing," Liz said with a smile.

"Thank you! I'll be right back." Jada headed for the door. She pushed it open and glanced into the hallway, and her breath caught. *Zack.*

At least six-one, with ridiculous broad shoulders and a wide chest that tapered down to a narrow waist. He was a sexy beast and his dark hair, which was normally spiked, looked as if he had run his hands through it a few times. His olive skin always looked as if he had a tan, and today was no different.

After her gaze traveled the length of him, her attention went back to his face...and those sparkling blue eyes that shone with love.

"Hey, beautiful," he said, his deep voice wrapping around her like a warm blanket.

"Zack," she whispered.

Jada's heart was beating fast enough to pound out of her chest. She finally darted out the door and leaped into his arms, knowing that he would catch her.

"Whoa!" he said with a laugh and wrapped his arms around her at the same time her legs went around his waist. "I guess you're happy to see me."

Instead of responding, Jada covered his mouth with hers, and the moment their lips touched, electric currents of pleasure pulsed through her. God, she had missed him...missed this. With each lap of his tongue inside her mouth, Jada's body came more alive as the sensation energized every nerve inside her.

Zack had the ability to turn her on with a look, but when his mouth and hands were on her, like they were now, she could barely contain herself. The way his large hands skimmed down the side of her body and cupped her ass had her ready to jump his bones right then and there. And the fact that he was there and not in Connecticut only turned her on more.

She loved that he'd been given an opportunity to work for ESPN, but she hated the distance. What started as a guest spot on the network had turned into a permanent position. Now they were trying to juggle their lives between two states.

Zack moaned and squeezed her butt tighter as he devoured her mouth, but Jada wanted more. She wanted to feel all of him. Sure, she was hugged up to his magnificent hard body, but she wanted them naked and the sooner the better.

Jada pressed her hand to the back of his head and deepened their lip-lock. Standing in a hallway backstage wasn't ideal, but she couldn't get enough of him. And clearly, he felt the same considering how he moaned against her mouth and squeezed her more.

"Ahem. Ahem!"

Jada jerked her head up when someone cleared their throat, and her gaze darted to Bryan who was standing to their right. She narrowed her eyes at him, wanting to wipe the smug look off his face.

"Sorry to interrupt this kissing fest, but your team needs some direction in packing up. Times a ticking," he said and pointed at his bare wrist as if there was a watch there.

Jada sighed as Zack slowly lowered her, he made a point of holding her close against his erection. Now she was the one moaning before her feet finally hit the floor. When she started to move away, he held her in place with his hands on her hips.

She frowned at her husband. "Let me..." She started but stopped when she realized the problem. "Go away, Bryan, and tell the ladies I'll be there shortly."

Jada heard him walk away as she stared into Zack's eyes and smiled as giddiness swirled inside of her.

"Thanks for covering me. Otherwise, your friend would've seen just how turned on I was thanks to you. It could've been awkward."

Jada grinned. "Anything for you, honey. Now what are you doing here?" She wanted to kiss him again but didn't. She needed to get back to the room to get her stuff.

Zack gently caressed her cheek with the pad of his thumb. "I had to be here for your show. Besides, I missed the hell out of you."

"I miss you, too, but now that this show is almost over, I can visit you more. It's Little Zack that I'm concerned about."

Zack lowered his forehead to hers. "Yeah, I know. I gotta figure all this out. I signed our boy up for that special session of peewee football not thinking that I'd miss some of his games." Normally, the kid's football team played in the fall, but the league he was a part of added a spring and summer session.

"Well, you could just take him out of football," Jada said. "Then we could both visit more, and you won't miss anything."

Zack lifted his head and chuckled. "You'd like that, wouldn't you?"

Jada hated the possibility that her baby might get hurt on the football field. On top of that, she despised how dirty he got during practice sessions and games.

"He's a boy, and he loves roughhousing and getting dirty." Zack shrugged. "Football is good for him. Besides, I love the idea of him following in my footsteps, and he's a natural."

Jada sighed, knowing he was right about their son loving the idea of playing around in grass. Even if he got knocked down, he popped right back up as if it was nothing.

She imagined Zack was like that when he was younger. He started playing when he was four and went on to be one of the best running backs in NFL history. He loved the game, and he was enjoying his new career as a sports analyst.

"So, when can you get out of here? I want to spend as much time as possible with my wife before I head back tomorrow."

"One night?" Jada grumbled. "That's all I get is one night?"

"You can have as many nights as you want if you come back to Connecticut with me," he said simply and planted a quick kiss on her pouting lips. "Actually, since the show is over, why not fly back with me tonight?"

Jada rested her forehead against his chest. Her arms were tight around his waist. "I wish I could spend a few days with you in Connecticut," she lifted her head, "but I don't like for both of us to be away from Little Zack. Besides, one of us needs to see him off to school on Monday."

When she spoke the words, Jada didn't mean for them to come out accusingly. She was just stating a fact, but by Zack's expression, she could see the guilt on his face.

"I know, babe." He lifted her chin with his finger, then lowered his head and kissed her sweetly. "I'm sorry that I'm putting so much on you, but we'll figure this out."

Jada knew they would. She laid her head back on his chest, ignoring all the commotion around them. Zack already knew she wasn't interested in moving to Connecticut. There was no way she wanted to leave Cincinnati and her family. But if it meant keeping them together in one city, she might have to consider it.

Chapter Eleven

Zack couldn't wait to get Jada into the hotel room and naked. He'd been semi-hard from the moment she stepped out of the dressing room after the fashion show. Looking like God's gift to man, she was wearing a low-cut blouse and a skirt that flattered her hourglass figure. If that wasn't enough, those sexy-ass knee-high boots sparked a need in him that only she could fulfill.

Yeah, it had been too long since he'd held his wife in his arms, kissed her sweet lips, and loved on her gorgeous body. Lately, Zack had been questioning his decision on signing the contract with ESPN. He'd been retired a few years, and the idea of talking sports with other sports analysts was too tempting to ignore. But he hadn't counted on how much he would miss Jada and Little Zack.

But right now, Zack had a one-track mind. And as fast as Jada was walking beside him in her high-heeled boots, it was safe to say that she was just as anxious as he was to be alone.

They finally arrived at her hotel room, and Zack waited impatiently for her to unlock the door. Once she did, he followed her in. The door had barely closed before he dropped his duffel bag on the floor and scooped her into his arms.

"Zack!" Jada squealed and slung her arms around his neck and held on tightly.

Surely, she didn't think he would drop her. She was petite in every way. Hell, back in his NFL days, he ran down football fields with men twice her size trying to drag him down. Compared to them, carrying her was like carrying a case of water.

A lamp on the nightstand next to the king-size bed was on, giving him enough light to see his way across the room. Zack set her on the bed, but she popped back up and clambered to her knees.

Jada fisted the front of his shirt and pulled him to her. "Don't say anything about wanting to take this nice and slow tonight. We're not! I've missed you too much, and I want it hard and fast."

Zack chuckled. "Is that right?" He toed off his shoes and kicked them to the side.

"Yes, it is."

Jada sat back on her butt and started unzipping one of her boots, but Zack grabbed both of her ankles and tugged her forward.

"Aaah!" she screeched, and her eyebrows shot skyward. "What are you—"

"The boots stay on," he said gruffly, and she graced him with a slow, wicked grin.

His gaze dropped to where her legs were spread just enough to give him a peek at the lace between her toned thighs. His heart rate kicked up.

"Cool with me," she said, and Zack undid the hook on her skirt and pulled the garment over her hips and down her legs.

His gaze didn't leave her incredible body as he dropped the skirt to the floor. "I'll admit I had planned to take my time kissing, sucking, and licking every inch of your body."

"*But...*" she said and propped herself up on her elbows. That wicked grin from moments ago reappeared when she let her knees fall open.

"But damn, woman." He was already hard as hell, and her lying on the bed, inviting him to take her, was like lighting a match to a pile of kerosene-soaked towels. "With you looking enticing and shit, I can't wait to be buried balls deep inside of you."

A naughty smile tugged up the corners of her raspberry-colored lips. "In that case, take off your clothes. Now!"

"Okay but don't move."

While Zack undressed, his gaze roamed over her gorgeous body and the hot pink, sexy underwear. From the day he'd met her, even when she was a sheet metal worker, Jada always wore sexy and expensive bra and panty sets.

That hadn't changed, and it was one of a million reasons why he felt like the luckiest bastard on earth. She loved all things pretty, and he loved to see her in them.

He wasted no time undressing and continued admiring the sight of his wife. He took in her more-than-a-handful breasts and her flat stomach, and his gaze slid lower to the V between her thighs.

Oh yeah, he missed her.

"I love when you look at me like that," Jada said as she sat up again and crawled to the edge of the bed. She ran her soft hands slowly over his pecs and up to his shoulders before slipping her arms around his neck. She nipped at his chin and smiled up at him. "Your pretty eyes go from a soft blue to almost a dark blue like the ocean when you're turned on."

He grinned at her as he backed her up and joined her on the bed. "Then they must be ocean blue all the time when I'm looking at you because you always have me in a state of arousal as you can see."

She grinned. His dick was standing at attention and was as hard as granite.

"Oh, I see," she said seductively and wrapped her hand around his erection and started stroking him.

Zack sucked in a breath and fisted a handful of the sheets as she slid her hand up and down his length, squeezing and teasing before brushing her thumb over the head of his penis.

"Damn, that feels good," he mumbled, and she picked up speed, making him struggle to keep his breathing under control. "Okay...okay, Babe..." He was barely able to get the words out as he eased out of her grip. "My first priority is to spend time worshiping your gorgeous body." Tonight was about her and all that he wanted to do to her.

Zack laid her back and hovered above her. He was glad that her bra opened in the front. Easy access. With two fingers around the clasp and a flick of his wrist, the lace and silk garment fell open, and her mouthwatering breasts spilled into his hands.

He groaned at the sight of them and cupped them before pushing them together. "You get more beautiful with each passing day," he said and sucked on one of her swollen nipples. He swirled his tongue around the bud while he squeezed and teased her other breast.

The way her beguiling scent of jasmine and sandalwood wrapped around him, Zack felt transported on a soft cloud. Desire pulsed through him, and that only increased his need to be inside of her.

Jada squirmed beneath him, moaning with pleasure as she gripped the back of his hair. He'd been wearing it just a little longer in the back than usual, and he had a feeling she liked it for just this reason.

He raked his teeth over her sensitive nipple, and drew a whimper out of her, knowing how much that turned her on. Zack gave the same attention to the other breast before he lifted his head.

Wanting her completely naked, he removed her lace thong and tossed it to the floor with the rest of their clothes before capturing her mouth in a kiss.

While their tongues tangled, he caressed every dip and curve of her body and delighted in the softness of her skin. But the erotic sounds she was making against his mouth had him growing harder.

She was right. There was no way they could take this first time slowly.

As his tongue continued exploring the inner recesses of her mouth, Zack moved his hand down the center of her body until he reached the apex between her thighs. Jada arched into him and moaned when he slid a finger, then another, into her damp folds.

He worked his fingers in and out of her as she moved frantically against his hand. No doubt nearing her release.

"Come for me, baby," he murmured against her lips. He picked up the pace, and her moans grew louder as she bucked against him.

She's close.

He smiled when Jada ripped her mouth from his. "Zack. Aww th—that feels so... Oh my goodness," she panted and rode his hand as he continued swirling his digits inside of her. He picked up the pace and went deeper while teasing her clit with the pad of his thumb.

"Zack," she cried, "I'm going to come. I'm...Zack!"

Her body stiffened as she screamed his name, and she dug her nails into his skin. Her interior muscles tightened around his fingers, and aftershocks rocked her body.

Zack didn't wait for her to catch her breath. He moved between her legs and nudged her thighs farther apart. He was so damn hard, he felt as if he was going to burst. The head of his penis bumped against her slick opening a couple of times before he slid into her sweet heat.

Jolts of pleasure blasted through him, and he moaned at the same time that Jada said, "Ahh, yes." He drove into her hard, going deeper with each thrust.

Watching her breasts bounce up and down turned him on even more, and he picked up speed. That, along with the erotic sounds she was making, pushed him closer to his release.

"I'm sorry, babe, but you feel too damn good. I'm not going to last if you keep squeezing around me like... Shi...Jada!" he growled her name and his body tightened when an orgasm took his breath away. Jada cried out at the same time, and they climaxed together.

To keep from collapsing on her, Zack held himself up on his elbows...barely, and rested his head in the crook of her neck. Their chests heaved, and they panted as their heavy breathing filled the quietness of the room.

With his eyes tightly closed, Zack shook his head. "Damn." Was all he could say for the next few minutes as he tried to get air into his lungs.

He eventually rolled onto his back and pulled Jada on top of him. Still breathing hard, she laid her head on his chest. Seconds ticked by before she readjusted and found his mouth.

Having her incredible body stretched out on top of him while they shared a passionate kiss stirred his desire. He loved her more than life itself, and he would never get enough of her.

"Can you tell I missed you?" Jada asked against his lips.

Zack chuckled. "Yeah," he said and repositioned her so that she was lined up perfectly with his dick. "And can you tell I want you again?"

She burst out laughing. "Uh, *yeah*."

"Good, 'cause I'm about ready for round two."

Chapter Twelve

Jada carried several paper bags into her kitchen and set them on the counter before she started putting the groceries away. It had been four days since the fashion show weekend, and she was still replaying a few highlights in her mind.

It had been a success, and as expected, she was approached by two individuals wanting to commission her for a few pieces. One was a B-list actress who needed an evening gown for a nationally televised awards show in the fall. Jada was thrilled, especially since the woman was known for seeking out African American designers. The fact that the eveningwear would get national attention was a bonus.

Life is good.

She was living her dream—a career in fashion and married to a sexy, wealthy man.

Thinking about her handsome husband, Zack's sparkling blue eyes flashed in her mind. Showing up at the event had been so sweet of him, but spending hours making love was definitely the highlight of the evening.

Jada smiled at the memory, and an electrifying shiver scurried up her spine at how Zack had rocked her world. Everything might not be perfect in their relationship, but their sex life was on point.

The doorbell rang, and she picked up her phone that was on the counter. Tapping the icon for the home security app, she quickly pulled up the camera at the front of the house.

Christina.

"What the heck? A visit in the middle of a workday?" she murmured into the quietness of the house.

Jada hurried to the door. "Hey, you. What are you doing here?"

"Hiding from my husband," Christina said as she breezed into the house despite looking like she had an over-inflated basketball

74

under her dress. Actually, it was more like she floated in, as if riding on some magic carpet where her feet didn't touch the ground.

Her cousin glided through life as if she didn't have a problem in the world. Rarely was she down about anything, and she definitely had the flower-child vibe going on.

"You're looking awfully cute," Jada said, checking out Christina's boho, floral dress that stopped just below her knees and the camel color boots that matched her short suede jacket. And the wide-brim, floppy hat she was wearing was adorable, but it was barely staying on because of her head full of curls.

Her cousin beamed. "Thank you. Coming from you, that's a real compliment."

"Okay, so what has that overprotective husband done this time?" Jada asked as she led the way to the kitchen.

"Nothing...and everything. He's hovering even more than usual, and it's driving me nuts. One minute I love him to death, and the next I want to strangle him."

Jada grinned and went back to putting away the groceries as she recalled how it was with Zack when she was pregnant. "Don't be too hard on him. He was protective even before you got pregnant."

Christina sighed and sat on one of the barstools at the counter. "I know, but sometimes he's too much. Oh good, you have food. I'm hungry. But I have to admit that I'm surprised you did something so menial like grocery shopping, especially in the middle of the day."

Jada stopped unpacking the bags and eyed her cousin. "Why would I grocery shop when someone else can do it for me? Do you even know me?"

Christina stared at her for a split second, then burst out laughing. "Well, I figured since you're a wife and a mom now, and not the pampered princess you used to be, that grocery shopping would be your thing. Clearly, I was mistaken."

"Clearly," Jada said dryly. Grocery shopping ranked up there with taking out the trash. She hated both tasks and didn't do either when she didn't have to.

Once she finished with the groceries, she made her and Christina grilled cheese sandwiches and vegetable soup.

"How's your part of the reunion planning going?" Jada asked as they ate.

"Magnificent," Christina said, her eyes lighting up with excitement. "I found this company that brings the party to you. They have several party packages, but I told the owner that we're looking for something a little more customized for this event. Something unique. She and I have been brainstorming ideas, and I think we're going to have a lot of fun activities for the family to choose from during their visit."

As they chatted about the reunion, Jada found herself getting more excited about it. Though she was like Martina when it came to preferring to be around their immediate family, spending time with their extended family might be more fun than she first thought. There were cousins they'd played with as kids who didn't live in Ohio, and she hadn't seen them in years.

"Wait, what time is it?" Jada asked but stopped and glanced at the slim, platinum watch on her wrist. It had been a birthday gift from Zack a couple of years ago. "My baby's show is on in twenty minutes, and I don't want to miss it."

Christina frowned as she rubbed her stomach. "Why? Since when do you watch anything related to sports? You barely own a pair of gym shoes. Don't tell me you're suddenly interested in anything athletic."

"Girl, please. I've changed but not that much. Zack told me he was going to send me our secret message while he's on the air," Jada said, trying to keep the giddiness out of her voice. It was no use. She couldn't help getting excited knowing that he thought about her as much as she thought about him.

"Oh, brother. This I gotta see, but first, can you grab the ice cream? I'm going to need a sweet treat to get through what is sure to be a nauseating experience with you and my cousin-in-law."

Jada stared at her.

"What?" Christina asked.

"For a minute there, you sounded like MJ. I had to look at you to make sure you weren't her."

"Ha, ha, ha. Funny. Just get the ice cream before your boo comes on TV."

Jada grabbed a tray and placed two pints of ice cream and spoons as well as bottled water on it before leading Christina into the family room. When they were old enough to live on their own, she and CJ shared a house together. They were roommates up until Jada fell in love and married Zack. They'd had plenty of nights of watching TV and chatting over a pint of ice cream.

Within minutes they were settled on the overstuffed sofa in front of the eighty-five-inch flat-screen television mounted on the wall. Despite them having a theater room that seated twenty, Zack had insisted that they have a ridiculously large television in the family room too.

Christina stuck a heaping spoon of Oreo cookie ice cream into her mouth and moaned. "This is *sooo* good, but ice cream isn't the same when I'm not eating it with you or eating it directly out of the container."

"I know, right?" Jada said.

She always kept pints in the freezer for whenever her cousins stopped by to just hang out. Zack and Little Zack had their own sweet treats and rarely touched her ice cream.

"Who's the hottie teamed up with your boo? I like her hair."

Yeah, Jada liked the woman's hair too. Actually, whoever styled Zack's co-host for the show nailed it. From her impeccably applied makeup to her shiny, blonde hair that fell in waves over one shoulder, she was well put together. The mustard-colored sleeveless top brought out her piercing green eyes, showcased her long graceful neck, and the deep V emphasized her perky breasts. The garment looked good against her sun-tanned skin, and it showed off her toned shoulders and arms.

The woman was cute, and Jada hated to admit it, but she looked good sitting next to Zack.

"Her name is Gina Weisenfeld," Jada finally said. "She's been working for the network for a while, but normally she's on one of the morning shows. She just moved to the afternoons a couple of weeks ago."

Jada was normally self-assured and never compared herself to another woman, but every now and then, that green-eyed monster made an appearance. She'd noticed how others checked her out when she attended events with Zack. They acted like they were surprised that he, a white man, would marry a Black woman, even in this day and age. No one had ever disrespected her, at least not to her face, but Jada didn't miss the whispers from females attracted to him.

She shook the thoughts free and zoned in on her handsome husband. A smile kicked up the corners of Jada's lips, and her heart swelled with the love swirling inside of her. She had always wanted to get married, but she had no idea that marriage could be as amazing as theirs was.

I have nothing to worry about, she told herself. *Zack loves me.*

Jada didn't take her attention off Zack as she waited for him to tap two fingers against his chest, right over his heart. It might've been cheesy to anyone else, but it was his way of saying *I'm thinking about you.*

She was watching him closely, but had she missed it? There were only a few minutes left in the show, and the only thing she noticed was how many times Gina touched him. They weren't sitting that close but close enough for her to reach over and caress his arm.

"What the hell?" Jada mumbled.

"Oh good. You noticed it too. It took you long enough," Christina said around a spoonful of ice cream.

Jada jerked her head to look at her cousin. "Noticed what?"

Christina's eyebrows dipped into a frown. "Umm, what were you talking about when you said, 'What the hell?'"

"The woman keeps touching him," Jada snapped. "Every time she laughs or says, 'Good point, Zack,' she puts her hands on him."

Christina stared at her. "Is that all you noticed?" she asked slowly.

Jada whipped her head back to the television and then lunged out of her seat. "Son of a..."

"Oh, good. So, you did notice that she looks at him like he hung the moon. I was starting to think that—"

"No not that," Jada said, her attention glued to the television. "Zack was getting ready to tap his heart, but that heifer messed it up by jerking on his arm!"

"Is this the first time you've watched the two of them on television?" Christina asked and placed the carton of ice cream on the tray. "Does she always act like this?"

"I've never watched them together before."

"Well, you might want to go back and watch the other days to see if this is a pattern. She might be nervous. Or she could just be a touchy-feely person."

Jada shook her head. "Nah, this skank ain't just touchy-feely. She's after my man," Jada said and headed for the stairs.

"Wait!" Christina called out before Jada made it out of the room. "Where are you going?"

"To pack a bag. I'm going to Connecticut."

Christina's mouth dropped open. "You can't be serious. JJ, it was one episode. At least watch the other shows. Or call Zack and ask him about it. You might be making an issue out of nothing."

Jada stood there with her hands on her hips and huffed out a breath. Seconds ticked by before she returned to the sofa. She couldn't just up and leave anyway because of Little Zack.

Her cousin was probably right, but everything inside Jada was telling her to catch the next flight out. She might've trusted Zack, but she'd seen how other women looked at him, and Jada couldn't much blame them. The man was gorgeous. He had the prettiest blue eyes and a body that fantasies were made of. And then there was his dimpled smile...a smile that could brighten the darkest day.

Yeah, he was eye candy attracting attention everywhere he went.

"Okay, you might be right. Maybe I am overreacting. I'll talk to him, but if that woman even thinks about touching him again, she's going to have to deal with me."

Chapter Thirteen

Zack dragged himself into his apartment as he tugged the knot of his tie back and forth trying to loosen it. After work, he and some of his coworkers had gone to a sports bar to watch a baseball game. He'd only planned on staying a little while, but when his boss showed up at the restaurant, Zack had hung out longer than he intended. Now he was dead on his feet and couldn't wait for his head to hit the pillow.

He flipped on lights and dropped his laptop bag in one of the upholstered wingback chairs in the living room. Then he headed down the hall towards the bedrooms. But as much as he dreamed of showering and going straight to bed, Zack needed to get in a quick workout. Since leaving the NFL, where his body had taken a beating, he couldn't go two days without exercising. At least not without waking up with stiff muscles and achy bones.

What he would rather do was curl up with his wife on the sofa and watch one of those mindless reality television shows that she enjoyed.

But he couldn't.

Jada was in Cincinnati, and he was in Connecticut.

And therein lies the problem.

It was also a problem that he had missed another one of Little Zack's football practices. It bothered the hell out of him when Jada's cousin, Jerry, had sent him a video. It was thanks to a couple of her male cousins that Little Zack was even able to play football. Because there was no way Jada would take him to practice or his games. While at the bar, Zack had viewed the video on his phone, and he almost cheered right there in the crowded place as he watched his son run down the field for a touchdown.

But his excitement had been short-lived. He should've been there. He should've been the one taking his kid to practice and cheering him on from the sidelines. He was missing everything, and for what? A job. A job that he didn't even need but a job he enjoyed.

At some point soon, he had to make a decision—continue in his position at ESPN, or go home and spend his mornings, noons, and nights with his family.

It was a no-brainer, but he hated the idea of breaking his contract. Still, he was seriously considering it.

"Alexa, call my wife," Zack said to the electronic device that was sitting on the dresser when he strolled into the master suite. She had left a voice message a couple of hours ago to say she was thinking of him. And though he had planned to call her back sooner, time had gotten away from him.

While the phone rang, he slipped out of his suit jacket and dress shirt and had started unbuckling his pants when Jada finally picked up.

"Hey, baby." Her sleep-filled voice flowed through the speaker and sounded sexy as hell. Zack could almost picture her hair mussed, and the long strands spread across her satin pillow. He could also imagine her wearing some skimpy lingerie...or nothing at all.

His body responded immediately to the vision playing around in his mind.

Dammit. This was another reason why the two of them living in different states didn't work for him.

They weren't meant to sleep apart. They were supposed to be naked in bed together with his arms wrapped around her and her fine ass pressed against the front of his body. No, better yet, she should be lying on top of him riding his dick. Or maybe under him with him buried deep inside of her. Then again, maybe she'd...

"Zack? Babe, are you still there?"

Zack cursed under his breath. What the hell was wrong with him? Why was he torturing himself with thoughts of her in his bed when that couldn't happen tonight? Clearly, their mini love fest the night of the fashion show hadn't been enough because his body craved Jada.

He needed his wife. And he wanted her more than anything.

"Yeah, sweetheart, I'm here." Frustration propelled him across the room, and he jerked open the bottom drawer of his dresser. Grabbing a T-shirt and running shorts, he definitely had to go to the gym and work off some sexual tension.

"Sorry I'm calling so late," he said. "How was your day?"

"Not bad. Just missing my man." She yawned loudly. "I assume dinner was good since you're calling after ten."

As he changed into his gym clothes, he told her about dinner and his day, and she talked about her day and the upcoming reunion. He wasn't sure, but something sounded off with her. He couldn't explain the feeling, but he knew her. She was holding back.

Then again, maybe he was reading too much into nothing. His brain was overly tired. If something was on Jada's mind, she'd tell him. She was a straight shooter and always said what she was thinking. Which was something he appreciated.

"By the way, have you talked to your son today?" Jada bit out.

"No, but I saw the video of his football practice. Impressive. Wait," he said, realizing her tone wasn't one of a proud mother. "What did he do?"

"He was fighting at school," she said with distaste in her mouth. "He shouldn't be allowed to play football or anything else if he's cutting up in school."

Zack frowned. His son was all boy, but they had never had a problem with him fighting. "Did he say what happened? He wouldn't fight for no reason."

"He said the kid was pushing on a girl in his class, and he didn't like it. So, he pushed him, and then punched him in the face."

Zack chuckled. Chivalry was not dead, even when it came to his grade schooler. He started to tell Jada that she should be proud that they raised a good kid who was protective of females, but he didn't. She still saw Little Zack as her baby and didn't want him doing anything that could get him hurt. No sense in saying something that would probably start an argument.

"I'll talk to him when I call in the morning."

"Yeah, do that," she said.

Silence fell between them, and that eerie feeling from a moment ago gnawed at Zack. Something was up.

"Jada, what's going on? Did something else happen? Are you—"

"Does Gina Weisenfeld know that you're married?" she interrupted, her voice just above a whisper.

Zack frowned. "Of course, she does. Why do you ask?"

Several seconds passed, and for a moment, Zack didn't think she would respond.

"Just wondering," Jada finally said. "I watched your show today, and I didn't like the way she was all over you. She kept touching you."

Zack sighed. He had temporarily forgotten he'd told Jada to watch the show for his secret message to her. "Babe, I'm not sure what you think you saw, but you—"

"I know what the hell I saw, Zack!" she snapped. "Don't try to act like I'm the crazy one here. The heffa couldn't keep her hands off of you!"

"Whoa. Sweetheart, let me make this clear. There is nothing going on between me and Gina. I'm sorry the secret message I had planned for you got screwed up, but I'm telling you, Gina is a coworker. Nothing else. You're it for me! Got it?"

She sighed loudly. "Yeah, I know. I guess I was—"

"Feeling insecure? Jealous?" he said, unable to stop the smile from spreading across his face.

"Hell no! That hussy ain't got nothing on me," she said, and Zack burst out laughing. Suddenly feeling a renewed energy, he finished dressing and headed out of the bedroom.

Jada wasn't the jealous type, normally. Sure, early in their relationship, she was concerned that he'd get lured away from him by some *"white woman—a groupie"*, her words, not his. But Zack squashed that frame of thinking really quickly. He never gave her a reason to feel insecure, and since then, she hadn't. At least as far as he knew. But he loved that possessiveness of hers that snuck out on occasion.

"Are we good?" Zack asked, grabbing a bottle of water from the refrigerator.

"Yeah, we're good. But if I catch that woman touching you again, I'm coming for her."

Zack grinned. "Duly noted."

Chapter Fourteen

A week later, Jada tiptoed out of her son's room and closed the door behind her. This time of day was the hardest. Though she loved tucking him in at night, she hated retiring to her huge bedroom alone.

Don't even go there, she thought as she made her way down the hallway. She had never obsessed over anyone, especially not a man, until Zack came into her life. Now he was a part of almost every one of her thoughts. It was maddening.

Jada entered their master suite and closed the door. Padding across the plush carpet, she headed to the bathroom thinking about Zack. She couldn't wait for the weekend because he would be in Cincinnati. She'd just have to get through the next few days which wouldn't be too hard since she had to make a quick trip to Columbus, Ohio for business.

After going through her nightly routine, Jada finished in the bathroom and entered her sanctuary. Their bedroom was one of her favorite rooms in the house. Not just because of the magic she and Zack created in the king-size bed, she thought with a grin. But she loved the space because of how relaxing it was with dark gray walls, mahogany furniture, and splashes of beige sprinkled around. The color scheme was carried through to the attached smaller room that was used as a sitting area.

Jada slipped out of her light blue satin robe, leaving her in a lace teddy in the same color. She had always liked pretty things, and that included underwear and sleepwear. Some things you just shouldn't skimp on.

She pulled back the comforter. Zack should be calling shortly, and she wanted to be snuggled under the covers when he did. He always called her and their son every morning before their days started. And he was always the last person she talked to before going to sleep. But now, like clockwork, he also called Little Zack right after school.

That was something Jada appreciated. It was bad enough that she felt like a single parent most days, but she wanted to make sure Zack stayed in touch with their son.

Jada climbed into bed and fluffed the pillow, and as if on cue, her cell phone rang.

"Hello," she answered on the first ring.

"Hey, sweetheart. How are you?" Zack's deep voice came through the phone line and wrapped around her like a gentle caress. That brought a smile to her face, and she snuggled into her pillow.

"I'm great. How's it going with you?"

"All is well, except I have some bad news."

Jada sat up in bed, unease coursing through her veins. "Are you all right?"

"Oh, yeah. I'm fine, but I won't be able to make it home this weekend as planned." He explained that his boss asked him to fill in on a weekend show for one of the sports analysts who had a family emergency. The man's wife had been in a car accident that put her in the hospital. Though she would be fine, the guy needed a couple of days off. He wanted to be able to get her situated at home after she was released.

"I'm sorry to hear about his wife, and I hope she has a speedy recovery," Jada said even though she was disappointed that she wouldn't get to see Zack in the coming days.

"Yeah, I hope so too, but I hate that I won't be able to make the trip home," he said. "Why don't you and little Zack come here instead?"

"I wish we could, but remember he begged to go camping with Jerry and his kids. And I have to go to the warehouse in Columbus. I'll be gone from Wednesday to Friday," she said, trying to keep the pout out of her tone. The warehouse space was where her designs were turned into outfits. She went there every few months to check on production.

"Something has to give, Zack. Both of our careers are important to us, but I didn't marry you for us to be apart for a big chunk of the year."

Zack released a long sigh. "Yeah, I know, sweetie. I want nothing more than to be wherever you are, but—"

"I know," she interrupted.

Jada didn't want to keep making him feel guilty about his job. It was a great opportunity to be a part of something he loved. He lived and breathed sports even if he wasn't playing football anymore.

Growing up, her family members couldn't deny her anything and called her the princess of the family. That had spilled over into her adulthood, and Zack learned quickly that she was high maintenance and even a little bougie. Yet, he loved her anyway, and he always tried to give her the desires of her heart...but not this time. This time she had to be willing to make some sacrifices so that he could be happy.

"I've made a decision," Zack said. "I won't be renewing my contract with the network. Just bear with me for a few months. I'll ride this contract out and will never sign anything that will take me away from you and Little Zack."

"I can't ask you to do that," Jada said. "I know how much you enjoy this job. I would never ask you to walk away from something you love."

"But I love you and our son more. Nothing means more to me than you two," he said with conviction, and warmth spread through Jada's body.

"I love you so much," she said, "but don't make any final decisions yet. There might be another way around this situation."

She didn't want to move, but there was nothing she wouldn't do for Zack. If it meant spending part of the year in Cincinnati, and the other part in Connecticut, she wouldn't rule it out. That's how much she loved her man. And that was saying a lot considering she was also known for being selfish.

They'd figure something out. In the meantime, they'd just keep going on the way they were going.

***

Days later, Zack climbed out of the rideshare vehicle and held the door open until Gina stepped out after him. A cold chill swept through him when the wind picked up, and he burrowed deeper into his wool trench coat to ward off the crisp chill in the air. It was April and still a little cold out.

"Geez, I think the temperature has dropped even more in the minutes that it took us to get here from the restaurant," Gina said, lifting the collar on her own coat.

"I know, right? Come on, let's get inside," Zack said, escorting her to the front entrance of the luxury apartment complex where he was staying.

He and some of his coworkers had met for a dinner meeting. During the conversation, he mentioned a book that had helped him prepare for his broadcasting role on the show. Gina wanted to borrow it.

"Good evening, Mr. Anderson and...Ma'am," the doorman, Jefferey, said cheerfully as he opened the door for Zack and Gina.

"Evening, Jefferey. How's it going?" Zack asked, motioning Gina into the building.

"Excellent, sir. Have a good evening."

"Will do. You too." Zack guided Gina across the open space, their heels clicking against the travertine floor.

As usual, there weren't many people down in the large lobby, which always surprised Zack since it had several cozy seating areas. He loved the place. It was in Avon, Connecticut and about thirty minutes from work, but he didn't mind the ride. Especially since the building and his apartment offered the luxury that he was accustomed to.

"How in the world did you get a place here? I heard that they rarely have vacancies," Gina said as she sashayed alongside him toward the bank of elevators. "When I started with the network, I tried getting in here, but they were full."

Zack grinned. He'd been asked that question by a few coworkers who knew where he lived. "I know people," he said with a chuckle. There was a waiting list, but a friend of his had been planning to move out and had helped him slide right into the place.

"Well, clearly I need to start hanging out more with people who have connections."

They chatted on the elevator and exited on the sixth floor.

"I appreciate you letting me borrow the book," Gina said. "I think I'm doing okay on set, but I want to get a little more comfortable in front of the camera. Listening to you and Kenny talk about the book, I figured I should read it," she said of Kenny, a former NFL linebacker who was now a sports analyst at the same network.

Zack pointed to the right, and he and Gina strolled down the hallway to the last door on the left.

"This is me," he said and pushed open the door. He disarmed the alarm and escorted her farther into the three-bedroom, two-bathroom apartment. "Give me a second, and I'll go and grab the book," Zack said and set his bag in one of the living room chairs.

"Take your time." Gina glanced around the open floor plan. "You have a lovely place."

"Thanks."

Zack strolled down the hall to the room that he used as an office. He was fairly sure he had shelved the book with his nonfiction, but he didn't see it. After checking several other shelves, he went to the desk, thinking that he hadn't put it back where it belonged.

Nothing.

It's probably in the bedroom. He headed that way. He finally found it on the small table next to the reading chair.

"Okay, here we go. Sorry it took so long, but the book wasn't where I thought it would..." The rest of Zack's words stalled in his throat, and his eyes almost fell out of their sockets at the sight before him.

"I guess you like what you see," Gina said with her hands on her hips and her megawatt smile almost as bright as the fluorescent lights.

She stood in the middle of the living room in only a white lace bra and matching panties. As well as the red pumps that she'd had on when they walked in.

Zack wasn't sure how long he stood there with his mouth hanging open. But when the book slipped from his hands and hit the hardwood floor with a thud, he snapped out of the trance.

"Where the hell are your clothes?" he roared.

Gina shrugged and smirked. "I figured they'd just get in the way. Why don't we..."

Zack tuned out anything she had to say as his shock quickly turned into anger. He couldn't believe this was happening. He glanced around the space until his gaze landed on her red pants suit that laid neatly over the back of one of the dining room chairs.

He stomped across the room and snatched up the clothes, then walked back and shoved them into her arms. "Get dressed, then get the fuck out!"

Gina's smile fell and her eyebrows dipped. "Why are you so mad? I thought—"

"I don't know what the hell you thought, but I never led you to believe that there was *anything* more than a working relationship between us."

Before Zack could back away from her, the apartment alarm beeped, signaling someone had entered. His pulse pounded loudly in his ears as keys jingled and high heels clicked against the hardwood floors.

"Zack, baby, are you..." Jada appeared at the opening of the living room, and Zack's heart stopped.

"I can explain," he blurted.

Chapter Fifteen

Jada's heart was beating fast enough to beat right out of her chest. When she decided to surprise her husband with a visit, never in a million years did she expect to find a half-naked woman standing in the middle of the living room.

She read about crap like this in romance novels. No way was this happening to her.

Her overnight bag slid from her hands and landed on the floor with a thud as her gaze bounced between Zack and the woman. Not just any woman—Gina. Anger boiled inside of Jada and her attention settled on the heffa who had the nerve to be glaring at her. The skank acted as if she had a right to be there.

Zack rushed across the room to Jada's side and started to slip his arm around her waist, but she stepped out of reach. "Sweetheart, it's not what it looks like," he hurried to say, worry in his voice.

Jada moved closer to Gina and stopped several feet from her for fear that she'd punch the woman. "You must be awfully stupid because no woman in her right mind would be standing in my home half naked." Jada moved a little closer. "What made you think it was okay to get *undressed* in front of my husband?"

"Jada," Zack started but stopped talking when she lifted her hand, effectively hushing him. "I'm talking to her." Jada's voice was eerily calm even to her own ears, and there was no doubt that was freaking Zack out. He was still in the same spot she'd left him, probably for fear of getting close to her or Gina.

A slow, wicked smile kicked up the corner of Gina's mouth as she stared at Jada with a self-assured expression on her face. Clearly, the woman didn't know who she was dealing with. Jada hadn't slapped a ho since high school, but now she was tempted to do just that and more.

Gina cocked her hip and stuck out her lace-covered breasts as if she was posing in a photo shoot. "I came home with Zack, and one thing led to another. I—"

"Oh, *hell* no!" Zack barked and charged toward Gina as if he was on a football field running toward the end zone.

Jada reached out and grabbed the back of his shirt, trying to slow him down before he did something that would make the situation worse. Zack didn't get angry often, but right now Jada was seeing a different side of him as she struggled to hold him back.

"You have lost your damn mind," he roared and jabbed his finger in the woman's direction as fury radiated through him like steam from a radiator. "What you're not going to do is stand there and act like something happened between us!"

"Zack, baby," Jada said, tugging on his shirt as hard as she could and grateful when he finally stopped pulling against her.

He whirled around to face Jada, and the fear in his beautiful blue eyes made her chest tighten. Again, this was a side that she'd never seen. He was one of the most self-assured men she knew. But right now, he looked so much like their son when he thought he was in trouble.

"Jada, I swear nothing happened. I would *never* step out on you. *Ne-ver!* You have to believe me. I would never cheat on you," he said in a rush.

"I do believe you. I know this ain't on you," she said, looking him straight in the eyes before turning her attention back to his unwanted guest.

Jada pointed a perfectly manicured finger at Gina. "Get. Out. Before I throw your skinny ass out," she snapped.

Gina huffed out a breath and poked out her ruby-red lips like a child being chastised. Jada took a step toward her, and the woman took a giant step back and started slipping into her pants.

"Oh no," Jada said while shaking her head and moving closer to the woman. "Not in here. You're not getting dressed in here. Take your shit and get the hell out of here!" she yelled and grabbed hold of Gina's pants, causing the woman to stumble and fall back on the sofa with one leg in the pants.

Gina let out a little scream. "Let go, you crazy bitch!" she said, desperately holding on to the pants and the jacket as Jada pulled her back into a standing position.

"You want to prance around half naked, you can do it in the hallway. Now get to steppin."

Gina gasped. She held on tight to her clothes despite Jada dragging her and the garments to the door.

"Stop it!" Gina screamed, her high heels slipping and sliding while struggling against Jada's pull.

Jada might've been petite, but she was stronger than she looked. As a former sheet metal worker, who lugged around ladders and ductwork with a tool belt hanging from her waist, her strength often surprised people. Anyone who didn't know her would never believe she used to work construction.

"Zack, do something!" Gina screamed.

"No! Zack, you stay right where you are," Jada ground out, and he didn't move.

He'd learned a long time ago not to go up against a Jenkins woman when they were angry. They could be scary as hell, especially when they were together. Yet, even by herself, Jada was a force, and if she didn't get this woman out of their apartment now, there was no telling what she would do to her.

When they reached the door, despite Gina still trying to get out of her grasp, Jada jerked it open and shoved the woman into the hall, clothes and all.

"Come near my husband again, and I will beat your ass!" Jada slammed the door closed and stormed back into the living room.

"You have lost your damn mind bringing that woman into this apartment! What the hell were you thinking?" she yelled at Zack.

"Whoa! Wait!" He held his hands out in front of him, and his eyes were wild with fear. "Baby, I told you, it was not what it looked like. I did *not* touch that woman, and *nothing* happened."

"That's beside the point," she snapped.

Zack dropped his hands and frowned, looking thoroughly confused. "That's exactly the point. I would never cheat on you. Never!"

"I know," Jada snapped again, practically growling the words. "But the fact that you put yourself in this situation is what I'm mad about, Zack. That woman can say that you lured her here. Or that you propositioned her. I can't believe you put yourself...or even *us* in this type of position! You were a pro athlete for years. You know better than anyone what some of these skanks are like."

Zack sighed and ran his fingers through his dark hair before letting his hand drop to the back of his neck. "Dammit. You're right. I do know better. I fucked up. I shouldn't have ever brought her home with me, but I never thought she would do something like this. She asked to borrow a book that we were talking about at dinner."

"Wait, you had dinner with her?" Jada moved closer, and her anger spiked.

"There were six of us, including our producer," Zack said quickly. "It was a work thing with coworkers. That's all it was. I sure as hell didn't think agreeing to lend her a damn book would result in her stripping out of her clothes."

Jada growled under her breath, then dropped down on the sofa, the fight fleeing from her as something else came to mind.

"What if Little Zack had been with me? Or anyone for that matter." She glanced up, and the anguish marring Zack's face was like taking a punch to the gut. "Seeing Gina like that in our home..." Her voice trailed off as other thoughts warred within her. He had put himself in a compromising position, and it could've gone wrong quickly.

Zack sat on the sofa next to her and wrapped his arm around her shoulder. Pulling her close, he placed a kiss on the side of her head. "I'm glad you showed up when you did, but more than that, thank you for believing me, for trusting me," he said into the quietness of the room.

Jada rested her head on his shoulder. "Always. But, Zack, I don't trust that woman. Anyone brazen enough to come to your home, knowing that you're married, and strip down to her underwear, is capable of anything."

He sat back, taking Jada with him and held her close. "I know, and I'll fix this first thing Monday morning."

***

Though Zack loved having his wife in town for the weekend, he'd been distracted and anxious about going into work. At first, his plan was to go to his boss and tell him what happened, but this morning, he thought better of it. He didn't know what Gina had been thinking the other day. Had he given off some type of vibe that made her think that he was interested?

No way.

There was no way she thought that he was interested in her. He didn't flirt. Hadn't ever complimented her. Nor had he led her on.

So, what happened?

How had they gotten their signals crossed?

It didn't matter. Zack needed to talk to her. He had to make sure she understood that nothing could ever happen between them. He was crazy in love with Jada, and nothing was going to change that.

When he arrived at work, Zack was surprised that Gina wasn't there, but he was also relieved. He had another day to think about how to handle the situation between them. In the meantime, he'd been glad to learn that Kenny was scheduled to fill in for her, and during the show, Zack had enjoyed the banter between them.

It was nice to cohost with someone who had actually played a professional sport. Zack wouldn't be surprised if the episode ended up being one of the highest-ranking ones that he'd had. The comradery was effortless. The two of them lived for football, but they could discuss any sport and did.

The next day, Tuesday, was much of the same. Gina had called in, and Zack had a great time hanging out on set with Kenny. Zack also realized he wasn't missing home as much as he'd been—mainly because he was having a good time at work.

Considering how uncomfortable it was going to be sharing a set with Gina, he wasn't looking forward to it. So much so, that he was thinking about talking to his boss and maybe even the executives about splitting them up. Maybe she was feeling the same way since she had called in two days in a row.

When Wednesday rolled around, Zack had barely made it to his dressing room before his supervisor showed up.

"Hey, Niles," Zack said, setting down his laptop bag. "What's up?"

Niles Moretti was one of the most laid-back executives, but at the moment, he looked a little frazzled. He'd clearly run his fingers through his short dark hair a few times, and his olive skin had a tinge of red. Normally, the man was clean shaven, but it looked as if he had skipped the task this morning. Still, he was dressed to impress in a crisp white shirt and a black Armani suit with faint gray pinstripes.

"Let's talk in my office," Niles said. "Bring your bag."

Zack frowned. "What's this—" he started but stopped when Niles put a finger to his lips and glanced around. He jerked his head toward his office and turned to walk away.

Worry swept through Zack. He was glad there weren't many people in the office yet because he had a bad feeling about this.

Once they were behind closed doors, Niles sat behind his desk and told Zack to have a seat.

Zack set his bag in one guest chair that was positioned in front of the desk. Then he unbuttoned his suit jacket and claimed the seat next to it.

"Okay, so what's going on?" Zack asked.

"Gina has accused you of sexual assault," Niles said without preamble.

Zack's heart slammed against his chest. "Say what now?" He'd heard the guy fine, but he couldn't believe what he was hearing.

"First of all, she came on to me," he hurried to say. "Secondly, she used the excuse of wanting to borrow a book to get me to..."

Suddenly, it was as if Zack could hear his attorney, Luke Hayden, Christina's husband, screaming in his ear saying *stop talking.*

"You know what?" Zack said and stood. "I'm not saying another word without my lawyer present."

"That's probably a good idea," Niles said, looking conflicted. "Man, Zack," he started, seeming to struggle with what to say, "The company takes these types of allegations seriously. I'm going to have to suspend you until further notice while the network investigates."

Zack nodded. Niles might've been his boss, but he also considered him a friend, but that didn't matter at this moment. The guy had a job to do.

Zack spied a pad of paper on Niles's desk and reached for it along with an ink pen. "This is my lawyer's number. Any further communication or questions you have for me, call him."

Niles huffed out a breath. "All right, and Zack, I'm sorry man. I..." His voice trailed off as if catching himself before he said something that he shouldn't.

Zack understood enough to know that his friend...his boss, couldn't take sides. But by the crestfallen expression on Niles's face, it was safe to say that he didn't believe the allegations.

At least there was that, but Zack planned to make sure Gina regretted ever coming after him.

Chapter Sixteen

Jada had planned to skip Sunday brunch, but her grandmother had called that morning to make sure that they'd be there. Of course, Zack nixed the idea. He had only been back in Cincinnati for a few days, and the last thing he wanted was to be around people. Actually, he had told Jada that he only wanted to spend time with her and Little Zack. He got no argument from her. She loved having him home. She just wished it was under better circumstances.

But instead of her staying home with him, she thought it a better idea for him and Little Zack to spend time together. When she left the house, they were playing video games and had barely said bye to her. She smiled at the memory. Hopefully, the time bonding with his son would take Zack's mind off the havoc that Gina had wreaked on their lives.

Jada balled her fists. Not only had Gina lied about Zack assaulting her, but the witch claimed that Jada had struck her in the face, leaving a bruise. She had even manufactured photos to go with the lies. Jada had wanted to hunt the heffa down and give her a real ass whooping.

Jada sighed as Lou, her driver, the one Zack had insisted on thanks to the paparazzi hanging around their home, neared her grandparents' mansion.

Her grandmother had started the Sunday brunch tradition when Jada was a child. She insisted that dinner together kept the family together, and over thirty years later, that was still the case. The family had tripled in size, and there were some days when the crowd was overwhelming. But everyone continued to show up because they knew her grandmother expected it and loved being surrounded by her family. They all might've got on each other's nerves, but they could always count on each other to come through whenever needed.

This is a bad idea. Jada thought as Lou pulled into the long, circular driveway. If it weren't for the family reunion meeting after dinner, she'd have Lou turn around and take her back home. But she had to face her loud, busy-body family at some point. They were good at getting into each other's business, especially if someone in the family was having a problem.

A short while later, Jada entered through the front door, and the noise level seemed to be at a hundred decibels. Kids were running through the halls, and based on the stomping overhead, some had made it upstairs.

Like usual, the family was spread all over the house. The men were probably in the basement where there was a game room as well as a theater. The older male family members often hung out in her grandfather's large office. And the women could be found in the kitchen, dining room, or the ballroom, also known as the piano room. The place was large enough to hold everyone and not feel cramped.

The smell of barbecue and a host of other seasonings wafted through the air and drew Jada toward the kitchen. She already knew there would be a ton of food on every flat surface, and she couldn't wait to dive in. Except her heart rate had picked up, and Jada slowed her steps.

She inhaled deeply and released it slowly as she neared the kitchen. She mentally braced herself before walking in. Thankfully, her grandmother was the first person she saw.

"There's my baby girl," Gram said and opened her arms to Jada who went willingly. "I'm glad you came," her grandmother whispered in her ear as she gave Jada one of her warm hugs.

Gram gave the best hugs. Being in her grandmother's arms was like a soothing balm that calmed Jada's nerves. Not even her own parents had this type of effect.

"Thanks, Gram. I needed this." As her grandmother continued holding her, Jada soaked up her love before saying, "I hope you didn't let them eat all the food," she joked, knowing there was enough food to feed an army.

"Of course not, baby," her grandmother kissed her cheek before releasing her. "And I made your favorite—short ribs."

Jada grinned. This was why she adored this woman. There was no other person like her.

"Well, well, well, look who decided to show up," Martina said as she leaned against one of the kitchen counters. "I'm surprised—"

"Don't start, Martina," Gram said, giving her one of those "I dare you to defy me" glares.

Jada licked her tongue out at her cousin. Childish? Yes. Felt good? Definitely. "Yeah, MJ, don't start. I'm not in the mood for whatever nonsense you have in mind."

"Hey, Pooh Bear," Jada's mother said and gave her a quick kiss on the cheek before she went back to slicing the ham. "Good seeing you."

Jada smiled at her mother. "You, too." Her parents had been her rock the last few days, and she was blessed to have them.

She strolled over to the sink to wash her hands, and she greeted some of her other cousins and aunts who were fixing plates. Some looked like they were on their second helping.

Right away, Jada was bombarded with questions about her, Zack, and Gina. Some had gotten information from the family's rumor mill, while others learned about what was going on through entertainment news.

As she fielded questions, Jada surveyed the food items. There was everything from collard greens and cabbage to fried chicken and grilled fish. Definitely something for everyone.

"These young women today have no shame," Jada's mother said about Gina while shaking her head and pulling a pan of dinner rolls out of the oven. She placed them on the center island. "She'll get hers in the end. God don't like ugly."

Jada didn't respond. She knew the situation would work out eventually, but in the meantime, her husband was being crucified by people on social media. Those jerks didn't know the truth about what happened. Yet, they thought it was okay to voice their opinion and side with Gina when they didn't know the whole story.

The anger that she'd managed to get under control before arriving was swirling inside of her again.

"Okay, that's enough on that topic," her grandmother said and placed short ribs on Jada's plate. "Focus on eating some of this good food, and everything else will work itself out."

Jada couldn't help but smile. Her grandmother thought food healed all ailments, and right now, as hungry as she was, Jada was willing to give it a try.

She usually ate light during the week and pigged out on Sundays, but even she couldn't eat all that was laid out. She finally chose collard greens and yams, and though she was sure she wouldn't be able to eat everything, she grabbed a piece of fish. With her plate, she went to the dining room.

"Hey, girl," Toni said and pulled out the chair next to her. Jada was glad that there were only a few people in the room.

"Hey, Cuz. How's it going?" Christina asked from across the table.

"About as well as expected," Jada said, and she told them about Gina's latest lies. The more she thought about the lying witch, the more Jada wanted to seriously hurt the woman.

"That's awful. Isn't there something Zack can do to gag her legally?" Charlee asked. She was married to Jada's brother, Liam, and had become one of her best friends. They'd bonded over their love of shopping.

"Or we can all go down there and give her an old-fashioned Jenkins beatdown," Rayne, sitting next to Charlee, said with a grin, and everyone laughed. She'd only been married to Jada's cousin, Jerry, for a few years. Yet, she had heard stories of how the "*Jenkins girls*" always stuck together. You fight one. You fight them all.

"Are the paparazzi still camped outside of the house?" Toni asked.

"Yep, they're still out there hoping to get a shot of Zack and ask him questions."

She and Zack had been trying to keep a low profile, and it worked for a while. The media didn't know if they were at the apartment or at the house. Too bad she'd had to go to an appointment yesterday. Otherwise, they wouldn't have known they were home.

"Okay, now that Gram isn't around, I can say whatever the hell I want to," Martina said as she entered the dining room carrying a four-layered chocolate cake. She set it in the middle of the table along with a knife. There were already small dessert plates on the table.

"What I don't understand is why Zack would let a woman who wasn't you into the apartment in the first place. He had to—"

"MJ, just stop," Toni said. Exasperation dripped from each word, and MJ had barely said much. Everyone knew that sometimes dealing with her was like getting salt in an open wound. It was irritating, stung like crazy, and overall was a pain in the ass.

"So, where's Zack?" Martina continued. "He wasn't brave enough to face the Jenkins's firing squad? I never thought my favorite cousin-in-law was a wimp."

"Damn, MJ. *Shut up!*" Jada snapped and slammed her fork down. Suddenly, she wasn't hungry. What she wanted to do was knock the girl upside the head with a plate. "Ain't nobody trying to hear your nonsense today."

Martina lifted her hands and dropped them back on the table. "*What?* I could see if I'd asked if he was in jail, but I didn't."

"You're an idiot."

"You talk too much."

"You have to be the most insensitive person in the family."

Everyone spoke at once, and Jada tried to tune them out. She knew Martina was joking around, something she did more often than not. But this situation was no laughing matter. Luke, who was a defense attorney at the Law Offices of Jenkins & Associates, was the best. She had no doubt that he could clear Zack's name, but Jada wouldn't be satisfied until this mess was over.

"Hey, I can't help it if I say what others are thinking," Martina said as she cut herself a ginormous slice of cake. "For instance, Christina, what's going on with you and the thug lawyer? You walked into the house looking like you wanted to pummel him."

"I did notice that," Toni said. "Is everything all right?"

"Yeah, everything is splendid," Christina said, sarcasm dripping from her words as she picked at her food. "He's just so...much. I don't mind his protectiveness, but he's taking it too far. He even thinks I should start maternity leave like now. That means no Jenkins & Sons and no commissioned work. The baby isn't due for another couple of months. I'd go crazy sitting around the house doing nothing."

"That dude is living in the dark ages if he thinks women can't be pregnant and work too," Martina said between bites. "As long as you feel okay, you should be able to do whatever you want."

"Finally, something we can agree on," Jada said. "But with that said, don't be too hard on him. He adores you. Besides, he's going to be a daddy soon. That can be scary even for the bravest of men."

Christina sighed. "I know, and I love him for taking such good care of me. But I have an art show coming up, and I know he's going to give me grief about it."

"Why? He's always been supportive of your art," Jada said. "I doubt if he'd try to keep you from participating."

Christina nibbled on her lower lip. "It's in Atlanta."

Silence fell over the room. Christina was in great shape and for the most part had had an easy pregnancy, but she had to be around twenty-nine weeks along. Jada could understand her hesitation in telling Luke about the trip.

"He doesn't know that I'm going," Christina said.

"CJ, it might not be a good idea to go by yourself," Toni said, appearing to weigh her words carefully. "And take it from me, secrets don't belong in a marriage. Talk to him."

Christina sighed heavily. "I will."

"Okay, now that we have that settled," Martina said, "let's get back to Jada and Zack."

The room exploded. Everyone went in on Martina, and Jada shook her head. MJ was never going to change. She loved getting under their skin. Yet, Jada knew her well enough to know that if needed, her cousin would be right there to help her out of any situation.

But just once it would be nice to get through a brunch without wanting to strangle her.

Chapter Seventeen

Breaking News: Zack Anderson, former running back for the Cincinnati Cougars and ESPN sports analyst, accused of sexual assault. The Hall of Famer has denied the claims but has been suspended during an internal investigation...

Two weeks later, the words from a national media outlet were still spinning inside Zack's mind. The whole situation with Gina had been a public nightmare. And having paparazzi hanging out in front of his apartment complex in Connecticut, as well as his home in Cincinnati, had only made matters worse.

Zack was back in Cincinnati for good, and he was currently sitting in Luke's office getting an update. But mentally, Zack was still in Connecticut, reliving bits and pieces of the situation that Gina had roped him into. He was exhausted and had experienced every emotion from shock to anger, and even despair at times, all because of her lies.

After leaving Niles's office weeks ago, the first thing Zack had done was call Luke and explain the situation. His best friend and lawyer jumped on the case and pulled Michael Cutter, Peyton's husband into the situation. He was one of the best private investigators in New York and could find information on anyone. He hadn't wasted time digging into Gina's background.

"Sit tight," Luke said, pulling Zack out of his thoughts. "I'll be right back. I need to check on something."

The moment he stepped out of the office, Zack released an exhausted breath and stretched his legs out in front of him. Gina would get everything she had coming to her. She had turned their lives upside down and had tarnished his stellar reputation. And for what? Because she thought he wanted her and then felt humiliated by the way Jada had dragged her out of the apartment?

Gina hadn't given a damn that she could be destroying his life with her accusations, and sadly, it wasn't the first time she had accused someone of sexual assault.

Thanks to Michael, they'd learned that back in college, she had falsely accused one of her professors. The case had been dropped with no charges filed, and there wasn't much information on what had happened. At least not until a few minutes ago, which was why they'd come to see Luke. Mike had informed them that Gina and the professor had been in a relationship. She'd wanted him to leave his wife, but when he wouldn't, she claimed that he had assaulted her.

If Gina felt humiliated by the way Jada had dragged her out of the apartment, it was nothing like what she was probably feeling now. The saying *don't get mad, get even* had become Zack's daily mantra. He wasn't normally a vindictive person, but he planned on making Gina feel his wrath. He didn't care how long it took. He wanted her to suffer the way he and Jada had.

Luke returned, followed by Jada who had stepped out earlier to take a call.

"Okay, as I was saying," Luke said, reclaiming his seat, "Gina is being charged with a misdemeanor for falsely accusing you. Even though she dropped the lawsuit against you, we're going to file a civil suit for malicious prosecution and slander. I'll be looping one of our civil attorneys in to handle the civil suit."

"Good. Whatever it takes to make her ass pay," Jada said from the chair next to Zack.

Gina had officially been fired from ESPN after they completed their investigation. She'll never work in the television industry again, but that wasn't enough for Zack. He wanted her to pay in every way possible.

"I want her to suffer—emotionally, financially, and mentally," he said. "I want her to experience the crap that she put us through, and I want my and Jada's names cleared publicly."

"I can't believe she thought she'd get away with this, especially since she cried wolf before," Jada said. "It's people like her that mess it up for women who have actually been assaulted on the job. I knew her skanky ass was up to no good."

"Yep, you called it." Zack brought the back of Jada's hand to his lips and kissed it.

He understood that the network had to take Gina's claims seriously, but he still hadn't liked the fact that he'd been suspended. Yet, the suspension had been just what he needed to walk away from the network and get back to what was most important. His family.

His supervisor at the network had apologized profusely and asked him back, but for Zack, the situation with Gina had been too painful. He learned quickly how one lie could turn his life upside down. It was an experience he never wanted to repeat.

So no, he wasn't going back, and he'd still get the money promised to him in his contract. Unfortunately, he would miss talking sports with other analysts.

"We'll make sure she gets what's coming to her," Luke said.

Zack glanced at his beautiful wife and squeezed her hand. His heart softened when her gaze met his, and all the love he had for her multiplied. She had been his rock through all this.

"I'm sorry for putting myself and our family in this position. It won't happen again. You have my word."

She leaned over the arm of the chair and kissed him. "I know, baby, and I hate that you had to go through this, but it's over. Now we can move on to better things," she said, and Zack didn't miss the twinkle in her eyes or the wicked smile on her face.

Yeah, he recognized the heated expression. He had to make up for the time that he'd missed with her. Including going on some romantic dates, providing her with a few extra kisses, and a whole lot of lovemaking. Starting the moment they got home.

Zack kissed her hand, which he'd still been holding, before releasing it and standing. Luke stood as well.

"Man, I appreciate all you and Mike did for us. I owe you both big time," Zack said, shaking his friend's hand and pulling him in for a one-arm man hug.

"That's what family does, but you just make sure you pay when you get my bill. None of that shit about you not having any money or that you have to wait until you get yo check on Friday."

"One time. I said that *one* time, and you never let me forget." Zack glances at Jada who was laughing. "It was in college when I hardly had two nickels to rub together."

He and Luke had been roommates and had quickly become best friends. They had also been so broke that they barely had a dollar between the two of them.

Times had changed. Now they were financially comfortable and living the lives they'd dreamed about.

"Yeah, whatever, man. Don't let me have to come looking for you," Luke said, sounding too much like a gangster rather than the polished, highly sought-after attorney he was, and Zack burst out laughing.

The Thug Lawyer nickname that Martina had given him was more fitting than she knew. Even in college, Luke had been a chameleon of sorts, able to adapt and soar in any environment or situation. He might've walked around in Armani suits all day and could hold deep conversations with the most brilliant minds. But he was also that guy who would shed his suit jacket, roll up his sleeves, and be ready to kick someone's ass. He always had Zack's back.

The man was a total badass, a loyal friend, and Zack was closer to him than his own brother.

"Luke, I had no doubt that you could fix this," Jada said as she hugged him. "We appreciate everything you and Mike did for us. Thanks for everything."

"Glad I could help," Luke said as his cell phone vibrated on the desk.

"Well, we're going to get out of here so you can get back to work," Zack said as they started toward the door.

"Oh," Jada said and pulled up short. "Tell CJ to call me before she heads to Atlanta for her art show. I have an outfit for her."

Zack didn't miss the surprise on Luke's face before he quickly schooled his features. If Jada noticed, she didn't say anything. Instead, she chatted about how proud everyone was of Christina's success.

"Yeah, I'm proud of her too, and I'll give her your message," Luke said a little too dryly for Zack to believe that he was proud of his wife. Zack made a mental note to give his friend a call later.

From the moment Luke found out that Christina was pregnant, he had been on edge. Of course, he was happy about the news, but there was something off about his friend. Zack couldn't quite put his finger on it. When questioned, Luke claimed he was just concerned about becoming a father, but Zack had a feeling it was more than that.

Chapter Eighteen

"What the actual hell?" Luke ground out the moment Zack and Jada exited his office. He tried hard not to slam his door as he thought about what Jada said.

Yes, he knew Christina had a show in Atlanta next weekend, but they had agreed that she'd let her agent represent her. Now, at thirty-one weeks pregnant, his wife promised she wouldn't do any more traveling until after the baby was born. Yet, she was planning on flying to Atlanta.

Not if I have anything to say about it.

Luke reclaimed his seat behind his desk and started to call her when he noticed a text. It had come through a few minutes ago.

Christina: *Thinking about you. I'm at J&S for a meeting but made dinner before leaving home–stuffed manicotti. Home late. Reunion meeting tonight. Love you!*

She added the emoji with the heart eyes at the end of the message.

Stuffed manicotti was his favorite. Was she trying to butter him up since she knew he'd be livid about her traveling next week? Had she even planned to tell him? Normally, she gave him her show dates in advance, and he attended her art shows with her. Maybe she didn't want him there.

Luke sighed. Some of his anger dissipated as he stared at her text, and he debated on how to respond.

On the one hand, he appreciated her making dinner, especially since he had been arriving home later than usual over the last few weeks. He was slammed with cases, and he couldn't remember the last time they had dinner together.

On the other hand, he was pissed and wanted answers about Atlanta. Why hadn't she talked to him about her change in plans?

Probably because she didn't know how you would respond.

His desk phone buzzed, and Luke pushed the intercom button. "Yes?" he said to his assistant.

"Sorry to bother you, Luke. Just wanted to remind you that you have a meeting in fifteen minutes. Ben said that he and the others will meet you in conference room B."

Luke glanced at his watch, surprised that it was almost three o'clock. Where had the afternoon gone?

"Thanks for the reminder, Ana," he said.

"No problem."

Luke sat back in his seat and rubbed his forehead as his mind went back to Christina and his concern about her traveling this late in her pregnancy. He loved the idea of them growing their family, but he was also terrified.

Was he ready to be a father? Absolutely, but that didn't mean that he would be a good one. But what scared him more than anything was that he could lose his wife and baby.

When Toni almost died last year after miscarrying her and Craig's baby, Luke feared the same could happen to Christina.

He couldn't lose her.

He had already experienced so much loss in his life. His mother died of cancer when he was ten, and his father, an NYPD cop, had been killed in the line of duty the year Luke graduated from law school. Then, Luke's half-brother had been killed by a mob boss.

Luke could admit to being a little paranoid, but he would never recover if anything happened to Christina or their unborn child.

That's why he'd been so overprotective of her, especially now that she was pregnant. She complained that he was driving her nuts with his constant need to know where she was at all times and asking how she was doing. He couldn't help it. She meant everything to him.

Luke picked up his cell phone, knowing he needed to respond to her text message. No sense in bringing up Atlanta. He knew why she hadn't told him. She didn't want an argument. If he was honest, neither did he, but he also didn't want her traveling.

He pinched the bridge of his nose and growled under his breath. He also didn't want her upset. They'd have to talk at some point, and instead of saying anything about Atlanta, he typed:

My love for you grows every day, and not just because you're a helluva cook. Thanks for dinner. I should be home by the time you get there. Be safe.

Now, all he had to do was keep his head when he talked with her tonight.

***

The calming scent of rose and lavender wafted from the diffuser near the entrance to the ballroom, and Christina inhaled deeply. It had been a long day of meetings, and she was ready to head home. But her grandmother had insisted on being brought up to date with the plans for the family reunion.

"We have a month left. How's everything looking?" Katherine asked just as Jada rushed into the room and took a seat.

There were at least twenty of them at the meeting. More than Christina had expected. The group included her mom, Velvet, Christina's female cousins, aunts, and some of the women who'd married into the family. The reunion committee also included some of the Jenkins men, but only a few were present.

"You all know I want this to be the best reunion anyone has ever attended," Gram said.

Christina smiled at her grandmother who had a notepad and pen in her hands as if she was in a classroom taking notes. She was serious about this reunion being the best. Especially since she and Christina's grandfather were investing a lot of money into making it just that. They hadn't charged a reunion fee since the event was last minute. People attending had to pay for the T-shirts they all planned

115

to wear during the picnic, as well as their housing. Except those who were staying on the estate, which included the main house and a four-bedroom, three-bathroom guesthouse.

"The cutoff date to confirm attendance and buy their T-shirts was last weekend. We have over two hundred planning to attend. Some of those will only be participating in parts of the reunion," Toni said, glancing down at the notes on her cell phone. "Oh, and it's good Peyton did a first-come first-serve regarding that Saturday night—the formal night. Otherwise, we would've had to try to find a hotel ballroom at the last minute. Even after the cutoff date, people were still trying to sign up for that event."

"You snooze, you lose. They shouldn't have waited until the last minute," Peyton said, her voice flowing from the laptop in front of one of the sofas. "There will be someone monitoring the door that night with a guest list for those who try to sneak in. I'm also glad we said no kids at the formal."

"What are the plans for the kids?" Katherine asked.

"We assured everyone attending the formal event that we'd have childcare available offsite."

Coordinating that night was going to be tricky. They'd need to get the children to the childcare center at Jenkins & Sons Construction. The new facility had been added on for the employees, but it was going to come in handy on the formal night.

"The ballroom at the house can comfortably hold a hundred people, and even that's pushing it once we add round tables for dinner and a dance floor," Peyton said of the ballroom that Christina and the others were currently meeting in.

Christina glanced around the huge space. The room was divided into three areas: They were currently sitting in the middle of the room where four long sofas were in a square and facing each other. The two other areas included a library space with a comfortable area rug, overstuffed chairs, beanbags, and floor pillows. And at the other end of the room held a baby grand piano, as well as chairs and tables that you would see in a jazz club.

The ballroom was grand with a two-toned, twenty-foot coffered ceiling and a wall of windows that overlooked their grandmother's park-like flower garden. Just beyond that was the guesthouse and extra parking.

"CJ, are all the activities for the weekend set?" her grandmother asked.

"Yes, ma'am. We even planned a game night for Thursday for those arriving early."

Christina was glad for the help she had received from her sister-in-law, Rayne, and a few others assigned to the entertainment committee. Shuttles were in place to get family back and forth to her grandparents' estate and anywhere else they needed to get to as it related to the reunion. Christina and the others had worked tirelessly to make sure they'd thought of everything. That included getting family to and from the park for the picnic and getting the kids to the center on the formal night.

For the next hour, they discussed every aspect of the reunion, including the menu.

"Gram, that's a lot of food that you and Gramps will have to pay for. Are you sure you don't want to scale back?" Martina asked. By not charging a reunion fee, they'd be expected to cover all food costs, as well as everything else.

"The food budget is huge," Peyton said. She was the only one who knew the full budget. Those over the individual committees, like CJ, had a set budget for their role in the family reunion. "So far, as long as Gram and the aunties don't get carried away with shopping, we should be fine."

By the time the meeting was adjourned, it was eight o'clock, and Christina was exhausted. She had alternated between standing and sitting since her back had been giving her problems lately. It also hadn't helped that the baby was pushing against her bladder. She couldn't wait to get home and stretch out.

Which reminded her. She glanced at her cell phone screen, noting that Luke hadn't called or texted. At least not since earlier when he sent her the text expressing his love and thanking her for cooking.

He knew he didn't have to thank her. She loved cooking for him, but she knew he felt guilty because of the late hours he'd been keeping lately. It wasn't his norm, and she knew one of the reasons for his long days was because he was trying to close a few cases before the baby arrived. He planned to take a month of family leave to be with her and their little one.

A smile touched her lips with that thought. It'll be like the blind leading the blind since they both were entering new territory. It was still mind-blowing that she would soon be a mommy. As if on cue, the baby started moving and kicking.

Christina settled her hands on her stomach. "Calm down in there," she mumbled, glad that he...or she, listened. She wanted a boy, but Luke was adamant that it would be a girl. They had decided to be surprised, but she was pretty sure they were going to have a junior.

One of the last to leave the room, she grabbed her large handbag and smiled as Jada approached her. The woman was a walking billboard for all things sexy and chic. The mustard-colored, one-shoulder dress hugged her curves and tapered in to show off her tiny waist. The small, dark gold feathers along the hem and bust line made the outfit unique. There was no doubt that it was a JJ original. Matching strappy sandals and silver jewelry round out the outfit.

"I know you didn't get all dolled up to come to a family reunion meeting," Christina said, giving her a hug. "Where you been?"

"Girl, it's been a busy day. I forgot about the meeting. It's a good thing Toni texted me asking where I was. At the time, Zack and I were leaving dinner."

"How could you forget? Toni only reminded us like a thousand times the other day during brunch."

"I know. I know. I've had so much on my mind, but at least the situation with Gina is almost over. That hubby of yours is a godsend," Jada said, filling Christina in on the latest. "Oh, shoot. I almost forgot I brought you something. Don't move."

Jada hurried out of the room, and within a few minutes, she was back with a white garment bag. She unzipped it, and Christina squealed when she saw the maxi dress tunic in beautiful, bold colors with a split up one side. Navy blue skinny pants hung beneath it.

"Oh, my goodness. This is stunning." And way dressier than Christina usually wore. "As big as I've gotten, I don't know if it'll fit."

"Girl don't worry. The material has some give in it, and it'll fit fine. Besides, it'll show off your cute baby bump."

"Oh, please. This is more than a baby bump. I'm at thirty-one weeks, and I can barely see my feet," Christina said, holding the dress across the front of her body. The abstract design and colors of blue, orange, purple, yellow, and red popped. She loved colors, especially when it came to her attire.

"Did you design this?"

"Yep, and this is the first one I've had made. I need you to rock it so that others will ask about the designer. And I know you're not a fan of heels, but because of the length of the tunic, you'll need to wear at least two-inch heels or taller."

"Jada, this is so generous. Thank you."

"You're welcome. I designed it with you in mind. I told Luke to tell you that I had it for you, but that was when I had forgotten about the reunion meeting."

"Yeah, I haven't seen him all day. I need to get out of here. Tonight, I'm going to tell him about Atlanta. I want him to go with me, but since I waited until the last minute to tell—"

"Wait. He doesn't know about Atlanta?" Jada said in a rush, her eyes suddenly big and round. "CJ, you were supposed to tell him a couple of weeks ago! Oh, no. This is not good." She covered her face with her hands before dropping them.

Christina frowned. "What? I'm going to tell him tonight."

"He knows," Jada mumbled, and then she told Christina about her conversation with him in his office.

Christina felt sick, and it had nothing to do with her pregnancy. Luke was going to be livid. He knew about the show in Atlanta, but he didn't know that she planned to attend.

This is so not good.

Chapter Nineteen

An hour later, Christina released a heavy sigh as she rode the elevator up to her and Luke's apartment. She was not looking forward to the conversation that she should've had months ago. The conversation that should've started something like—*I changed my mind. I'm not done traveling.*

But no. She had agreed with him that she wasn't going to Atlanta, and she would let her agent attend the show without her. She vowed that she wouldn't do any more traveling until after the baby was born.

What had she been thinking? Painting was her career. It was the one thing that gave her a creative outlet. The one thing that gave her a sense of purpose. The one thing that she had control over. Instead, she was having a baby in a couple of months, and she was scared silly.

How could she explain to her husband that taking a break from painting and traveling to art shows was stifling a huge part of her?

He would never understand.

The elevator stopped on the top floor. This was something else that was changing in a few weeks. They were in the middle of searching for a house, a place that would give them more space than the loft that she'd purchased before they'd gotten married.

Everything was changing, and she wasn't sure she was ready.

Christina stilled her nerves as she entered the loft. The open floor plan gave her a view of the kitchen, dining area, and great room. Luke was sitting at the dining table eating. He was also totally engrossed in the basketball game that blared from the sixty-five-inch television hanging over the fireplace.

While he cursed and talked back to the TV, she studied him. He had shed his suit for a T-shirt and sweats and looked more relaxed than she'd seen him in days. It didn't matter how long they were together, each time she looked at him, she fell deeper in love.

Christina had always been attracted to dark-skinned men, and from the first time she'd seen Luke, she'd been hooked. They'd met at one of Zack's parties. Right away, she recognized an edginess about Luke that spoke to her soul. He was such a contradiction. He could recite the U.S. Constitution in one breath, then spit the lyrics to any rap song in the next. He gave Renaissance man a whole new meaning.

Christina's gaze ate him up. Luke had smooth skin the color of mocha and an athletic body that looked good in and out of clothes. He might've been a prestigious lawyer, but his rugged handsomeness and swagger were better suited for the cover of Esquire magazine.

The man was *fine*.

Luke glanced up, and his eyes widened in surprise. "Hey, baby," he said, wiping his mouth with a napkin and then turning down the TV volume. He moved across the room toward her with the grace of a panther. She loved his walk. Or a better description would be—his swagger. The man was the total package...still.

He wrapped his strong arms around her and kissed her sweetly. Jada might've been mistaken. Maybe he didn't know about the trip. She thought he'd be sitting in the dark, brooding while waiting for her to come home. Or maybe his calm demeanor was a test to see if she'd bring up the topic of Atlanta.

"You doin' okay?" he asked, then moved his hands down her body and rubbed her stomach.

"Yeah, I'm fine, and our little athlete in here has been active today."

Luke bent down and kissed her belly so lovingly, Christina almost whimpered. Apparently, she wasn't the only one affected by his gentleness. The baby chose that moment to act as if he was playing kickball or maybe boxing.

Her husband met her gaze and smiled. Feeling their baby move still left her and Luke in awe.

Christina grinned back at him. "He was probably giving you a high five."

"*She* was probably trying to hug me and kiss me back," he said.

They shared a laugh, and as Luke stood to his full height, her heart melted. Christina loved this man with her whole being, and she felt so blessed to have him in her life.

Emotion gripped her, and she reached out to cup his cheek.

"I love you so much," she said just above a whisper.

She caressed the soft stubble on his jaw with the pad of her thumb. His expression was serious as he stared into her eyes. Then he covered her hand with his, turned his head slightly, and placed a kiss inside her palm.

"I love you too," he said, his stoic expression remaining the same as he eased away from her.

She released a quiet sigh. *He definitely knows about Atlanta.*

That anxiousness from earlier returned, and Christina knew she had to bring up the subject. But Luke left her standing between the kitchen and great room while he headed to the refrigerator.

He pulled out a beer and asked, "Are you hungry? Did you eat anything?"

"I made a cranberry pecan and sweet potato casserole earlier. I ate a little of it before I left."

Over the years, she had wafted between pescatarian and vegetarian and had recently settled on pescatarian though she didn't eat a lot of seafood.

"I also snacked some at my grandparents' house."

Christina sat her handbag in one of the dining chairs and leaned on the back of it. She and Luke had always been able to talk about anything, but lately, they'd been having more disagreements. That was another reason why she'd kept postponing the conversation about Atlanta.

"So, you heard I'm planning on attending the art show."

She tried to sound nonchalant even though inside she was a nervous wreck. No excuse for not telling him seemed strong enough, and thoughts of what to say fluttered through her mind.

Luke set the beer bottle on the kitchen island and braced his hands on top of the granite countertop. He didn't look at her right away, but when he did, her chest tightened. He wasn't angry. What she saw in his gaze was disappointment. For her, that was worse than him being angry.

"I'm sorry I didn't mention it earlier. I was planning on talking to you tonight because I wanted to see if you'd be able to travel with me next weekend."

He released a humorless laugh. "Oh, so now that I know that you're going, you want to invite me along?" The bitterness in his tone made Christina stiffen.

"Luke, I honestly planned on discussing this with you tonight. I hadn't said anything sooner because I was trying to avoid an argument."

"Christina, we've already talked about this. You're over seven months pregnant. We agreed that you wouldn't do any more traveling until after the baby was born. Traveling at this point is not safe."

"My doctor said that I'm fine to travel." She moved to stand next to Luke in the kitchen. "You know what? The trip can be a babymoon for us. We haven't taken one, and it could be fun. We can attend the show, then add a couple of days to our stay, and—"

"I'm preparing for trial and will be in court all next week. This isn't a good time for a babymoon."

"Well, how about we attend the art show together and—"

"Christina, I can't just drop everything. You know my job doesn't work like that."

She threw up her hands. "Fine. Forget I asked. I'll go alone or see if Peyton can meet me there."

Actually, maybe those would be better options. Peyton was already planning to attend the show. Maybe they could share a...

"Dammit, CJ!" Luke pounded on the counter, startling her. When she glanced at him, his handsome features were twisted in frustration.

She didn't like upsetting him, but she'd be lying if she said that the heat radiating off of him wasn't turning her on. Crazy? Probably. But Luke had a bad-boy side that did wicked things to her, and that side of him was showing.

Or maybe it was her hormones. She had always had a healthy sexual appetite, and Luke's matched hers. Their sex life had been on another level during her pregnancy. She couldn't get enough of him and vice versa.

"You don't get it, do you?" Luke said, snapping her out of her thoughts. "I don't want you traveling right now, especially if I can't be with you. What if something happened while you were away? I wouldn't be able to get to you fast enough."

Christina sighed and leaned her hip against the kitchen counter. "Luke, I love that you're concerned about me and our baby, but lately it's been too much." At first, she thought it was sweet—him hovering and the constant *are you doing okay*—now it felt almost suffocating. The closer she got to her due date, the more protective he got.

Instead of responding, his sharp, assessing eyes held an intensity that served him well in the courtroom. But not here. Not now. They had a problem, and she didn't know how to fix it. Seconds ticked by as she held his gaze, but then she took in his chiseled jaw and juicy lips that had brought her more pleasure than any woman deserved.

Christina was tempted to whip out a canvas and paint him. She had several of him, even in the nude. Those were for her private collection, and no one would ever know they were of him...except for her. The man's body was a work of art. If she'd ever had a mind to sell paintings of him, she'd make a killing. But she'd never sell them—even if no one could tell they were him, she'd know.

When he still didn't speak, she said, "I wish I could make you understand that being pregnant is not a disability. I can still do everything I usually do." Well, mostly, but she didn't add that part. She'd always kept a healthy weight and was in great shape. Yet, the bigger she got, the slower she moved. And if she was honest, the simplest activities tired her out—like grocery shopping and climbing flights of stairs.

Still, she wasn't helpless, and she needed him to understand that.

He remained silent and Christina sighed again, louder this time. "Luke, I'm sorry. I'm sorry I didn't tell you that I wanted to attend the art show. More than anything, I'm sorry I went back on my word. I promised no more traveling for a while, and this is my last art show for the foreseeable future. Knowing that is not easy for me, and I'm going to miss this part of my life. A part that means so much to me. Of course, none of this means more to me than you and our baby, but...I need to attend this show."

Still, he didn't respond. Only stared at her.

Fine. She turned to leave him standing there.

If he can't understand that, to hell with it and him.

Chapter Twenty

Luke couldn't leave the conversation like this. He hated when they argued. He hated it even more that his wife felt that she couldn't talk to him. Any other time, she would've told him about her travel plans the moment she knew them.

So, this was bad, and he needed to get over himself and fix it.

When Christina started moving away, Luke stopped her by sliding his arm around her midsection. She stiffened, but relaxed as he pulled her against the front of his body.

"I'm sorry," he whispered, burying his face into her mass of curls and breathing in the lavender scent of the shampoo she used. He placed a lingering kiss against her cheek, and they stood rooted in place while he held her tightly.

She was the most important person in his life—his only family left. Of course, he was protective. He was afraid of losing her like he'd lost his parents and brother. Not much scared him, but he hated this fear that crept through him from time to time. Abandonment issues? Probably. Therapy after his father was killed had helped, and overall, Luke felt like he was fine. But if he didn't get his shit together, he'd have to consider going back.

He gently caressed Christina's stomach, and his heart did a little jig inside his chest.

They were bringing a baby into the world, and Luke was scared to death for more reasons than one. There were days that he still couldn't believe that he was going to be a father. *A father*. He was going to be responsible for another human being, and he wanted to get it right.

He was looking forward to fatherhood, but it wasn't something he thought he ever wanted. He hadn't ever planned to settle down, get married, and have a family. Hell, for a while, he thought he was incapable of letting someone get that close. But then Christina came along and blew down all the barriers he had built around his heart.

He loved this woman.

That meant trying to see things from her perspective and supporting her in every way possible. No, he wasn't comfortable with her going to Atlanta, but he didn't want her unhappy.

Minutes ticked by without a word, and though they'd just argued, the silence was comfortable. Unfortunately, Luke knew they needed to finish their conversation.

"You and this baby are all I have, and sometimes...I...I get possessive. I let fear get in the way and become unreasonable." He tried to keep the emotion out of his voice, but he heard it, and he was sure she had too. "But I only want the best for you, and I want you happy."

"Oh, Luke." She started to turn in his arms to look at him, but he needed to finish his apology.

"I'm sorry for the way I've been treating you and the way I've been acting," he said, meaning every word. "I'm sorry that you felt that you couldn't talk to me about the trip. I never want you to feel that you can't tell me anything. And I'm sorry that you have to give up a part of yourself to have our—"

"No!" Christina hurried to say and turned in his arms. "Stop right there. First of all, you make me extremely happy. I love the life I have with you. Secondly, I am thrilled about having your baby. It's all a little scary, but it's one of the most exciting times of my life. What I love most? I get to share this experience with you."

She kissed his lips and caressed his cheek as she stared into his eyes. The love he felt in that simple gesture made his heart beat a little faster. Luke felt beyond blessed that she was his, and he hoped he never had to experience the world without her in it.

He needed to figure out how to stop pushing his fears, specifically fear of losing her, onto her. He'd always been overprotective of those he loved, and he couldn't help it. That's just the man he was. But he needed to make some changes. No more hovering. No more smothering, and no more being afraid that he was somehow going to lose her.

"I'll eventually figure out how to have it all—my career, our family..." she said. "But you and our baby are my priority. Still, I need to go to this art show. I need to be there in the midst of it all, soaking up the energy until I can return to painting."

It wasn't that she had to stop painting, but early in her pregnancy, some of the smells of paint made her sick. Lately, she'd been hanging out in her art room, but she was doing more sketching than painting.

"Will you be okay with me going to Atlanta?"

"Yes," he said without hesitation.

What else could he say? She was going with or without him. He knew she'd keep painting once the baby was born, something he wanted her to do. He just didn't like the idea of her traveling without him. "I'm going to figure out how to go with you."

Christina smiled, and suddenly the room seemed brighter. She had that type of effect on him. Actually, she had that effect on everyone who knew her.

"Thank you for understanding." She gave him a quick kiss. "I know work is busy for you right now, and if you can't go with me, no worries. It's only for a weekend. I'll talk to Peyton."

"If she can spend that Friday with you, I'll catch a flight out Saturday morning. I'll figure something out. I like the babymoon idea and want to make sure we do that." He had never heard of such a thing, but they needed time away together before they became parents.

"Now, onto another subject. Sumeera lined up a couple of houses for us to tour on Sunday." He opened his mouth to speak, but she placed a finger on his lips to keep him quiet. "Before you say you're too busy, this is important. I need you to make time."

Luke dropped his arms from around her and released an exaggerated sigh. "Damn, woman. You're just trying to hog all my time."

Christina laughed and slapped his chest. "Quit playing. You know you're just as excited as I am about finding a bigger place."

He hated house hunting, but she was right. Knowing they were looking for their forever home to raise their growing family was exciting.

"You're right. I'll make time. We need to find a place soon. Otherwise, my daughter will be born before we've set everything up for her."

Christina laughed. "You are not slick. I see what you did there. I don't know why you think we're having a girl. This little guy inside of me is a boy."

Luke smiled and pulled her close. She wrapped her arms around him and stared up at him with a grin on her tempting lips. Sometimes he wished they hadn't agreed to wait to find out the sex of the baby. He wanted to know, but he would be fine with either a boy or a girl. He just liked the idea of being a girl dad.

"My gut tells me it's a girl," he said and covered her lips with his, slipping her a little tongue in the process. Christina moaned against his mouth, and all thoughts of houses and babies flew from his mind. "I think we should officially make up...in the bedroom...with you naked," he said when the kiss ended.

Christina palmed his butt with both hands, making him laugh.

"I've always loved the way you think," she said as she squeezed his ass.

"Yeah, right," he said, still laughing, but he sucked in a breath when she cupped his dick. The way she massaged his package made it clear what she wanted, and he was here for it. "Come on my little freak." He swung her up into his arms. "Let's go make up."

Christina looped her arms around his neck as he carried her to their bedroom. "Like I said, I love the way you think."

He hated when they argued, but he loved the way they made up.

***

Christina was lying flat on her back. Her knees were bent, and her hand rested on her chest as if that would help get breath into her lungs. Sex with Luke was always mind-blowing, but it seemed her orgasms were even more intense now that she was pregnant.

Her man had worked her into a frenzy with his mouth, tongue, and hands. He'd kissed, licked, and brought pleasure to every inch of her body before waves of ecstasy sent her tumbling over the edge of control.

She swallowed hard. Luke wasn't done. He kissed his way back up her body, the stubble on his face tickling her heated skin. He didn't stop until he reached her breasts.

Her nipples were so sensitive. It didn't take much to get her fired up again. He squeezed her breasts together and swirled his tongue around one pebbled peak before showing the other the same attention. With each tug and lick, he had her toes curling and desire pulsing through her veins.

When she released a long moan, Luke's gaze met hers and he lifted his head to stare down at her. "You okay?" he asked, his voice deep and raspy.

"I'm wonderful," she murmured, her body rebounding as she looked into his dark eyes. "I'm better than wonderful, and I'm ready for round two. On your back, Loverboy."

She pushed against his chest, and he flashed that hot, sexy grin that always made her want to ride him until he couldn't take anymore.

Once he was lying down, she lifted up on her elbow and swept her gaze over his muscular chest and his six-pack abs that looked as if they'd been drawn onto his stomach. Then her gaze went lower to his erection that stood at attention waiting for her. Instead of taking him into her mouth, she straddled him, and slowly, inch-by-inch, she sank down on his long, thick shaft.

He cursed under his breath and slammed his eyes shut as his fingers dug into her hips. Luke held her steady while Christina placed her hands on his hard chest. She used it as leverage while she slid up and down his length.

She had always loved being on top, and these days it was the most comfortable sexual position for her. The problem was she usually lost control faster than she preferred.

Luke felt too damn good. His penis pulsed inside of her, filling her completely while she barely hung on for the ride.

Christina wanted to take her time and savor every minute with him inside of her. But when she rocked her hips, what started as a slow grind quickly picked up speed. She couldn't help it, especially when Luke matched her stroke for stroke.

"Damn, you on top does something to me. And when your beautiful breasts bounce up and down like that..."

Luke groaned with pleasure and showed off his powerful abs by lifting slightly. With one hand on the bed and the other on her lower back, he slowed her moves and sucked one of her nipples into his mouth.

"Luke," she breathed, her eyes tightly closed as pleasure zigzagged inside of her. She wasn't going to be able to hang on.

"Aww, shi..." Luke growled through gritted teeth just as she was about to tell him she was coming.

He fell back against the pillows, lifted his hips, and drove in and out of her like a piston. Christina lost it, screaming his name as her release plowed through her with more force than the previous one. Luke was right behind her.

Oh my goodness.

Exhaustion gripped her, and she almost collapsed on top of him, but Luke caught her. He lowered her to the bed on her side as they gasped for air. He lay beside her with his hands on her stomach as their heavy breathing filled the quietness of the room.

Seconds ticked by, and Christina knew what was coming next when he lifted up on one elbow and stared down at her.

"You okay?" he asked, concern in his voice.

She sputtered a laugh that evolved into full-blown laughter. He was being such a worrywart, but she loved him anyway.

"I'm fine, baby. Just trying to catch my breath." His expression turned concerned, but before he could say anything, she said, "Luke, stop worrying. I'm *fine*, and I can't wait to do that again."

His eyebrows knitted together, and he shook his head. When he dropped back down on the bed, he flung his arm over his eyes. "I could barely keep up with you before we got pregnant, and now I'm sure I can't. What the hell type of hormones do you have charging you?"

Christina laughed so hard that tears filled her eyes. "I don't know, but you're doing just fine keeping up with me." She snuggled against him. "Now get some rest. I might want to do that again before the night is over."

Within seconds, Luke's snores rumbled near her ears, and Christina smiled as she drifted off to sleep.

Chapter Twenty-One

"Have I mentioned today how glad I am that you're my husband?" Christina asked when Luke pulled into the driveway of a home that her cousin-in-law, Sumeera, planned to show them.

Luke chuckled and parked. "I don't think you have, but the feeling is mutual. I'm glad you're my wife."

He undid his seatbelt and reached over, cupped her neck, and claimed her mouth. He tasted of peppermint, and the scent of his woodsy cologne surrounded her like a warm embrace. With each lap of his tongue, Christina wanted more...more of him.

An involuntary moan slipped through as he deepened their lip-lock. The man was good at everything, and that included kissing. She loved the way he took his time and worshiped her mouth the way he usually did her body—completely and thoroughly.

His fingers tangled in her curls as their kiss grew more intense. They needed to get into the house, but she didn't want to stop. Hell, if it was left up to her, and if she was as flexible as she used to be, she'd suggest they climb into the back seat for a quickie. But they didn't have time. Besides, though he usually went along with her sexual desires, he would nix that one. Mainly because she was pregnant. In the past, they'd had sex anywhere and everywhere.

A loud whistle pierced the air, and Christina jerked her head up. Just over Luke's shoulder, she saw Sumeera standing in the walkway with one hand on her hip and the other near her mouth, ready to whistle again.

Luke glanced behind him, then turned back to Christina and grinned. "It's a good thing she stopped us. Otherwise, I would've taken you right here and right now."

Christina laughed and gave him a quick peck on the lips. "I so love the way you think, but we should probably get in there. Let's hope this is the house of our dreams."

"Yeah, let's hope."

When they climbed out of the car, Sumeera was shaking her head and grinning. "Well, it's about time. For a minute there, I thought you guys were going to climb into the back seat."

"You know us so well," Christina cracked, and Sumeera laughed.

Christina and Luke walked hand in hand as they slowly strolled up the walkway.

"Like I mentioned on the phone. This is a five-bedroom, three-bathroom home that sits on an acre lot. The HOA fee I told you about on the telephone covers the front lawn, the community pool, and snow shoveling. You guys will be responsible for the backyard and the exterior of the home."

She gave them a few more details before she reentered the house, leaving them outside.

Christina took in the front of the home. It was ticking off some of the items on their wish list, including a three-car garage, two-story brick, and perfectly manicured grounds.

"This is beautiful," Christina said. "So far, based on the outside, I like this house better than the others we saw today."

"Yeah, me too," Luke said but slowed before they reached the front door. "I'd want these bushes cut back or removed. I don't like that you can't see around them. That's not safe for you and our baby, especially if I'm not here and you're coming in at night."

Christina smiled. Always the protector. The last place had trees in the yard that he would've wanted cut down for the same reason. She didn't respond. She appreciated how he looked out for her well-being, even in cases like this.

When they entered the house, Christina's breath caught.

"Impressive, isn't it?" Sumeera said, grinning.

The two-story foyer had sparkling dark hardwood floors and deep gray walls. Off to the side was a wide, spiral staircase that led to the second floor. Christina always appreciated a good paint job, and from what she could see, the color scheme throughout the open floor plan was on point.

"It's gorgeous," she said as she moved farther into the house. "You did good, Meera."

She took in the large kitchen with stainless steel appliances and a long center island. The first floor also had a family room, a spectacular office for Luke, and a half bathroom. She liked that one of the bedrooms was on the main level and included an attached bathroom.

It was nice having a real estate agent in the family. Sumeera, who was married to Christina's cousin, Nick, knew what they wanted, and her cousin-in-law nailed it with this home.

"I like that we could just move in without doing renovations," Luke said.

The other places they toured came close but were fixer-uppers. Christina wouldn't have had a problem with a few renovations since her family owned a construction company. But Luke didn't want them to have any projects so close to the baby's due date.

"I'll let you both head upstairs, and let me know if you have any questions," Sumeera said.

After Christina climbed the stairs, she rubbed her back, which was bothering her again. There was just enough of an ache to be irritating. She was sure it was because she'd had a restless night, unable to get in a comfortable position.

Without a word, Luke placed his hand on the small of her back and began rubbing it. Damn, the man. He didn't miss anything, which probably added to him being such a good lawyer. "That feels good. Thank you," she said and started checking out the second floor. "Five bedrooms seem to be a lot."

"Five bedrooms might seem like a lot, but by the time we have a couple of kids the space will shrink," Luke rationalized. "One room will be your art studio, one room will be a nursery, and another will be a guest room. Then there's the master bedroom. That only leaves one extra bedroom."

"Mmm, that's a good point," Christina said as they entered the room next door to the master bedroom. It was a nursery decorated in yellow, mint green, baby blue, and white. There was a mural on the far wall of hot air balloons of various colors and sizes. The space was so beautifully done that Christina fell in love with it.

"This would be a perfect space for our son," she said wistfully.

Luke *tsked*. "Our daughter will love it."

Christina grinned up at him, then returned her attention back to the gorgeous space. She loved everything about the house and could totally see them raising their kids there.

"I think we should make an offer," Luke said before she could say anything, and Christina laughed.

"I was thinking the same thing. I've seen enough. This is our new home."

Luke moved behind her and wrapped his arms around her midsection. "I agree. Now we have to come up with an offer they can't refuse."

"Good thing I'm married to a powerful attorney who *insists* on giving me everything I want. I have complete faith in you getting us this house."

"Oh, the pressure," he quipped and kissed the side of her head. "Let's get Sumeera on it. Then I'm taking you home so that you can get off your feet."

"Is that your way of trying to get me naked and into bed?" she joked.

Luke laughed and held her tighter, kissing the side of her neck. "Yeah, let's go with that. Come on. Let's go buy this house."

Chapter Twenty-Two

Luke strolled into the Law Offices of Jenkins & Associates with renewed energy. It was always a good day when he won a case. Throughout the trial, he had poked holes in the prosecution's case and felt confident that he could win. But he hadn't been positive until the jury spoke those two magic words—*not guilty*.

It's been a good week, he thought.

A few days ago, he and Christina learned that the seller accepted their offer on the house and agreed to a quick closing. Luke had hoped to be in the place before the baby was born, but they were cutting it close. At least they had finally found a home and could scratch that off their list of things to do.

Now, if he could get through the rest of the day without thinking about how Christina was traveling alone, he might be able to maintain his sanity. She was at the airport, and he was trying not to text her...again. It gave him a little peace, knowing that she and Peyton should arrive in Atlanta around the same time. Knowing her sister would be there made him feel a lot better, and it would give Christina a day and a half to hang with her.

After greeting his assistant, Luke entered his office, flipped on the lights, and rounded his desk. He dropped down into his seat and released a long sigh of relief. Instead of addressing the messages on his desk, he took a moment to lay his head back and closed his eyes. Not even a minute had passed before his cell phone vibrated in his pocket.

So much for taking a break.

He opened his eyes, pulled out the device, and glanced at the screen.

Michael: Call me when you can.

There were a few people in Luke's life who he always made time for, and Michael Cutter was one of them. But this text was a bit ominous. Rarely did his friend send messages without including some details.

Curious, Luke called him, and Michael picked up on the first ring.

"What's up, man?" his friend said. There was rustling in the background, and it sounded like Mike was moving around, then Luke heard a door close. "I wasn't expecting to hear from you so quickly. I assumed you'd still be in court."

"Nope. I just returned to my office," Luke said as he skimmed a document that his assistant had left in a folder on his desk. "What's going on? I don't usually hear from you in the middle of the day."

"Randolph Cray is out of prison," Michael said without preamble, and shock blasted through Luke.

"What?" he croaked out, unable to say more than that. He dropped the stack of papers and slammed back against his seat.

"I just found out and figured I'd let you know in case you hadn't heard," Michael explained.

Running a shaky hand over his mouth and down his chin, Luke's brain raced as memories of Randolph flooded his mind. The gangster, also known as Lefty, used to be an enforcer for the L'Arco crime family out of New York.

A few years ago, the guy had gotten arrested for a double murder and had tried to hire Luke to defend him against the charges. After reviewing the case, Luke had refused, and that hadn't gone over well.

"Shit," Luke spat and lurched out of his seat. He paced behind his desk as fifty-million thoughts ricocheted around in his mind. He hadn't expected to ever hear from the man again. But months after Lefty had been sentenced to life in prison, he had gotten a message to Luke.

When I get out of the joint, and I will, I'm coming for you.

Luke rubbed the back of his neck as those words rolled through his mind. "How the hell is that motherfucker out of prison?" he mumbled under his breath more to himself than Michael. "When was he released?"

Luke huffed out a breath and dropped back down in his seat, feeling as if he was carrying the world on his shoulders. He needed to get as much information on Randolph and his case as he could. Last he'd heard, Lefty had appealed the ruling, but it had been denied.

"This morning," Michael said, sounding distracted. "He got a new lawyer, and supposedly there were some procedural errors, and—"

"That's bullshit! I followed that case, and it was airtight," Luke said. "If he's out, there's something bigger at play, and I'd bet my life's savings that it has something to do with the L'Arco family. He had to have cut some type of deal... maybe he gave them some information on the L'Arco family." The same family that Luke believed was involved in his own brother's murder, but it had never been proven.

"You might be right, but let's be cool about this. Lefty might—"

"Are you tracking him?" Luke interrupted. "I want to know where he is at all times, and I'll pay whatever your fee."

He and Michael had met while Luke lived in New York and had been friends for as long as Luke could remember. They'd had each other's back during some of the most horrendous times of their lives. Outside of Christina, there was no one in the world that Luke trusted more to have his back.

"Right now, he's lying low. He's staying at a woman's house in Harlem. Rumor has it, he's changed. He found Jesus while locked up and was a model prisoner for the last four years."

Luke half expected his friend to say, *Just kidding*, but that never came.

"You're serious?" Luke asked after a few seconds. "He's had a come to Jesus moment, and you actually believe that shit? You don't think he's going to make good on his threat?"

"To be honest, I think he has more pressing issues to think about," Michael reasoned. "If the L'Arco family didn't get him out, they're going to think that he talked...that he cut some type of deal that could incriminate them in some way. Let's not panic until we know more."

Luke's heart rate inched up as his mind whirled a hundred miles a minute. He didn't scare easily, and he knew how to handle himself. That was thanks to growing up with a cop for a father. But it wasn't just his safety at stake. He had a family now, and he would bury anyone if they even thought about going after Christina and his unborn child.

He rubbed his chest as if that would ease the tightness that he suddenly felt. Lefty was one of the most ruthless men Luke had ever met. He wouldn't put anything past the bastard, and knowing Christina was on her way to Atlanta wasn't helping Luke's mood. She was unprotected. Even if Peyton knew self-defense and knew how to handle a gun, something that Michael taught her early in their marriage, it wouldn't be enough. If he wanted to, Lefty wouldn't hesitate to kill them both.

"I have eyes on him, but I'm telling you, man, I don't think you're going to have any trouble out of him. Based on my sources, Lefty is not like he used to be. If it'll make you feel better, I'll see what I can do about getting close to him. At least close enough to get a read on him."

Luke might trust Mike, but he couldn't make himself believe that Randolph had changed. He thought the worst of the guy back then and even more so now.

"Until then, I need some protection on me, but especially for Christina and Peyton. I hope you're right in thinking that we have nothing to worry about, but just in case..."

"I have a friend in Atlanta who works for a security firm. I'll give him a call now."

"Is this firm any good? I want the best protecting my wife, Mike, and I don't care about the cost."

Michael snorted. "And what? You think I don't want the best for Peyton? Your ass is lucky you're too far away for me to smack you."

If Luke wasn't so anxious, he'd laugh. He knew how protective Michael was of Peyton. If anyone so much as looked at his wife the wrong way, they'd regret it. So, it was a good sign that his friend didn't sound worried, but still, Luke wanted security in place when CJ landed.

"I'm sorry, man. I didn't mean to imply that you weren't worried about Peyton," Luke said. "I'm just... This has caught me off guard. Who do you have in mind as far as providing protection?"

"My guy, Myles Carrington, is former CIA, and he works for Supreme Security—Atlanta. I've told you about them. They're also known as Atlanta's Finest, and they are the best of the best. Trust me on this."

Luke did trust him, and he also recalled Mike mentioning Atlanta's Finest in conversation. They also had a firm in Chicago. "Yeah, I remember, and I just thought of something else. I don't want to tell Christina about Lefty unless I have no other choice. She's anxious about the show, and I don't want her worrying unnecessarily."

Michael agreed. "When will you get to Atlanta?"

"Not until Saturday," Luke said. "See if you can get a few people on our women without them knowing."

Luke hoped he was overreacting and that they had nothing to worry about. But he wasn't taking any chances with his wife and their baby.

Chapter Twenty-Three

Christina had arrived at Hartsfield-Jackson Atlanta International Airport and was slowly making her way through the terminal. She could see why the place was dubbed the busiest airport. There were travelers everywhere. Some had just deplaned and were anxious to get to baggage claim, while others were rushing with carry-on luggage trying to get to their gates.

She only traveled with a carry-on and a handbag, but she still needed to get to the baggage claim area. Thank goodness there was a train to take her there because she couldn't imagine walking to it. She hated to admit it, but Luke might've been right about her traveling right now. The turbulence had been horrible, and her back was bothering her. Add in swollen ankles and exhaustion, and she was tempted to find a corner in the terminal to take a nap.

But she couldn't.

One: because a ten-minute nap might turn into a three-hour one. And two: Peyton had already arrived and was meeting her near baggage claim.

Christina smiled at the thought, and knowing her sister was already there gave her a little burst of energy. She hadn't seen PJ in person in a few months and couldn't wait to spend time with her. Sure, she was looking forward to the art show, but more than that, she couldn't wait to have a slumber party with her big sister.

"Excuse me. Sorry," a woman said when she bumped into Christina as they exited the train. Christina was heading toward the two-story escalator that would take her to the baggage claim area. While the woman was making a beeline to an elevator. She was pushing a large stroller with two kids inside and pulling a carry-on suitcase behind her.

God, that might be me one day.

Christina shivered at the idea of traveling with kids. She could barely handle traveling alone, and this trip was showing her that she wasn't in as good of shape as she thought. She was huffing and puffing with every step. How the heck was she going to get around with a baby, stroller, and diaper bag along with everything else?

Before she could go down that mental rabbit hole of fearing that she wasn't cut out for motherhood, she thought she heard someone call her name.

"CJ!"

Christina slowed and glanced around, recognizing Peyton's voice but she didn't see her right away. Once she spotted her, she had to stop herself from squealing and running toward her. Instead, she walked a little faster. Her heart was so full of love as Peyton closed the distance between them.

Tears pricked Christina's eyes. Damn, hormones. These days, she teared up whether happy or sad, and she felt like such a dweeb for doing so.

"Oh, my God. You are too cute," Peyton gushed and engulfed Christina in a big hug. "Let me look at you," she said, pulling back and touching Christina's belly. "How's my niece or nephew?"

"Busy. This kid has been moving around more than usual and wearing me out. At least she or he doesn't have their foot pushed up against my bladder like earlier."

Peyton chuckled and linked her free arm through Christina's. "Ahh yes. The joys of being pregnant."

Christina rolled her eyes. "Yeah, the joys, and speaking of the joys, can we get a bite to eat before we leave? I'm starving."

Peyton grinned and pointed at a chain restaurant that was near baggage claim. "How about there?"

"As long as they have food, it works for me."

A short while later, they were seated at a table eating.

"Do you have to meet with Mandy today?" Peyton asked Christina's agent. "I assume you guys will need to make sure everything is in order at the art gallery."

Mandy Gibson was a godsend in so many ways. Christina had signed with her a few years ago, after firing her first agent, Valerie, who had betrayed her trust. She had wanted Christina to be more in the spotlight—something CJ hadn't been ready for. Christina painted under an alias, and Valerie wanted her to reveal herself. She'd claimed that with Christina's talent and good looks, she'd sell even more of her work.

Christina had refused, not ready for the public to know her, even under her alias—Sasha Knight. But Valerie had taken the choice from her by leaking her identity to a magazine. Luke had been livid. The first time he'd met the agent, he'd called her shady. Then Valerie went on to prove his assessment of her was correct. By the time Luke was finished with her, and other clients found out about her betrayal, Valerie had lost most of her clients. Christina hadn't seen or heard from her since.

"She's going to meet us in the morning, but I've worked with this art gallery before, and they are extremely organized. They're great at displaying artists' work."

And if they didn't, Mandy would set them straight. Luke had been the one to find her, and Christina could admit that he'd chosen a winner. She was amazing, and Christina couldn't have made a better choice herself.

She went back to eating but stopped when the hairs on the back of her neck stood at attention. She hunched her shoulders at the weird sensation. It felt as if she was being watched, but as she glanced around, she didn't notice anyone looking at her.

I'm probably just tired, she thought.

"How's everything at home?" Christina asked as she moved her salad around with her fork. "Have you told Michael how you've been feeling about leaving New York?"

Peyton blew out a slow breath. "Not yet. His number one priority has been to keep me and the kids happy. I think if I want to relocate, he'll go along with it even if he doesn't want to."

"And that's why you haven't said anything," Christina surmised.

"Exactly. He loves Brooklyn and thinks there's no better city in the world. I'd hate to uproot him and the kids just because I'm a little homesick."

"Maybe it's more than just being homesick. Maybe you need a change. It happens. You guys could always split your time between Brooklyn and Cincinnati."

Peyton shook her head. "Not with the kids and their schooling. I want their lives to be as stable as possible."

Christina nodded. *No one ever said that adulting would be easy.* She remembered her mom saying a few months ago. Christina had been complaining about how hard it was going to be juggling marriage, a baby, and work. But women have been doing it for years, and she knew that somehow, she'd figure it out too.

Christina shivered as that weird sensation of being watched returned. Trying not to be too obvious, her gaze bounced around their surroundings. When she returned her attention to Peyton, her sister was frowning.

"What's wrong with you?" She started looking around the way Christina had just done. "You're acting strange. Did you see something?"

Christina leaned in. "No, but have you ever felt like you were being watched?"

Peyton slowly nodded. "I have, but I don't feel like that now. If someone was watching you, wouldn't they be watching me too? Are you feeling okay?"

"Besides a little tired, I feel fine." Except for that sensation of being watched was still hovering over her.

As they cleared the table and strolled away from the restaurant, Christina shook off the strange vibe. Once they got to their hotel and she got a little sleep, she'd be fine.

But that didn't stop her from glancing back toward the restaurant.

***

Saturday afternoon, as the driver neared the art gallery in Midtown Atlanta, Christina inhaled deeply and released the breath slowly. Anxiousness swirled inside of her even though she'd attended plenty of her shows. It never got easier. She put her heart and soul into each piece of art, and knowing that people would critique them, good or bad, made her nervous.

Painting as Sasha Knight helped, though. Some knew what she looked like, thanks to her former agent's betrayal. Yet, there were still a few individuals who didn't recognize her. That gave her a chance to stand back and watch the attendees from a distance.

Okay, here goes, she thought when the driver pulled up in front of the gallery.

A short while later, she and Peyton strolled into the building. There were already quite a few patrons there, and Christina's chest expanded with pride. Though she had seen the set-up, she was pleased with how well everything was displayed. Her abstracts were hanging toward the front of the gallery, and the landscapes were in the middle of the large space. Her nudes were located toward the back of the building, where it appeared the biggest crowd was located.

"I know I said this yesterday," Peyton reached over and squeezed Christina's hand, "but I am so proud of you. It still blows my mind that my little sister is a world-famous artist. Sometimes it doesn't seem real."

Christina smiled, happy that her sister was proud of her. That hadn't always been the case, especially when Christina had started painting nudes. Peyton had expressed her displeasure more than once, and it had nothing to do with Christina's talent. But it had everything to do with her feeling that Christina was sullying the Jenkins family's name. Never mind that she painted under an alias. But over the last few years, Peyton had become one of her biggest cheerleaders.

As they roamed around the huge space, Christina covertly watched the patrons' reactions. For the most part, everyone seemed to appreciate what they were seeing, and she even heard a few *oohs* and *aahs*. This part of the art business never got old. Knowing that people appreciated her work had Christina sticking her chest out with pride. She was living her dream. It didn't matter how many shows she did or how many paintings she sold. The feeling was surreal.

I made it, she thought to herself. She had finally reached a point in her career where she felt like she had accomplished more than she'd set out to do.

"I have always loved this gallery. Darlene, the owner, has a gift of presenting the artwork in the best..." Christina's voice trailed off when she noticed Peyton's frown. "What is it?" she asked.

"Why is there security here?" Peyton asked as she glanced around as if looking for someone. "I thought the guy at the front entrance seemed familiar. Now I know where I remember him from. He's a friend of Michael's."

"You think Michael put security on you?" Christina asked and recalled the creepy feeling she had experienced at the airport.

"Who knows with my husband, but I remember the guy at the front door and the one near the rear of the building. The last time

Michael and I were in Atlanta for an event, the guy at the entrance was a part of the security team. And they weren't just some fly-by-nighter team. They were the best in the business."

Christina glanced back and made eye contact with the guy at the front of the building. She'd seen him the night before when she and Peyton arrived at the gallery. He was hard to miss. Well over six-feet tall, with beautiful dark skin, and a well-toned body that looked as if he spent plenty of time in the gym. But last night, like everyone else, he was roaming around checking out the art. Apparently, he'd been looking at more than paintings.

"I'll ask Darlene," Christina said and looked around for the owner. Darlene was taller than most women, especially wearing heels. So, it shouldn't be hard to find her.

"Okay, and I'm calling Michael," Peyton said, pulling her phone from her small handbag as she strolled away.

Christina spotted Darlene near her office door staring down at an electronic tablet that was in her hands. Dressed in a black, sleeveless cocktail dress with her long dark hair pulled up on top of her head in a bun, she looked regal and sophisticated.

As Christina headed in her direction, the woman glanced up, and her ruby red lips tilted into a smile, while her dark, almost black eyes, glimmered with excitement. "Hey, there. I was coming to find you. At the rate we're going, we'll sell out by the end of the weekend."

Christina couldn't help but smile. "That's amazing! Thanks for everything you've done to make this show a success," she said, unable to express how much she appreciated the woman's hard work.

Darlene grinned. "It's my pleasure."

"Hey, I noticed there's security here today," Christina whispered. "What's that all about?"

Darlene's eyebrows dipped into a frown. "Umm, I assume you had something to do with that. Your husband contacted me yesterday morning and told me that he'd hired security for the show."

Luke? Now he's gone too far.

"I didn't ask why," Darlene continued. "I assumed that since some of the nudes were priced at five figures that you were concerned about some walking away."

"Yeah, that's probably it," Christina said, knowing there was something more going on.

Luke had some explaining to do.

Chapter Twenty-Four

Christina glanced at her watch. She had received a text from Luke saying that he was en route from the airport. She'd wanted to call and ask him about the security team he had hired but decided to wait until he arrived.

When Peyton asked Michael what was going on, he told her that Luke would explain. Christina knew deep down that this had nothing to do with her being pregnant and traveling without him. No, there was something else going on, and she had every intention of finding out what.

"I'll be back. I need to empty my bladder," Christina said, trying not to do the pee-pee dance that kids do when they've waited too long to get to the bathroom.

"Okay, I'll be by the refreshments," Peyton said, nodding her head toward the side of the room where finger foods and drinks were stationed. "I'm hungry, and I don't think I can wait until dinner to eat. See you in a few."

They went in opposite directions. Christina hurried to the back hallway only to find three other women in line. Maybe they'd have mercy on her and let her skip, but she remembered there being another bathroom on the lower level. Only the staff and artists knew about it since it was where the artwork and props were stored.

She turned on her heels and headed to the back of the building and down the stairs to the basement. Thankfully, the space wasn't creepy like some basements, but it was nothing fancy either. Crowded, but in an organized way, the space was sectioned off.

There were several rooms on each side as she strolled through the open space. Towards the back on the left was a temperature-controlled room where her paintings had been stored for a few days.

Christina picked up the pace as she neared the workroom in the back that had a small bathroom inside. She entered, flipped on the light, and barely took in the long table, chairs, and supplies that made up the workstation. Her focus was straight ahead where she'd spotted the door to the bathroom.

Good. It's empty, she thought and hurried inside.

Christina patted the wall to the right until she found the light switch. Once the tight space was illuminated, she locked the door and handled her business.

Noise sounded outside of the room. It was faint, but she was pretty sure she heard someone dragging something heavy.

While she washed her hands in the tiny, metal sink, she thought she heard someone talking in the distance. She hurried out of the bathroom and went to the other door.

It wouldn't open.

She turned the knob and played with the lock, but the door didn't budge.

What the...

She turned the knob again and put her shoulder against the door, trying to open it. When nothing happened, she banged the side of her fist against it. "Hello! Can anyone hear me? Hello!"

Christina growled under her breath. "Just great." She pulled her cell phone from her small, brown, crossbody purse and texted Peyton.

Christina: Hey. Come downstairs. Locked in room. Need help.

Before she could glance away from the screen, a *Not Delivered* message popped up in red.

Christina frowned and started to text again, but she noticed she barely had one bar. Then it disappeared, too.

"Oh, you got to be kidding me!"

No internet service.

***

Luke glanced around the gallery while Peyton fussed at him. "Where is my wife?" he asked with a little more bite than intended. He missed Christina and wanted more than anything to just hold her. "I don't see her."

Peyton folded her arms over her chest. "She went to the bathroom. I hope you have an explanation regarding the extra security because CJ's not too happy."

"Yeah, I know. I just didn't want her to have to worry about anything more than the show. I'll explain everything once I find her. I'll be back."

Luke strolled around the gallery, and his heart swelled with pride. He knew how talented his wife was, and seeing all the red *SOLD* stickers on most of her paintings proved that he wasn't the only one. He didn't even have to go to the section that contained her nudes. Those always went quickly. They were breathtakingly good, and no doubt others would agree.

Luke headed toward the hallway that led to the bathrooms. When he rounded the corner, he practically ran into Kenton Bailey.

"Looking for Christina?" he asked.

Kenton was one of the security specialists that Michael recommended. A giant of a man, he stood well over six feet and looked more like a defensive lineman than a former FBI agent.

They shook hands in greeting.

"Yeah. Her sister said she went to the restroom," Luke told him.

"I saw her less than ten minutes ago when she got in line, and she was standing behind that woman." He nodded toward the first person in line. There were two women behind her. "I have a lady inside checking to see if she's in there."

Kenton explained that he had stepped out of sight of her for a second, and then she was gone. He assumed that the others in line had let her skip, but he wanted to make sure.

Seconds ticked by before the woman returned. "She's not in there," she said and pushed the stylish, red oversized glasses farther up on her nose. "I called out for her, but there was no one in there by that name."

"Okay, thanks," Kenton said before talking to someone through an earpiece. "She hasn't left the building. So, she's here somewhere."

"Hey, Luke! You made it," Darlene said as she strolled toward him.

"Yeah, but I can't find my wife. Her sister said she went to the ladies' room, but she isn't in there."

"Are there other restrooms in the building?" Kenton asked quickly, concern in his dark gaze.

"Only the one in the storage area, but I doubt she would've gone down there. Then again, there's been a line out here off and on for the last twenty minutes. Maybe..."

"Darlene, you're needed up front immediately," someone said through the walkie-talkie she was holding.

"I'll be right there," she responded into the handheld radio. She started to say something else to Luke, but she was called again.

"Tell me where it is, and I'll go and check," Luke said. His patience vanished as his concern for Christina increased. He didn't want to think the worst, but when it came to her, his protective instincts stayed on high alert.

Darlene pointed towards a closed door and told him how to get to the other restroom.

"I'm right behind you, but I want to check one area up here first."

As Luke took off toward the basement, he heard Kenton instructing his team to check the rest of the building.

"Christina!" Luke called out once he was on the lower level and started moving through the space. The front part was well lit as he skirted around equipment, furnishings, frames, and numerous props.

He called out for her a few more times as he moved farther into the space.

"Christina!"

"Help! I'm in here. Help!" The words sounded like they were far away, and he jogged toward the voice and the pounding he heard.

"Christina?" Luke called again, not sure where the yelling had come from. There were several rooms with closed doors and even more furniture scattered about. "Baby, where are you?"

"Luke? Oh, my God! I'm in the workroom."

He followed her voice and frowned when he saw a long table with a ton of chairs stacked on top of it blocking a door to the room she was in.

"What the hell?" he mumbled and glanced around frantically. Had Lefty found her? Was he behind this?

"Luke?"

"Are you okay, sweetheart?" he asked in a rush.

"I'm fine. I just want out of here," Christina said.

She sounded fine, but he needed to see her with his own eyes. He also wanted answers, but first, he needed to move the furniture.

"Hold on, baby. I'm going to get you out of there."

Luke turned his back to the door and the furniture stacked in front of it, and glanced around while he pulled his phone from his pocket. Whoever had done this might be hiding out down there somewhere.

Lefty. The man was well-connected. Was he behind this? Had he found Christina?

Luke's anxiety was off the charts as every horrible scenario played out in his mind. If the guy was behind this, Christina wasn't safe, and Luke was silently freaking out.

As his gaze bounced around the space, he shot off a text to Kenton. He needed backup...just in case.

A second later, he got a message that the text wasn't delivered.

Son of a...

No service.

Not seeing or hearing anyone, Luke hurried and started unstacking the furniture. He had taken a few chairs off of the table when he heard movement behind him. He swung around and automatically got in a fighting stance before really thinking about it.

"It's just me," Kenton said, and Luke explained that Christina was barricaded in the room. Before Kenton could speak, he seemed to pull a gun out of thin air and whirled around.

"Whoa!" two guys said at the same time with their hands up. They were wearing baseball caps low over their eyes. The T-shirt and the jeans the first guy wore were both black, and dusty work boots covered his feet. The second guy, who was a few inches taller than the first man, was dressed similarly.

"Who are you?" Kenton barked. His deep voice was like a whip cracking through the air. Sharp and impossible to ignore.

"We—we work here," the tallest guy said.

"Someone open this damn door!" Christina yelled.

"We're working on it, babe," Luke said, not missing the way both men's eyes went wide at hearing her in the room.

"Oh hell. Someone's in there?" the shorter guy said and dropped his eyes. His eyebrows dipped into a frown as confusion marred his face. "We blocked the door, but we didn't realize anyone—"

"Just get this stuff moved," Kenton demanded.

They all worked together.

Apparently, the space next to the room that Christina was locked in was used for storage. The men needed to get to several props for a smaller showing happening in another area, but they were blocked by furniture. With limited space to work with, they moved the tables and chairs in front of the door, not realizing that Christina had been in the room.

Luke gritted his teeth to keep from saying anything because he couldn't understand why they'd block the door. Then again, considering the limited space, maybe they didn't have anywhere else to move the furniture to, even temporarily.

The moment the long table was slid away, Luke jerked the door open, and Christina practically fell into his arms.

"God, I'm so glad to see you," she mumbled, her arms tight around his neck despite her large belly between them.

Her breath was warm against his neck, and Luke tightened his arms around her waist. He wasn't sure how long they stayed that way, but he needed to look at her. He needed to make sure she was okay.

Luke eased back and his gaze slid over her. "Are you okay? Do you feel all right?" he asked.

The words flew from his mouth like a rapid-fire machine gun. He still had one arm around her and with the other, he slid his hand along her stomach. He wasn't a crying man, but when his kid kicked his palm, he felt like he was going to lose his shit.

He didn't.

He sucked it up and sent up a silent prayer of thanks. Still, the boulder-like weight he'd felt the moment he realized she was missing remained. He had thought the worst—that Lefty had somehow got to her...that he had taken her.

Luke wrapped his arms around her again and closed his eyes, then breathed in her scent. Anything could've happened to her, and no one would've known. Granted Supreme had the entrances and exits covered, and for the most part, had kept eyes on her, but...

"I'm so glad you're okay," he murmured against her ear, trying to ignore the talking and moving of furniture behind them. "I was so worried."

He wasn't sure what she heard in his voice, but she stiffened, then said, "Oh, baby, I'm fine. I'm sorry I scared you."

She tried to pull away, but he couldn't let her go.

Not yet.

Not ever.

Chapter Twenty-Five

"Let's get out of here," Luke finally said.

The men, including Kenton, had left him and Christina downstairs, and for that, Luke was grateful. It had taken him a little longer than expected to pull himself together. He'd gotten himself worked up, thinking that Christina had been kidnapped or worse. The situation was nothing like he had imagined, but still, his heart was beating faster than usual.

Now he had to tell her about Lefty. It wasn't going to be an easy conversation, but it had to be done. He didn't want secrets between them. Besides, he needed to make sure she was aware of her surroundings.

When they were halfway up the stairs, his cell phone rang.

"Great. Now we get service," Christina said. She shook her head and kept climbing the stairs as Luke pulled the device from his pants pocket.

Michael.

"Hold up, baby. I have to take this." Luke reached for her hand the moment they were at the top of the stairs. "Hello," he said, his voice gruffer than intended.

"Shit, man, you sound like a damn grizzly bear," Michael said by way of greeting.

Luke gripped Christina's hand tighter as he moved them to an empty corner near the back exit. Thankfully, she didn't protest. They needed to talk, sooner than later. First, he needed to see if there was an update on the Lefty situation.

"Maybe this will make you feel better," Michael continued. "Lefty was found dead this morning in a vacant lot on the edge of town."

Shock roared through Luke, and he slumped against the wall.

"Luke?" Christina placed her hands on his chest as her troubled gaze searched his eyes. "Are you okay? What's wrong? What happened?" she demanded.

He wrapped his arm around her neck and pulled her close, placing a kiss on her cheek. "It's okay," he said to her, and then to Michael, he said, "Are you sure?"

"Positive. A detective friend sent me photos. They're still investigating, but it looks like a hit. One shot in the center of his forehead. My guess is that the L'Arco Family took him out. Like us, they assumed he had cut a deal with the prosecutors to get out of prison early. That hasn't been confirmed, but it would explain the hit. They'd want revenge and to make sure he could never testify against the family. That's assuming he had actually cut a deal."

At this point, Luke didn't care. As long as the man was out of the picture, that's all that mattered.

We're safe. The words played around in Luke's mind as relief flooded him. If it weren't for the wall holding him up and Christina gripping the front of his shirt, he was sure he would've slid to the floor. The boulder-like weight had finally lifted, and he shut his eyes and released an audible sigh.

Michael gave him a few more details before they disconnected the call.

"You need to tell me what the hell is going on," Christina snapped. "And I want to know now."

***

"You should've told me," Christina said once Luke had explained everything to her.

They were holding hands as they sat on the sofa in Darlene's office. They'd been in there for the last twenty minutes.

Though Christina knew she needed to get back to the show, Luke needed her more. There had been something in his eyes earlier.

Even in the way he'd held her felt off...almost desperate. He'd been a man on the edge. There had even been a moment when she saw him swipe at his eyes.

Now she understood why. He'd been truly afraid for her life. Christina couldn't believe that there might've been a killer out there gunning for one of them or both, and he thought it best to keep her in the dark.

"You should've told me," she repeated.

"I know." He rubbed his free hand over his head and exhaustion showed in his eyes. "I thought I was doing the right thing by putting security on you until I was able to get here. I had every intention of filling you in after your show."

They talked for a few minutes longer. Christina couldn't be mad at him. She appreciated him looking out for her. Not just physically, but she often got anxious before a show, and he hadn't wanted to add to that.

"You look tired," she said. "Why don't you head to the hotel and get some rest? I'll be there in a couple of hours." They had a two-bedroom suite, and she was looking forward to curling up with him later.

"There is no way in hell that I'm leaving here without you. I'm not that tired, but what about you? Is your back still bothering you?"

Christina smiled and rubbed her hand over the light stubble on his cheek. "Actually, I feel good. No, make that great. The show has been a success so far, you're here, and we get to spend the next few days together. What more could a girl ask for?

Her cell phone rang, and she dug it from her small purse. Glancing at the screen, she frowned at seeing Martina's name on the screen.

"Who is it?" Luke sat forward with concern on his face.

"Martina. Let me see what she wants." Christina answered the call. "Hello?"

"What is this I hear about the Thug Lawyer having gangsters after him?" her cousin asked.

Christina's mouth dropped open. "What are you talking about?" she asked. As far as she knew, Luke and Michael were the only ones who knew about that. Peyton didn't even know the details. Then again, Martina always had a way of finding out information, and she never revealed her sources. If Christina didn't know better, she'd think her cousin was somehow spying on everyone in the family.

"Don't play dumb, CJ. I can tell by your tone that you know exactly what I'm talking about. Now spill!" Martina said a little too enthusiastically.

Christina sighed. She wasn't in the mood for whatever Martina was up to. Besides, if she shared anything with her cousin, the whole family would know everything by the time she and Luke arrived home.

"Like I said, what are you talking about?" Christina asked, and glanced at Luke who had an eyebrow raised questioningly.

"Ah, come on CJ. Tell me. You know I live for this shit! Gangsters? Dude, you have to give me something," Martina insisted.

"Goodbye, MJ." Christina disconnected the call and turned to Luke.

"I swear that woman is like a damn bloodhound," Luke said standing. He grabbed Christina's hand and pulled her to her feet. "I'm starting to think she has someone tracking every move that you and your family make."

Christina grinned. When it came to Martina, anything was possible. Not only was her cousin nosey, but it was spooky how she learned things about everyone in the family. Personal stuff that they assumed no one knew. She didn't know who MJ's sources were, but usually they were spot-on. Actually, she probably didn't want to know.

"Come on," Luke said and wrapped his arm around Christina's waist and guided her to the door. "Let's go see if you sold out yet. The sooner you do, the sooner we can start our babymoon."

"*Ohh*, I can't wait," Christina gushed.

Peyton was flying home after the show, and then Christina and Luke would have the luxurious suite to themselves for the next five days.

"I have big plans for you over the next few days," she said, wiggling her eyebrows and causing them both to laugh. "Are you sure you don't want to go and rest up?"

Luke stopped before they walked out of the office and pulled Christina in front of him. He stared her in the eyes, his expression serious. "I never knew I could love someone as much as I love you," he said. "Today gave me a taste of what it would be like if I ever lost you, and I don't think—"

Christina placed a finger over his lips to keep him from continuing.

"Luke, I'm not going anywhere," she said. "I love you, too, and I need you to stop worrying so much. Don't always expect the worst. I know you've lost a lot."

Heck, he had lost all his family. So, she understood where he was coming from, but...

"You can't walk through life in constant fear that you're going to lose me. It's not healthy—physically or emotionally."

Luke nodded. "You're right. If I keep this up, I'm going to make us both crazy. I promise you, I'll do better."

"Good." She kissed his lips and slipped her arm in his before tugging him out of the office. "Besides, we don't want our son to live in fear. He's going to need his daddy to be fearless in every aspect of life."

There wasn't much that scared Luke. So, she had no doubt that he'd get himself together and turn back into the strong, powerful man she had fallen in love with.

"You mean *she's* going to need her daddy to be fearless," he said with a smirk on his tempting lips.

Christina grinned up at him, and her heart felt as if it would burst as she stared into his dark eyes. "Our baby is going to be the luckiest kid in the world."

"I couldn't agree more," he said, kissing the top of her head.

Christina's cell phone dinged with an incoming text, and she slowed and glanced at the screen.

Martina: Come on. Give me details!

Christina growled under her breath. "Remind me to strangle MJ the next time I see her," she said to Luke while shooting off a quick text.

Christina: Get a life Martina and stay out of mine!

Martina: Fine be like that!

Christina slipped her hand into her husband's larger one. "Now that's taken care of, let's go and enjoy the rest of our evening."

Chapter Twenty-Six

"P—Paul, I—I'm coming," Martina panted, struggling to hang on as her husband tightened his hold on the back of her thighs. His fingers dug into her flesh when he lifted her higher against the wall and thrust into her with more intensity.

Damn, this man knew how to make her feel good. The way he was buried deep inside of her, his dick bumping against the back of her core, had Martina inching closer to her release. And knowing they were getting busy in one of his parents' bathrooms while trying to be quiet only added to her sexual desire.

She loved when her man was like this. Sexy, uninhibited, and totally out of control. Normally buttoned up tight, this was a side of Paul she didn't get to experience often enough. But when he brought the heat...

"Yes! Oh yes!" Pressure mounted inside of her as an orgasm drew near. "Baby, th—that's it. Right there. Ri—right there," she chanted close to his ear, getting louder with each word as her inner muscles tightened around him. "Paul that's, *ohhh*..."

Martina stiffened and then bucked against him as her body vibrated with liquid fire, and a scream flew from her lips. Paul slammed his mouth over hers, drowning out her cry of pleasure as he pistoned in and out of her.

His kiss was hard and commanding and only added to the out-of-control orgasm that tore through her body. Heat rippled over her skin, and she struggled to suck in enough oxygen as Paul pounded into her.

Seconds later, he growled his release as his grip on her tightened to the point of almost being painful. Martina wouldn't have it any other way. She enjoyed sex a little rough and out of control. As usual, her man didn't disappoint. Paul was one of those guys who was good at everything, and he knew how to put it down in the bedroom...and apparently the bathroom too.

He was breathing hard near her ear and still had her pressed tightly against the wall while she rested her head on his broad shoulder. Neither of them spoke.

This was a first for them—sex in one of his parents' bathrooms. At least Paul had had the mind to find one away from prying ears. Had it been up to her, she would've chosen the first one they found. Which would have been the powder room near the front entrance.

"The tricky part will be leaving this room without being spotted," Paul said, his voice deep and sexy as he slowly set her on her feet.

Martina kissed his lips. "Well, I personally don't care if we get caught. As a matter of fact, maybe we should do it again but without you covering up my scream." She punched him in the shoulder playfully. "I didn't appreciate you smothering my attempt at letting the whole house know how good you were putting it on me."

Paul shook his head and chuckled. "You're such a troublemaker. We'll pick up where we left off once we get home. Then you can scream all you want," he said, lowering his head and kissing her passionately.

Martina savored the sweetness of his mouth as their tongues tangled and divine ecstasy flowed through her. "I love you," she mumbled against his juicy lips.

She never knew she could love anyone as much as she loved this man. Her family might've thought she was nuts most of the time, but when it came to Paul, there was no playing around. He meant the world to her, and she couldn't imagine him not being in her life.

"I love you more," he said when the kiss ended.

With one hand still on her hip, he used his other to dig into a nearby drawer and grabbed a hand towel. Wetting it, he made quick work of cleaning her up.

This was one of a thousand reasons why she adored this man. Despite her lack of filter and big personality, he took such good care of her. She knew he was blessed to have him in her life. Let her cousins tell it, she was a hard woman to love. Yet, Paul's love for her never wavered, and for that, she would be forever grateful.

Martina took in his smooth dark skin, beautiful brown eyes, and his irresistible full lips. Since he knew how much she loved a little scruff on his cheek and chin, he didn't shave every day. Today was one of those days, and she ran her palms over his cheeks and smiled.

By the time she and Paul pulled themselves together, Martina was fairly sure that most of the dinner party guests had left. At least she hoped. If they were gone, then maybe Paul would be okay with them leaving too.

She might've loved her husband, but she wasn't a fan of his parents—specifically his mother, Angelica. They were from old money, and his mother took every opportunity to flaunt that fact. She hosted events so that she could show just how well-connected the family was, and it bugged the hell out of Martina. She wasn't jealous. No, it had everything to do with how Angelica often made her feel as if she was beneath them.

"Ready?" Paul asked before he opened the bathroom door.

He had slipped his gray, tailored suit jacket back on and she admired the way he looked. The man had a spectacular body covered in the finest material that highlighted his broad shoulders and wide chest. Martina couldn't wait to get him home so that she could strip him down to nothing.

"I was born ready," she said, her head held high—the way his mother typically walked around.

If Paul recognized the pose, he didn't say anything. Of course, he didn't notice. Whenever she complained about his mother's high-and-mighty attitude, he blew it off saying, "That's just how she is."

He opened the door and peeked out before reaching back and grabbing Martina's hand.

"Let's make a run for it," he joked and pulled her into the hallway quickly.

"Um, let's not. I've been in these four-inch heels for almost three hours. They might be cute, but they are as uncomfortable as hell. There is no way I'm running in these things."

What had she been thinking, letting Jada dress her for this cocktail party? Her cousin lived for this crap. But the only reason Martina was there was because Paul asked her to attend with him.

"Psst," Martina heard someone whisper and knew who it was without turning around.

When she and Paul glanced back, Martina smiled at seeing their daughter, Janay, at the end of the hallway. She was peeking out from around the corner. Part of her face was covered by her long, wavy hair that she must've taken out of the ponytail holder.

Janay ran down the hall toward them, then leaped into her dad's arms, and Paul grunted from her weight. Their preteen was getting so big. Too big to be carried around.

"What are you doing up here?" Paul asked and kissed their daughter on the cheek before setting her on her feet. "I thought you were hanging out in the kitchen with the cook making s'mores."

"I was, but after I finished eating them, there was nothing to do. So, I came upstairs to play in my room."

Though Janay wasn't their only grandchild, she was the only girl, and Paul's parents had a bedroom designated for her.

"Then when I heard mommy, I came into the hallway."

Martina frowned. "I was whispering. How could you hear me?" Martina asked as they all headed toward the spiral staircase that would take them to the main level. She might not think much of her in-laws, but their mansion was gorgeous and had more bedrooms than she could count.

"Mommy, I heard you and Daddy in the bathroom. Are you hurt?" Janay asked, looking Martina up and down critically. "Why were you crying?"

Paul snorted but covered it up with a cough, and Martina pulled up short.

"What?"

"I said, why were you crying?" Janay repeated.

Not much embarrassed Martina but knowing her daughter might've heard them had her cheeks heating. She struggled to come up with a good response. Lying to her kid didn't appeal to her, but anything would be better than saying, "Your daddy was screwing my brains out against the wall". Her family insisted that she didn't have a filter, but there were some things Martina could keep to herself.

"It's these shoes that JJ made me wear. They are killing my feet," Martina said honestly.

The dress was an original that Jada had designed and gifted to her for Christmas. Martina didn't wear dresses often, but this one always made her feel beautiful and feminine. It was also perfect for this pretentious cocktail party that the Kendricks had thrown. The outfit had her blending in easily. She'd even given out Jada's contact information to a few women who'd asked about the designer.

"Why didn't you take them off? You always tell me that when I wear my patent leather shoes that hurt my feet."

Martina sighed, knowing that if she didn't nip this conversation in the bud, it was never going to end. "I thought about it, but I figured I'd look a little weird walking barefoot around your grandma's hoity-toity friends." The moment the last words were out of her mouth, Martina regretted them.

"What does hoity-toity mean?"

"Nothing," Paul piped in and glared at Martina. "Your mother is joking. Do you have all your stuff? We're leaving soon."

"Oh, I gotta go back and get my game," Janay said.

The moment their daughter bolted back down the hall, Paul pounced.

"Why do you always do that?" he whisper-shouted as he pulled her away from the stairs. "We agreed that you wouldn't talk about my mother like that around Janay. Yet, here you are, doing it again. You can dislike her all you want, but don't even think about filling my baby's head with your nonsense."

Martina lifted her hands. "You're right, I misspoke. I'm sorry. It slipped out." She didn't apologize often, but this was one time that she was in the wrong. Janay adored all her grandparents, and Martina didn't want to change that with her own prejudices. "I'm sorry, okay? It won't happen again."

She covered his lips with hers, only planning to soothe his hurt feelings. But when he slid his hand behind her neck, he deepened their lip-lock.

"Eww, gross!" Janay's high-pitched voice was like being doused with a bucket of ice water, and they pulled apart. Instead of their kid walking with them, though, she hurried down the stairs ahead of them.

Martina slipped her hand back into Paul's. "I'm sorry about what I said."

"It's all right, but babe, you got to watch what you say around her. We don't want her repeating some of the stuff that comes out of your mouth."

Martina wasn't offended. He was right. Some of the crap that came out of her mouth over the years wasn't for young ears, and she had to try to do better.

"Let's go. The sooner we get home, the sooner we can pick up where we left off in the bathroom."

No other words were needed. Hand in hand, they hurried to the stairs.

"Oh, there you two are. I'm glad you're still here. Paul, I forgot to tell you that we're celebrating your dad next Sunday with a Father's Day brunch. Don't you think that'll be wonderful?" She gushed.

It was taking everything within Martina not to tell her what she could do with her brunch. There was no way she was attending. Instead of saying that, she plastered on a smile that was as fake as her mother-in-law's smile.

"What time are you thinking?" Paul asked.

Martina didn't miss the fact that he had tightened his hold on her hand. No doubt he was trying to make sure she didn't say anything. It was a struggle, but her lips were sealed. She'd say all she needed to say by not showing up. Besides, the woman was a horrible cook, and the person in her kitchen pretending to be a chef was no better.

Why would I torture myself with bad company and horrible food when my family's brunch is second to none? she thought.

The Jenkins family got together for brunch every Sunday. It was a tradition started by her grandmother over thirty years ago. Paul's mother knew that, and Martina wouldn't be surprised if she was planning her little brunch to cause an argument between her and Paul.

If that was the case, she was going to be disappointed. Paul already knew that she never missed a Jenkins Family brunch, and she sure as hell wouldn't start now.

Chapter Twenty-Seven

As they drove home, Paul divided his attention between the road and his beautiful wife. She might not like spending time with his family, but she had come through for him tonight. He didn't particularly enjoy the parties that his mother hosted. He'd had enough of them while growing up and even during his stint as a U.S. senator. But having Martina by his side made the events less boring.

His wife was stunning. When he first met her, she wore her naturally curly hair short. For the last year, she had let it grow out and the long strands usually brushed her shoulders. Tonight, she had it in an updo with a few tendrils framing her face. Her makeup looked professionally done and only added to her beauty.

But it was the dress that made his mouth go dry when she'd glided down the stairs of their home to tell him she was ready. It was a wrap dress that hugged her body and brought attention to her full breasts, narrow waist, and hips that only added to her hourglass figure. He had considered keeping her home and having his way with her luscious body, but their daughter had urged them out of the house. She'd been anxious to see her grandparents.

Paul reached over and linked his fingers with Martina's. He was glad that she hadn't automatically shut his mother's idea of brunch down, but he knew she wanted to. Holding her tongue wasn't one of his wife's strengths, especially where his mother was concerned.

"I think Angelica is starting to warm up to me," Martina said of his mother, and Paul snorted.

They were two of the most important women in his life, but they couldn't stand each other. Their relationship was a little better than it had been before he and Martina married, but not by much.

"She only glared at me once over dinner. Then again, that might've been her usual evil look," she said with a laugh, but Paul growled under his breath.

He glanced into the back seat to make sure their daughter had her headphones on. The kid rarely left home without them or her handheld game.

"Not even a half hour ago, you promised to watch what you say about my mother, especially around Janay."

Martina mumbled a curse and glanced into the back seat. She squeezed his hand before releasing it. "I'm sorry. I slipped, but Janay can't hear us while she's playing that game. Besides, you have to admit, your mother does look at me as if she smells something bad. She's all high-and-mighty, looking down at others as if her shit don't stank."

"Only because she knows you don't like her. Martina, this has been going on for years." At least she wasn't calling his mother names, but still. "I need you to try harder where she is concerned. She's set in her ways, and I need you to be the bigger person. It's hard being around you two when you're both snarling at each other for no reason."

The last thing Paul wanted to do was argue, but that's what usually happened when his mother was the topic of conversation. Granted, Martina wasn't wrong. His mother was a bit pretentious and could sometimes be unyielding. She could also be disrespectful, but he had noticed her effort in trying to get along with Martina.

But this conversation wasn't just about his mother. Martina didn't have a filter and often said too much in every situation, and it had been a bone of contention in their marriage from day one. Rarely did she think about the consequences of how her words affected others. Granted, most of the time she was joking or trying to get a rise out of people by being argumentative, especially with her family, but she often went too far.

"Fine. I'll try not to say anything else bad about your mom. I'm probably wrong about her warming up to me anyway. After downing two shots of tequila with your sister earlier, my memory is a little sketchy."

This time, Paul laughed and recognized her attempt to lighten the moment.

"I should've known alcohol had something to do with you dragging me into the bathroom. I barely had a chance to lock the door before you jumped me."

Martina smiled. "Hmm, I remember it a little differently. All I did was give you *the look*, and then you dragged me around the house trying to find some privacy."

Paul laughed. "Okay, maybe it was a little bit of both of us, but I'm not complaining. I had fun with you in there." He squeezed her thigh, remembering their quick tryst.

"Yeah, it was a lot of fun, and I can't wait to do it again."

They rode a few minutes in silence before Paul said, "Thanks for not shooting down my mother's idea of a Father's Day brunch. I'll talk to her about maybe having it early in the day. That way we'll still be able to make it to your grandparents' home in time for—"

"Hold up," Martina said, turning fully in her seat to face him. "I'm not attending that brunch. Seeing Angelica twice in a month is too much for me, especially back-to-back weekends."

Paul divided his attention between her and the road. "What if I want you to attend with me and Janay?"

Martina sighed dramatically. "I agreed to attend this cocktail party with you. That's enough. I'd rather gouge out my eyes with a screwdriver or stick my head in an oven and turn it to broil than attend the brunch.

"I can't believe you thought I'd consider it," she said, incredulous. "Why would I wanna be around people who don't like me?"

Paul released a long, drawn-out sigh. "They don't hate you, Martina. You just make it hard for them to totally embrace who you are." He suddenly regretted bringing up the subject of brunch. "So, you won't reconsider even though I'm asking you to go along with me and Janay?"

"Nope. Like I said, I'd rather stick my head in an oven."

"Fine. Don't go," he snapped.

So much for ending the night on a high note.

Paul was done. Most days he could tolerate his wife's argumentative attitude, but right now, he just wanted to get home and put some space between them.

***

Without opening her eyes, Martina patted her hand back and forth on the other side of the mattress. Cold.

Figured.

Paul was an early riser, but she was fairly sure that he hadn't bothered to come to bed. He had probably slept in the guest room. Normally, when they had a disagreement, they could work it out before going to bed. Not this time. Paul had shut down. The moment they had arrived home, he showered and headed to his home office.

She hadn't seen him since.

Martina opened her eyes and picked up her cell phone from the nightstand to look at the time.

Six o'clock.

It was too damn early to be up on a Saturday. Except Paul didn't care. He stuck to a routine no matter the day. Some Saturdays he went to the gym before heading to one of his restaurants. On others, he often chauffeured Janay around to gymnastics, dance class, or soccer, depending on the time of year.

Today, Martina wasn't sure of his plan since he wasn't speaking to her. They probably needed to talk, but she'd said all that she needed to say. She wasn't going to his mother's brunch, and that was final. If Paul didn't like it, he'd just have to deal with it.

At least that's what she told herself.

But if she was honest, she could admit that she hated when they fought. There was no doubt that she got on his nerves *all* the time. Yet, he was always there for her—no matter what. Any other man would've left her years ago, but not Paul. He offered her more grace than she deserved. He had always accepted her as she was, flaws and all.

Martina covered her face with her hands and growled as guilt charged through her body. She loved that man more than she ever thought she could love anyone. He was such a loving, kind, and patient man. So why did she do and say stuff that often drove a wedge between them?

She shook her head and sighed. Martina didn't know why she was such a loudmouth. It was how she was wired. Just because she spoke her mind didn't mean that she didn't feel and love the way others did. She just had a different way of showing love. She was the type to pick on the people she cared about. As twisted as that might be, she'd always been like that.

One of these days, that mouth of yours is going to get you into trouble that you might not be able to get out of, her grandmother often said.

"I hope this ain't one of those times," Martina mumbled and sat up.

She slipped her feet into her slippers and slid on the short, red satin robe that lay on the bench at the foot of the bed. It was time to make things right with Paul.

Martina tightened the belt around her waist as she strolled out of the room and headed for the stairs. The smell of strong coffee met her in the middle of the staircase, and she almost groaned. She loved when Paul made coffee. It was way stronger than the crap they had at work, and she could barely wait for her first sip.

She rounded the corner into the kitchen, and Paul glanced up. He was standing at the counter with a mug to his mouth while he read something on his electronic tablet.

"Morning," he said dryly.

"Good morning. Are you still mad at me?" she asked as she approached. Normally, he'd greet her with a kiss, but it didn't look as if he planned to do that today. His attention was back on his tablet. "For what it's worth, I'm sorry."

He glanced up, and his gorgeous dark eyes bore into her. "What are you sorry for?" he asked. "You made it clear that you're not attending the brunch." He shrugged. "What's there to apologize for?"

That was a trick question.

No matter how she responded, it wouldn't be right in his eyes. Was this him lawyering her? Paul was a lawyer by trade, but instead of practicing law after graduating from law school, he had gone into politics like his father and forefathers before him had done.

Just thinking about him and his politics made her itch. Despite being on opposite sides of the aisle per se, they'd managed to fall in love and hopefully live happily ever after. But by his grim expression, she wasn't so sure.

"I'm sorry for my behavior on the way home. I know I was indignant in the way I talked about your mother, but I can't help it."

Martina batted her eyelashes, trying to look and sound contrite, but was probably failing. She was sorry about the way she spoke to him and how their night had ended. However, she meant every word she said about Angelica.

"Babe, you had to know that I wouldn't be interested in going to your mom's stu..." Her words trailed off and they both knew what she was about to say.

Dammit. I need to stop talking.

Instead of saying more, she moved to the coffee pot and poured herself a cup.

"I'll try to do better with my choice of words," she said and stood next to him, hoping that he'd forgive her like he usually did.

After a long hesitation, Paul shut down his tablet and finally looked at her. "Be who you are, Martina. I wouldn't want you to choke and die on your hurtful words by keeping them bottled up inside."

"Well, *damn*. Tell me how you really feel," she said with a chuckle. She must be finally rubbing off on him because that sounded like something she would say. But his expression was as stoic as it had been since she walked in.

"I'm heading to the club and then to the office," he said.

By club, he meant the athletic club that he, Craig, and some of the other men in the family were members of. By office, he meant the one at the first restaurant that he'd opened. It was home base for him.

"Oh, tell Janay I'll call her later about that movie she asked me to take her to this evening."

Instead of kissing Martina goodbye, like usual, Paul walked out of the kitchen, and seconds later, she heard the garage door go up.

Crap. He's not just mad. He's pissed.

"Great," she mumbled and lifted her coffee mug to her lips. "Now I have to figure out how to make things right."

"Mommy."

Martina's gaze darted to the opening of the kitchen where Janay was standing. She looked as if she'd just rolled out of bed with the ponytail on top of her head askew and her black and white puppy pajamas wrinkled.

Martina set her mug down. "Hey, sweetie. What are you doing up so early?"

Had she heard her and Paul talking? Normally, Janay slept in late on the weekend. Or she'd be in the den watching cartoons, but never this early.

"I have to tell you something," she said in a whisper and entered the kitchen with a troubled expression.

Unease swept through Martina and all her protective instincts kicked in. She clowned around and talked trash with people, but when it came to her child, she took her role as mommy seriously.

She met Janay midway and wrapped her daughter in a hug. "What's wrong?"

She might not be the most empathetic person, but from the day Janay was born, Martina had vowed to be a better mother than what she'd had growing up.

Janay's arms were wrapped around Martina's waist and her head rested just below her breasts.

Martina placed a kiss against her daughter's forehead. "Did you have a bad dream?"

"No. I—I started my period," she said barely above a whisper and Martina froze, surprised by the news. They'd had a prelude to *"the talk"* about a year ago when Janay questioned her about the feminine products in the master bathroom's linen closet. Her daughter was a preteen, but Martina thought she had a little more time before she had to go into detail about becoming a woman.

Times up.

She hugged Janay tighter and smiled. "My baby has become a woman. This calls for a special celebration."

Janay lifted her head and perked up when she looked at Martina. "It does?"

"Definitely. Today is women's day. Come on," Martina said, and they walked hand in hand out of the kitchen. "First, I'll tell you all about becoming a woman, then we'll get dressed and get our big day started."

Chapter Twenty-Eight

"I'd like to call this meeting to order," Paul said, trying to keep a straight face as he tightened the white terry cloth towel that he was wearing around his waist.

Sighing loudly, he laid his head back against the wall and felt the stress of the last twelve hours melt away. He, Craig, and Zack were lounging in the steam room at the athletic club after a rigorous workout.

I need this, he thought. He'd been wound tighter than a tension spring threatening to snap, and it was a state he never liked being in. But this was helping—a good workout, hanging with friends, and now winding down.

"What are you talking about? What meeting?" Zack asked.

"Our support group," Paul said and lifted his head to glance at each of them. "More than once, we've talked about starting a support group for the men married to a Jenkins woman. Well, I'm starting it, and I want to begin with the first item on the agenda."

Craig chuckled. "Where was this group when I needed it a couple of months ago?"

"Hell, where was it when I needed it years ago?" Zack asked with a laugh. "All this time married to my strong-willed wife, I've had to go it alone."

They all laughed, mainly because they'd all been in some sticky predicaments with their wives.

"Okay, so what's the first item on the agenda?" Craig asked and laid his head back against the wall and closed his eyes.

"Martina," Paul said without preamble and couldn't blame the guys when they groaned. "I know. I know. My wife is..."

He tossed around a few words in his mind to best describe Martina Jenkins-Kendricks. Amazing. Smart. Passionate. Hardworking. Those were just a few, but then there were plenty of others that weren't as complimentary, like headstrong, nosey, and selfish.

"She's driving me crazy," Paul finally said.

"What? She just started driving you crazy?" Craig cracked, and he and Zack burst out laughing.

Paul couldn't help but chuckle. Sure, she'd been driving him nuts since the day he met her. It was during his stint as a U.S. senator, and she opposed his politics. He loved her tenacity, her compassion for those less fortunate, and he appreciated the way she spoke her mind.

At least most of the time. Other times she went too far.

She drove everyone crazy. It was part of her charm. At least that's what she always claimed.

"I adore the woman," Paul continued. "And I can't imagine my life without her in it, but lately she's been nudging me closer to my breaking point. I'm tired. I'm tired of trying to get her to watch her words. I'm tired of the disagreements, and I'm tired that though she claims she'll do better, she doesn't."

He told them about the Father's Day brunch argument and went on to tell them about some of the disagreements over the last few months. There'd been several, but they'd managed to move past the others. Yet, the conversation with her the night before plagued him like an irritating splinter in his finger that he couldn't dig out.

Zack *tsked*. "I'm not sure what to tell you, man. You knew what your wife was like before you married her. I guess you're going to have to ask yourself what's different now?"

"Or remember why you married her in the first place," Craig added. "Do you still love her?"

"Yes," Paul said without hesitation.

There was no doubt in his mind that he loved Martina, and he enjoyed spending time with her. Because of her potty mouth and lack of filter, so many people didn't get to know her gentler side.

She was always doing nice things for people, but she did it without fanfare.

Her charitable contributions went beyond financial support. The month before, one of their neighbors underwent surgery, and it took her awhile to recover. Martina prepared meals for the family twice a week for a month. She was an amazing cook, and Paul loved that she cared enough to share that gift. Or how she mentored two female carpenter apprentices who were thinking about leaving the trade.

As a master carpenter, one of the best in the city, Martina was active with the union. Through them, she had set up a support system for apprentices who were struggling. Whether it was with their schoolwork or grasping carpentry techniques, she shared her knowledge.

Paul could think of so many instances during the years of their marriage where her selflessness shined. Unfortunately, there were just as many times when her mouth and lack of filter caused more headaches than he preferred.

"You need to tell her how you're feeling. Sit down with her and talk it out," Craig suggested.

Zack snorted. "I think we all know how that conversation would go. She'll keep interrupting him before he can complete a sentence. Then she'll call him a damn fool."

"And she might throw something at him," Craig added and laughed while pointing at the scar near one of his temples.

Paul smiled. His friend was right. Their women were not only beautiful, but they were sassy and hotheaded. The three of them just happened to be married to the ones who were more liable to fight first and ask questions later.

"Yeah, I need to talk to her, but maybe I'll call her instead of having a face-to-face with her," Paul joked. "Wouldn't want her to throw a pot at my head."

He and Zack laughed, and though Craig tried to keep a straight face, he joined in.

For the next few minutes, they discussed everything from relationships to sports. They'd all joked about having a support group, but Paul was thinking that maybe he should consider formalizing what they did naturally.

But first, he needed to deal with his wife.

***

This is just what I needed, Martina thought as the nail technician started her pedicure. Relaxing music played through the speakers and added to the calming atmosphere.

She and Janay's *women's day* was a success.

They'd started with breakfast, shopping, and then lunch at a new taco joint. Now they were ending the day with a mani-pedi at a boutique salon owned by Ella, a friend of Martina's. They'd gotten lucky that she was willing to squeeze them in. Even better, they had the small salon to themselves.

Ella had space and equipment to accommodate two customers at a time, but she typically only allowed one at a time. That made the experience more intimate and special for her clients. When Martina explained women's day, Ella made an exception and called in another nail tech to do Janay's mani-pedi.

"This has been a fun day," Janay said grinning, and Martina's heart squeezed.

Her daughter was a happy child by nature, but Martina loved when she could put a smile on her face.

"I agree. I've enjoyed hanging out with you," Martina said. "We'll have to do this more often, but I'm surprised you're having a good time even without that ridiculous handheld game. Sometimes, it seems like it's glued to your hand."

Janay grinned. "It's weird not having it. Even though you told me I couldn't bring it, I started to sneak it into my purse."

Martina laughed, thinking that when she was Janay's age, that's exactly what she would've done. But her daughter wasn't like her. She was sweet and a girlie-girl who followed rules and just happened to like video games.

"I still can't believe my baby is growing up."

Janay sighed. "Mommy, I'm not a baby. I'm a woman now."

Martina smirked. "Well, I don't care if you're a *woman*. You'll always be my baby."

"Okay, but can you stop calling me that when we're around my friends?"

"What? And miss the opportunity to embarrass you? I don't think so, *baby*, my little sugarplum who I love so much." Martina reached over and cupped Janay's chin. "Give your mommy a kiss," she said, trying to pull her daughter closer.

"Mom! You're embarrassing me," Janay whined.

"I'm embarrassing you?" Martina said in amusement. "Good, then I'm doing my job."

"Well, if that's your job. You're doing it too well."

Martina chuckled, and for the next few minutes, they nibbled on cookies and chatted with the nail techs while also sharing a few laughs. After a while, silence fell between them, and Martina had a moment to think about how lucky she was to have such an incredible daughter. She hadn't been kidding when she told Janay that she was enjoying hanging out with her. Now that her child was getting older, it was time they had more women's days.

"Did you and Grandma Carolyn have women's day when you were my age?"

A bolt of sadness jabbed Martina in the chest. It was the same sensation she felt whenever she thought about her childhood.

"No, sweetie. Me and your grandmother didn't have the type of relationship that you and I have," Martina said of her mother. "You remember I told you that I practically grew up at Gram and Grampa's house?"

"Yeah, I remember. I thought it was because Grandma Carolyn worked all the time."

"That might've been part of it, but I was mostly at their house because me and my mother didn't get along, and she was always...busy."

She wasn't ready to tell Janay everything. Especially the part about how Carolyn couldn't be bothered with Martina because she was out trying to find herself or sow her wild oats and, at times, chase men. For years, Martina resented Carolyn which was why she spent most of her days with Gramps and Gram. At times, she even pretended that Gram was her mother.

"Most of my childhood was spent with Gram. She's the one who gave me *the talk* and took me on my first women's day adventure."

"What did you and Gram do during your women's day?"

Martina smiled recalling that day. "Well, you know she doesn't like to eat at restaurants," Martina said with a laugh and Janay smiled.

Katheryn Jenkins didn't think anyone could cook better than her and refused to spend money at restaurants when she could prepare her own meals.

"After she made me a huge breakfast, we went shopping. That's when I got my first real purse. Then instead of lunch, we went to a tea shop. At first, I thought it was dumb." Martina laughed again, remembering how she'd griped about going to the tea shop when the tomboy in her had wanted to go bowling instead. Her grandmother had ignored her complaints and told her that bowling wasn't a part of women's day.

As Martina recounted the experience to Janay, warmth spread through her at the memories. Though the tea shop was frilly with flowered curtains, small tables with tablecloths, and real China, including dainty teacups, she'd ended up having a good time. They had munched on teacakes and tiny sandwiches while drinking tea. The place had been like something straight out of a children's fairytale book.

"That sounds cool. Maybe you and I can go to one and invite Gram to go with us," Janay said.

Martina loved this kid so much. "Gram would absolutely *love* that."

They chatted for a few minutes longer until Janay asked, "Why is daddy mad at you?"

Martina sighed. Apparently, Janay had heard them in the kitchen, but this was the first time she'd said anything about it.

"Ella, can you two give us a minute?" Martina asked the owner.

"Of course," she said, flashing Martina a sympathetic smile. "We'll take a break and come back in about fifteen minutes."

"That's perfect. Thank you." That would be more than enough time because this wasn't something Martina really wanted to talk to Janay about.

Once the nail techs were in the back of the building, Martina turned to her daughter. Janay was a beauty with the perfect mix of her and Paul. Martina's gaze roamed over her, and her heart melted. Her baby looked like a little lady.

Martina had straightened her daughter's hair that morning, and it hung past her small shoulders in waves. The yellow blouse Janay wore was gorgeous against her dark skin, and she'd paired it with black shorts and black sandals with a two-inch heel.

There was an innocence and a sweetness about her that Martina wanted her to maintain for as long as possible.

"You know how I clown around and say whatever is on my mind sometimes?" Martina asked, and Janay nodded. "Well, that drives your dad nuts, especially when I get carried away."

"Like when Gram tells you that you need to listen more than you talk? Or when she threatens to wash your mouth out with soap when you say bad words."

Martina laughed. "Exactly."

"I think you're funny, mommy. Especially when you're picking on CJ, JJ, and TJ," she said with a giggle talking about Christina, Jada, and Toni. "You don't hurt their feelings. They be laughing too."

"Well...sometimes I probably hurt their feelings, but they know I love them. The problem is, there are times when they aren't in the mood for my nonsense. In addition to that, everyone doesn't get my sense of humor. It can be offensive even though I don't always mean it to be."

"That's why daddy's mad," Janay said as more of a statement than a question.

"I think he's more frustrated than mad, but yeah. I promised him I was going to try to do better. Especially since I want to be a good role model for you, and I don't want you to pick up my bad habits."

Janay shrugged. "You are a good role model and the best mommy. Don't worry, I won't pick up your bad habits, and I'm not funny like you. Besides, I don't want Gram to wash my mouth out with soap. Sounds yucky."

Martina burst out laughing and reached over to pull her child close. She placed a kiss against Janay's temple. "I love you so much."

"I love you too, Mommy, and thanks for women's day. This is the best day ever."

Martina's chest tightened with emotion. She might not always say or do the right thing, but there was one thing in her life that she'd done right, and she was looking at her.

Chapter Twenty-Nine

Hours later, Martina leaned against the kitchen counter and stared out the window that overlooked the backyard. She was waiting for Paul to get home. He had called shortly after she'd left the nail salon asking if they could talk later. Martina agreed and had dropped their daughter off at Toni and Craig's house a few minutes ago, and now she was waiting for her husband.

Martina wasn't looking forward to the conversation. Normally, if they had an issue, they dealt with it immediately. This time was different. Paul had pretty much given her the silent treatment for the last twenty-four hours which was so unlike him.

Was this it? Was he going to tell her that she had one more chance before he called it quits?

Martina hoped that wasn't the case, but she was prepared to fight for her marriage. People sometimes thought she was heartless and lived to pick on folks. It was an act. Well...mostly. She did enjoy messing with people's minds and getting a rise out of them. Hell, it was her way of having fun at their expense.

Those who knew her well knew she didn't mean anything by it, and they also knew that even though she was a troublemaker, they could always count on her if needed.

Family first. That had been drilled into all of them from a young age, and she still felt that way.

But there was one area in her life that she took seriously—her marriage. It meant everything to her.

Martina glanced up as Paul entered from the mudroom.

"Hey there," Paul said, looking more energetic than he had that morning. Apparently, his time with the guys helped.

"Hey, yourself. Are you hungry?" she asked.

She had made homemade fries and had grilled burgers and brats. There was also a tossed salad to go with the meal.

188

"Yeah, I am." He strolled across the room and kissed her on the lips as if all was well between them. Maybe it was, and she was worrying for no reason.

"Let me put my stuff up. Are you eating too?"

"I was planning to. Why?"

He gave a slight shrug. "Just asking. Maybe we can talk over dinner."

Well, so much for all being well between them. "Okay."

Fifteen minutes later, they were sitting at the round kitchen table eating. Martina wasn't sure what else there was to discuss about his mother and their Father's Day plans. She had apologized for her words and attitude during their conversation on the way home.

"I'm sorry for what I said to you this morning," Paul started, and Martina racked her brain trying to remember what he'd said that would require an apology. "I shouldn't have made that comment about not wanting you to choke and die on your hurtful words and... Anyway, I was out of line, and it was disrespectful. No matter how mad or upset I might be, I *never* want to disrespect you in any way."

Martina released an unladylike snort and waved him off. "Oh, please. I didn't think anything of it. As a matter of fact, I thought it was funny. It actually sounded like something I would say."

Paul set his fork down and rubbed the back of his neck. "See, that's just it, Martina. Some things should never come out of your mouth. You are a grown woman, a wife, and a mother. Yet, your behavior is often like that of a high schooler or college student."

"I—"

"Wait. Let me finish," Paul interrupted. "I love you. I love you more than the day we got married. But through the years, it has bothered me when you talk about people in a degrading manner. It eats at me that you have more negative things to say about a person than positive ones. And I *hate* the way you disrespect my parents, specifically my mother. Granted it's usually behind her back, but

189

that's just as bad. I don't want to hear that crap, and it's not just what you say, but how you say it."

A bitter retort dangled on her tongue, but Martina kept her mouth shut. Barely. She could take criticism, and nothing he said was untrue. But as it related to his mother, he made it seem like she was the only one at fault.

Instead of saying anything right away, she did something she didn't usually do. Martina weighed her words before letting them fly out of her mouth. She respected Paul more than he probably knew and that meant his opinion of her mattered. However, there was no way in hell she was going to sit there without defending herself.

"Listen," Paul said, "I don't want you to—"

"No, you listen," Martina snapped, then caught herself. "I'm sorry if my way of expressing myself brings you pain. Whether mentally or emotionally, I don't speak the way I do to embarrass you. The way I talk is," she shrugged, "just the way I talk. I'm not trying to impress anyone, and I do and say what I want. Sometimes I'm clowning around, and other times I mean what I say."

"And that's—"

"As for your mother," she talked over him, "it is no secret that she can't stand me, but do you ever come to my defense? Have you ever told her to watch her mouth where your wife is concerned?"

"Most definitely. All the time. I love you both. I don't want to hear either of you talk negatively about the other. But you two are more alike than you realize, and I often feel like I'm caught in the middle. All I ask is that you both be respectful and don't bring that shit around me."

"Fine!" Martina yelled. "I'll try to do better."

He pounded the side of his fist on the wood table. "You always say that, but nothing ever changes! It's been years, and we keep having the same conversation."

Martina threw up her hands. She wasn't making empty promises. She planned to try harder at keeping her big mouth shut. Yet, that didn't seem to be enough.

"What do you want from me?" she asked. "Clearly, my apologies mean nothing to you. So... What. Do. You. Want?"

Paul sighed and planted his elbows on top of the table and rubbed his forehead.

When he didn't respond, unease crept through Martina.

Was this it? Was he done with her? Was her marriage over? This couldn't be the end of them, but she didn't know what to do or what else to say.

They sat in silence until she said, "I'm going to do better. I love being wherever you are, but maybe it'll be best if I stay away from your parents' home. You're right. I say too much, and I speak before thinking most of the time, but I never want to do anything to disappoint or embarrass you."

He reached under the table and squeezed her hand that was resting on her thigh.

"I know, and I know you're just being you, and I love who you are, sweetheart. I just wish that you'd try harder and watch what and how you say things. As for not ever going to my parents' house...I don't want that. I'm not saying that you have to attend everything they host, but I want you with me as much as possible."

Martina's heart melted. He hadn't given up on them. Her loud and, at times, raunchy mouth had always been a source of contention between them. Paul had every right to be tired of it all, but she was so glad that he was giving her a chance to get her act together.

"With that said," Paul continued, "If you don't want to attend the Father's Day brunch next weekend, no problem. But since it'll be Father's Day, I'd like for Janay to be with me."

"Of course."

Martina squeezed his hand and wished she could make herself go to the damn brunch with him. But that wouldn't be good for anyone involved.

"I meant what I said, Paul. I'm going to do better. I'm sorry for verbally disrespecting your mother. That'll stop, but I hope you give me time to change. I've been like this a long time, and I know I won't change overnight, but I'm going to try."

Holding her hand, Paul stood from the table and pulled her to her feet. "That's all I ask."

When he lowered his head and covered her mouth with his, Martina sighed against his lips and kissed him back. Considering how much she enjoyed arguing with people, she hated when she and Paul argued. Changing wasn't going to be easy, but if it meant keeping peace in her marriage, she was going to try.

Chapter Thirty

Paul stole a glance at Martina. She was sitting in the passenger seat as he drove his SUV up the long, circular drive that led to her grandparents' estate. She hadn't said much since their conversation the day before, and it was starting to freak him out.

He'd be the first to admit that a quiet Martina was nice and peaceful, but it was also unusual and a bit unsettling. Granted, he'd be lying if he said he didn't enjoy the peace and calm. She'd been downright pleasant, but at the same time, it was...strange.

Paul parked behind a row of vehicles that belonged to other family members, and he shut off the car. He reached for Martina's hand just as she was about to exit the vehicle.

"Are you okay?" he asked.

Before she could respond, Janay piped up from the back seat. "Can I get out?" she asked though she had one foot out the door.

"Yes, we'll meet you inside," Paul said and waited until his daughter left. He watched her enter the front door before he turned to Martina. "What's wrong?"

"Nothing," she said, barely sparing him a glance as she adjusted her small crossbody bag. "I'll grab the cake if you can get the doors."

Paul didn't release her, and she didn't pull away.

"Talk to me," he said. "Does your silence have anything to do with our conversation yesterday?"

She hesitated. "Maybe a little. You almost have me afraid to say anything. I told you I was going to try, but I can't change overnight."

"Sweetheart, I asked you to start being mindful of what you say and how you say things. I'm not trying to change you. I want you to be yourself. I just want—"

"I know what you want," she said with a bite in her tone, then ran her hand over her hair that was pulled back into a ponytail. "You want me to keep my trap shut."

She rarely looked troubled, but her beautiful brown eyes had lost some of the mischief he usually saw in them. Paul wasn't sure what to say or how to snap her out of the funk she'd sunk into.

"You know what? Be yourself, Martina," he said and ran the back of his fingers down her cheek. "I know what I said yesterday, but more than anything, I want you happy."

She glanced at him, and her perfectly arched eyebrows dipped into a frown. Then she sighed. "You make me happy. I know I have a big mouth, and I need to work on that. I just have to find a happy medium between being myself while also toning down my personality."

Now, Paul was the one sighing. He was glad she was serious about making changes, but he was also concerned.

"Now, can we get out of this car? It's getting hot in here...and I mean hot as in heat, not sexually. I'm sweating like a pig, and that damn cake has probably melted."

Before Paul could respond, Martina eased out of his grasp, and he chuckled.

She's back. Actually, his little spitfire had probably never left.

***

"Move it or lose it," Martina said as she carefully maneuvered around one of her aunts. The large cake was heavy, and having it in a box made carrying it a bit awkward.

As gently as she could, she set the cake on the kitchen table. Peeling the cardboard box away, she prayed that the dessert hadn't shifted.

Martina smiled as she admired her handiwork. The three-layered buttercream cake was decorated with colorful puzzle pieces around the sides with Toni, Craig, Bailey, and Kimani's names on the individual pieces. Across the top read: *Congratulations Craig & Toni. Welcome to the family Bailey and Kimani.*

She'd spent much of the night baking and decorating the cake, and it had turned out perfectly. Thanks to her grandmother, Martina had been baking since she was a kid. Cakes were her specialty, and the year prior, she'd taken a cake decorating class. She loved when she had an opportunity to use what she'd learned.

She gave the cake another once over. Toni had notified the family on Friday that the adoption had gone through, and Bailey and Kimani were officially their kids.

Martina might've given Toni a hard time about her obsession with trying to have more children the natural way. But honestly, she was glad that Craig had put his foot down. When Toni almost died the year before, Martina had fallen apart. Her cousin was one of her best friends, and she couldn't imagine a world without her in it. Though she'd never tell her that. She hated mushiness and being around overly emotional people.

"What's all this?" Jada said as she approached and so did others who'd been standing around the huge kitchen.

"Oh, wow. This is beautiful," Christina said, and Martina turned to her cousin and almost made a crack about her running from gangsters, but instead bit her tongue.

As hard as it was going to be, she needed to practice keeping her mouth shut. Not only would Paul be happy when she made some changes, but her grandmother would be thrilled. Ever since Martina was a kid growing up in her grandparents' home, Gram had been on her to watch her mouth.

If you don't have anything nice to say, don't say anything at all.

She'd heard that practically every day of her youth. Yet, it had the opposite effect. She spoke her mind, and oftentimes, her thoughts weren't nice.

There were at least ten people crowded around the cake, including her mother, Carolyn. The two of them had come a long way in their relationship over the last few years, especially after her mother married Lincoln.

While they were dating, Martina had seen her mother change for the best, and during that time, Martina learned about her father. Something her mother never talked about. Turned out, he wasn't a good guy. He was a man who had used, mistreated, and even abandoned Carolyn when he learned she was pregnant. Granted he'd been married, so that didn't help the situation.

Martina shook the troubled memory free and focused on the people around her. Her family. The people who loved her unconditionally.

"This is beautiful, baby. So talented," Carolyn said, squeezing her arm lovingly. "Mama, come look at this cake."

Martina hadn't seen her grandmother when she walked in, and she glanced over her shoulder. Wearing an Afrocentric housedress, Gram strolled over to the table smiling. She was the only one who knew that Martina was planning this surprise for Toni and her family.

"Hey, Gram. I didn't see you," Martina said and kissed her on the cheek.

"Hey, honey," she said as she moved closer to the cake and smiled. "You always make me so proud. Toni is going to love this."

"She'll probably be shocked and afraid to eat if she finds out Martina made it," Jada said with a laugh, and Martina glared at her.

"You're not funny." Martina shoved her, almost knocking her off of her four-inch heels. "I came planning to be on my best behavior today, and here you are trying to start some mess."

A few people chuckled and Christina said, "Yeah, right. Like there's such a thing as you being on your best behavior. Tell it to people who don't know you."

Martina reared back. "Oh, so you tryin' to jump in this. How about we talk about your—"

"Somebody go and get Toni and Craig," Gram interrupted and looped her arm with Martina's.

When her grandmother smiled up at her, Martina remembered that she was trying to be a better person. Did her grandmother know? Probably not. She just didn't want any nonsense started, and that was her way of shutting it down.

"Craig is in the middle of playing dominoes, but Toni's on her way," someone said near the opening to the kitchen.

"Here I am. Here I am. What's going on?" Toni asked as she moved closer. "What's this I hear about Martina making me and Craig a cake?"

Toni gasped when she saw the dessert, and she placed her hand on her chest. "Oh, my goodness, MJ. This is gorgeous. I can't believe you did this for us."

"I don't care what people say about you, Martina. Sometimes you're all right," Jada said with a laugh, and Martina rolled her eyes. That sounded exactly like something she would've said to one of them.

"Don't listen to her, MJ. I appreciate you doing this for us," Toni said. "Thank you, Cuz. I love it."

Toni turned and hugged her, holding on longer than Martina preferred. She didn't mind Paul, her daughter, and her grandmother hugging her, but it was always weird when her cousins got all mushy and teary-eyed the way Toni was now.

"Yeah, yeah, yeah. Just cut the damn cake. Geez," Martina said before thinking, and Gram elbowed her in the side.

Son of a...

This being sweet shit is going to be a lot harder than I thought.

Chapter Thirty-One

The following Wednesday, Martina entered her grandparent's piano room expecting to see others who were attending the family reunion meeting. There were plenty of cars outside, but she was first to arrive in the meeting space.

Good. Now she had first dibs on the fluffy sofa.

The huge area doubled as her grandparents' ballroom and with its calming color palette and comfortable furnishings, it was one of Martina's favorite rooms in the home.

She dropped down on one of the sofas that faced another one and propped her feet up on the coffee table.

"Gram was just asking if you had arrived yet," Jada said as she floated into the room wearing a white, off-the-shoulder jumpsuit that complemented her petite body. She looked as if she was heading to a Vogue magazine photo shoot.

"I came right in here since the meeting should be starting now. Where is everyone else?" Martina asked. "I've had a long day, and I'm ready to go home."

"Me too," her cousin said, sitting next to her and crossing her legs. "I'm sure they'll be in here soon, but what's gotten into you? Sunday, you didn't dole out one insult, and then you come in today without stopping by the kitchen. Usually the moment you walk in, you try to start some nonsense with at least one person."

"No, I don't," Martina lied weakly.

"MJ, yes you do. Are you sick or something? By now you would've said something like, *why are you walking in here looking like you should be on a street corner selling your body.* Or *look who's here—the Jenkins family's black Barbie doll,*" Jada said, making a funny face and almost sounding exactly like Martina.

198

Martina grinned. "That does sound like something the old Martina would've said, but I'm trying to change," she said, surprised that she'd volunteered anything.

Jada's eyebrows dipped into a V. "Change what?"

"Myself. My funky attitude. Now stop asking so many damn questions," Martina snapped and was now pissed because she let her cousin goad her.

Jada uncrossed her legs and turned fully to face Martina. "You?" she said with a smirk. "You're trying to change? After thirty-plus years of being a pain in the ass to everyone who knows you? *Now* you're trying to change? Why? Did you make a bet with someone?"

She was dead serious, and Martina couldn't help but laugh. Her family knew her too well. Normally, a bet would've been the only way she'd consider toning down her personality and adding a filter to her mouth. She lived to harass family and friends. It was her way of showing them that she loved them. Besides, it was entertaining as hell getting a rise out of them.

"No, I didn't make a bet. I promised Paul that I would stop running off at the mouth and try to be kinder with my words."

Jada stared at her for a long moment, and once she realized Martina was serious, she burst out laughing.

Most times, her cousin acted like she was too cute to laugh. She didn't want to mess up her makeup, clothes, or her always perfectly styled hair. But right now, she was literally rolling around on the sofa.

"What's wrong with her?" Christina asked when she, Sumeera, and Liberty strolled in followed by several others. "What did you do?" her cousin asked accusingly.

"I didn't do anything. She's just an idiot who—"

"See!" Jada pointed at her, barely able to speak from laughing as tears rolled down her face. "That right there tells me that you're never going to change. You can't. It's impossible."

Irritation swirled inside Martina. She was tempted to knock her cousin upside the head with a sofa pillow like she used to do when they were kids.

But she wouldn't.

Being around her family was the best time to practice the *new* her, and she refused to be distracted. She was going to prove to everyone and herself that she could keep her mouth shut. She didn't have to harass them for kicks.

For the next few minutes, Martina didn't say anything while Jada told the others about how Paul had convinced Martina to change her ways. Of course, no one believed she could do it and said as much.

"Can we just get this meeting started?" Martina snapped.

"Oh, so now you want to start on time?" Sumeera said with a laugh. "During the last meeting, we had to wait until you finished pranking my husband before we could start."

Everyone chimed in, sharing stories of some of her shenanigans. Martina had to admit that she'd gotten creative with some of them. She was going to miss being an asshole. It was definitely going to take her some time to clean up her act.

"All right, that's enough," Toni said and sat on the other side of Martina. "There's good in MJ. She just doesn't like for people to see that kind, gentler side of her, but it's there. We've all experienced her coming through for us at one time or another."

"True," Liberty chimed in, "but then she blows her kind gestures by doing or saying something that makes us want to strangle her."

Once again, they all chimed in with stories, and Martina was barely able to keep her mouth shut. The other reason she picked on them was because they gave her so much ammunition. All of them often had some type of drama going on in their lives, and because she had so many connections, she found out about them. She couldn't help shining a spotlight on their issues. Like now, she could tell everyone about how Liberty and Nate were caught...

Nope, I'm not saying anything. Just keep your mouth shut, girl, she told herself.

"That's enough. Let's settle down and get started," Grams said as she sat in the upholstered chair that reclined.

Several other family members strolled in, pulling up seating and forming a circle. There were at least twenty-five people gathered around.

"We only have a few weeks to make sure everything is in place before the Fourth of July," Gram said. "Where do we stand on everything?"

For the next hour and a half, they discussed everything from menus to transportation for getting the large family around town. There were so many moving parts, but everyone was taking their roles seriously. It sounded like they just might pull off a successful reunion.

Martina found herself looking forward to the event, but she also couldn't wait until it was over. She'd have to talk to Gram about not waiting until the last minute the next time.

By the time Martina left her grandparents' home, it was almost eight o'clock at night. She couldn't wait to get home since she and Paul would have the place to themselves. Janay was at a friend's house.

Martina smiled at the thought. Paul had to work late and wouldn't make it home until after nine. That would give her enough time to create a romantic evening with candles, some strawberries and whipped cream, and a bubble bath for two.

As she mentally planned what she'd need to do once she got home, her cell phone rang. She almost growled when her mother-in-law's name showed on the car's dashboard.

"She's the last person I want to talk to," Martina mumbled and started to let the call go to voicemail. Then again, the woman rarely called. Maybe it was something important.

Sighing, Martina answered. "Hello."

"Hello, dear," Angelica's haughty voice boomed through the speakers, and Martina turned down the volume. "I'm surprised you answered. I was planning to leave a voicemail."

"What can I do for you, Angelica?" Martina asked, proud that she was able to keep the irritation out of her tone.

"I just wanted to let you know brunch will be at one o'clock on Sunday. Paul told me that you decided to attend. You're going to love Chef Enrique's dishes. I know you're used to that unhealthy soul food stuff, but he's an award-winning, certified, executive chef who used to cook for three different U.S. presidents. He's masterful in the kitchen and thrilled that we asked him to cater our brunch."

Martina gripped the steering wheel tighter and gritted her teeth as anger rolled through her. She was going to kill Paul. She never agreed to attend and never would.

"Angelica," she interrupted the woman's ramblings. "Apparently there's been some mis—"

"Oh, hold on a minute, dear. I have another call."

The moment the woman clicked over, Martina disconnected. She started to call Paul and curse him out. Instead, she made a U-turn at the next intersection, causing another driver who was turning right to blare their horn at her.

Martina didn't care. The tongue-lashing she had planned for Paul needed to be done in person.

Chapter Thirty-Two

Paul leaned back in his office chair and slowly swiveled back and forth as he listened to Governor Whitehall. The man's raspy voice, from years of smoking, flowed through the speakerphone on Paul's desk. They'd been on the call for the last ten minutes, and Paul knew it wouldn't be a quick conversation. It never was. The man loved to talk.

"Okay, enough of my rambling," Whitehall finally said. "I'm sure you're curious about why I'm calling. I heard that you've been keeping yourself busy since leaving the Senate. I trust the restaurants are doing well."

Paul was curious as to where this conversation was going but played along. "Yes, they're doing well. I can't complain."

He talked about how fulfilling his new-ish career choice had been for him. He was in the process of assuming ownership of what would be his third restaurant, and Paul was excited about the challenge it would bring.

The governor asked him about the boards that he sat on, and Paul didn't have to wonder where the man had gotten his information. No doubt his father was bragging about his accomplishments. He wanted Paul to return to politics, but Paul had no intentions of doing that even though he had a feeling that was the reason for this phone call.

He had put distance between himself and the political world that had been a huge part of his life for years. He came from generations of political figures, and his father assumed that Paul would someday be president.

That was his parents' dream, not his. Still, even after leaving the Senate, he ran into colleagues at various fundraisers and other events. Many, like the governor, often asked if he'd consider returning, while others assumed he would.

"I'd like for you to consider running for governor when I leave office in two years. Only one other person, my wife, knows that I'm not planning to run again."

"I'm surprised to hear that. Is everything all right?" He was only two years into his first term and had the option of running for another four-year term.

"I've served in politics for over forty years, and according to my wife, it's time for me to retire," he said and chuckled. "You're married. I'm sure your wife has *told* you a thing or two. I've learned to pick my battles, and this is one I know I can't win."

Paul laughed. "Yeah, I know exactly what you mean."

He thought about his and Martina's disagreement regarding the Father's Day brunch. Sometimes arguing with her wasn't worth the stress that came with it. It was better to just concede and keep the peace.

"I know you left the senate years ago," the governor continued, "but your family has a long history..."

Paul listened as the man laid out all the reasons why Paul should return to politics and run for governor. Whitehall was wasting his time. Paul wasn't interested.

"Governor, I'm honored that you'd think of me, but I have..."

Paul's office door burst open, and Martina stormed in looking ready to kill.

"You have lost your mind if you think I'm going to your parents' house Sunday. I told you I'd rather gouge out my eyes with a screwdriver than attend that brunch. Yet, you told your mother that I'd be there. What the hell were you thinking? I wouldn't sit across from that woman even if you paid me a million dollars."

Anger clawed through Paul. He leaned forward in his seat and reached for the base of the phone as he glared at his wife. "Governor, let me give you a call back."

Martina's eyes grew round, and she cursed under her breath before turning her back to him.

"No problem, Paul. But, if possible, I'd like to know your answer soon."

"I understand, sir. I'll be in touch." Paul pushed the end button and leaned back in his seat struggling to contain the fury raging inside of him.

"Baby, I am so sorry," Martina hurried to say and approached the desk. "I didn't realize you were on the phone. I was so pissed at the call I received from your mother a few minutes ago. I just came over here and—"

"I'm done, Martina," Paul said, suddenly exhausted. "I have never been so embarrassed in all my life."

"I know, and I'm sorry, but you shouldn't have told your mother that—"

"I never told my mother you were attending. I told her Janay and I would be there, but you would've known that had you asked me. Instead, you burst in here like a crazy woman accusing me without getting your facts straight."

"Paul, babe..."

He held up a hand to quiet her, then sucked in a breath, and released it slowly. He repeated the action, willing himself to calm down.

"I'm tired of us having the same conversation over and over again, but what I'm really tired of—is your mouth."

Martina gasped and leaned back as if he had slapped her. "*Excuse you?*" she snapped. "I'm not one of your little flunky employees that you can talk to any—"

"Just...just be quiet for once!" Paul yelled and jerked out of his seat, causing the back of his chair to hit the wall. "I can't keep doing this with you, Martina. God knows I love you, but I've had enough of the arguing over the same damn thing. And I've had enough of listening to you bad mouth my mother and... Hell, I'm just tired of it all. I'm done."

Martina narrowed her eyes and moved closer to the desk. "What are you saying?"

"I'm saying I need a break."

The words were out of his mouth before he had a chance to process them, but it was true. A day, a week, Paul wasn't sure how much time he needed away from her, but he really did need a break.

"Come on, Paul. I said I'm sorry. Let's just—"

"Show yourself out, Martina, and close the door behind you." His voice was eerily calm, calmer than he felt.

Martina opened her mouth to speak again but quickly shut it. Whatever she saw on his face or heard in his tone got through to her. She turned and walked out of the office, slamming the door behind her.

Paul dropped back against his seat and ran his hands down his face. He didn't know what he'd do next, but he sure as hell planned to put some space between him and his wife.

Chapter Thirty-Three

Late Sunday morning, Martina sat at the kitchen counter as her grandmother made them both a cup of coffee. In less than two hours, the Jenkins clan would start rolling in for Sunday brunch.

"I really messed up this time, Gram. Paul is never going to forgive me." And Martina didn't blame him.

She had been horrified the other day when she found out he was on a call, on speaker phone no less. Each time the moment played back in her mind, she cringed. She might've embarrassed him, but she was equally embarrassed and was glad she didn't know the governor personally.

She recounted the incident to her grandmother, and the more she shared about that night, the worse she felt. Shame had practically strangled her over the last few days, and today was no different.

I'm sorry wasn't enough to fix the mess that she'd made, and if she didn't think of something soon, she was going to lose her husband for good.

It was a miracle that he hadn't left her years ago because she had definitely given him reason to. But this time... The anguish she'd seen on his face the other night crushed her. What had she been thinking? No, actually, that was the problem. She hadn't thought before speaking...again.

That night, after she'd left Paul's office, he had arrived home twenty minutes later. He had packed a bag quicker than she could form a proper apology. At least he'd told her where he'd be staying—a hotel, and that he'd be in touch.

That had been four days ago. Martina hadn't heard from him until he texted her late last night. He told her that he'd be picking up Janay and she'd be spending today, Father's Day, with him.

"When will you learn?" Gram murmured angrily, pulling Martina back into the conversation as she set the coffee mug in front of her. "I have warned you too many times about that mouth of yours. Now you might've lost the best thing that ever happened to you."

"I know, Gram, and I feel awful. I don't know how to fix this."

Gram sat next to her. "You said your in-laws won't eat until one, right?"

"Yeah." Martina dragged the word out and narrowed her eyes at her grandmother.

"Good. You still have time to go home, change into something pretty, and get there on time."

"But Gram, what about our brunch? I never miss a Jenkins family brunch. I'm sure as hell not going to miss it because of Paul's parents. They know that we always have Sunday brunch here. Besides, his mother can't cook worth a shit, and she's hired some... Ow!"

Martina gasped and leaped from the bar stool away from her grandmother who had just pinched her arm. Not just pinched, but she had twisted enough of her skin to rip it from the bone.

"What was that for?" Martina screamed, her arm stinging like she'd been severely burned.

"I am so sick of that mouth!" her grandmother yelled and pounded on the counter.

It took a lot to make Katherine Jenkins angry and right now she looked as if she was going to attack again.

"And if I have to tell you one more time about cursing in my house, I'm banning you from here, and I mean it! Do you hear me?" she demanded.

"Yes, ma'am."

Martina rubbed her arm. The furious scowl marring her grandmother's sweet face made Martina's heart crack. Once again, she'd gone too far. Normally, she didn't give a damn about anything anyone said to her, but what Gram thought of her meant everything.

The woman was her *shero* and the one person who put up with her crap and loved her despite it.

Well, her and...Paul.

Paul.

Tears pricked the back of Martina's eyes, and she batted her eyelashes to keep them from falling. Wednesday night had been the first time in a long time that she'd cried. Her tears had been falling off and on ever since. Her heart hurt.

Martina reclaimed her seat. "Gram, I don't know what to do," she said, tears falling faster than she could wipe them away. "I've been like this all my life. I can't just snap my fingers and change. What do you want me to do, stop talking?"

Her grandmother snatched a few napkins from a nearby holder and handed them to Martina before wrapping her arm around her.

"Sweetheart, I know you're hurting, and I know you're sorry about the other night. I just wish you could tap into that gentle, sweeter side of you that I see so often. I don't know where we went wrong with you, but you're going to have to do better, MJ."

"I know, Gram, and I've tried."

"Try harder. Paul adores you, but I understand how he can get tired of your slick mouth. You talk too damn much," she said. Martina's mouth dropped open, and then she couldn't help but laugh. She could count on one hand the number of times her grandmother cursed.

"Wait. I can't curse but you—"

"This is my house, and I can do whatever I want to. Besides, sometimes you bring out the worst in me."

Martina didn't miss the way her grandmother's lips twitched as if trying to stifle a smile.

"Now what was I saying?" Katherine asked. "Oh, I know. You can't say everything that pops into your head, especially to your man. Paul is not only your husband, he's a grown man. Respect that and stop taking for granted that he'll always forgive your nonsense. There might come a time when he won't."

That time might be now, Martina almost spoke aloud, but didn't. Instead, the words weighed heavily on her chest.

"You can't keep carrying on like this and expect to have a loving and successful marriage," Katherine continued.

"Gram, I was like this when he married me," Martina shot back. Yes, he complained about her saying the wrong things, but he loved the way she used her big mouth in other ways.

Crap. No way am I telling Gram that.

"I don't think Paul will ever forgive me," she said instead.

"You've messed up plenty of times, and he forgave you," Gram said and patted Martina's hand before standing.

"Yeah, but he never left me."

"That's true, but I know he still loves you so there's hope. Now...I need to make you a pan of banana pudding. Oh, wait, I made an extra peach cobbler last night. You can take that with you."

Martina frowned, and worry settled in. Her grandmother was getting up in age, and there weren't any signs of dementia, but... "Gram, I don't need to take any food home. I'm planning to eat here once everyone arrives."

"The cobbler is not for you. It's for your in-laws. You're going to their Father's Day brunch, and you're going to get your man back," she said with conviction. "But you can't go empty-handed."

She was one of those people who believed that when you went to someone's house, you took a gift to the host.

"I can't, Gram. Paul is so mad at me that he probably won't even let me into their house."

"Trust me. He'll be thrilled to see you. But in the future, when your husband asks you to go somewhere with him, go. You're his wife, his better half, his arm candy. I'm sure he doesn't ask you to attend every event with him. So clearly, he really wanted you at this one. The least you could've done was go."

She was right. Paul never complained about attending the Jenkins family brunch weekly. Not one time had he complained in all the years they'd been together. Yet, she couldn't be bothered to attend one stupid brunch with his family.

She shook her head. *I have to do better.*

Martina glanced at the peach cobbler that her grandmother set in front of her. It looked so good. She was tempted to stick a fork in it and start eating it herself.

"Even if I did go, I can't take that."

Her grandmother frowned. "Why not?"

"Because the Kendricks are not your typical Black folks. There's no way they'd eat that no matter how good I know it is. They are more of the green bean casserole, cranberry sauce with actual cranberries, and maybe pumpkin pie type of people."

Gram nodded. "Ah, okay. No soul food. Well, we should be able to whip up something you can take with you."

Feeling more encouraged, Martina stood from her seat. Yeah, she was going to swallow her pride and go to her in-laws' place and beg Paul's forgiveness. Then she would sit at the dining table with his family and friends and be on her best behavior.

"Sit down and take a load off, Gram. I'll make something. I'm just not sure what."

Actually, instead of food, maybe she'd take some hard liquor. Martina had a feeling she was going to need a shot of something strong before the day was over.

Chapter Thirty-Four

Paul had been at his parents' home for the last thirty minutes, and already he was ready to leave. There were at least twenty people there, and his mother was expecting more. She looked like royalty in a long, gold summer dress that complemented her dark skin as she floated around being the perfect host. Her hair was piled on top of her head in an intricate updo, and her makeup was as flawless as ever.

She was in her element talking to a couple of women. One was married to the mayor, and the other was the fiancée to a man who owned one of the largest manufacturing companies in the state.

While his mother entertained the women, Paul's father was on the back deck, smoking a cigar with some of his friends—a few senators and former senators.

Paul was near the foyer, leaning against the staircase railing, observing.

Why am I here? He thought. He wasn't in the mood for socializing, and he couldn't stop thinking about Martina. She might've driven him nuts, but he missed her like crazy. She also made his parents' events more tolerable, mainly because she talked about everyone.

Paul shook his head. He tried not to encourage that type of behavior, but the woman was funny even when she wasn't trying to be.

Stop. I have to stop thinking about her.

All he was doing was torturing himself with thoughts of her. What he needed to do was go find Martina, forgive her, and then ask her to forgive him. Walking out on her was a punk move. He'd vowed to love her through the good and bad. Yet, when things got beyond bad, he cut out.

Paul pushed away from the railing and strolled into his father's office. He'd barely made it to the patio doors that overlooked a large side yard before his mother entered the room.

"Why are you in here? You should be outside with your father and his friends," she said, strolling over and lifting up on tiptoes to place a kiss on his cheek.

"I'm not in the mood for socializing. I'll stay for brunch, but I probably won't stay much longer than that. I'll leave Janay, though, so that you can spend time with her."

His mother shook her head. "You've been sulking from the moment you arrived. Surely, you're not thinking about Martina. I don't know what happened between you two, but I've said it before, you can do better."

Paul ignored her comment, and asked, "Why did you call Martina the other night?"

Angelica frowned. "To let her know what I had planned for today. I wanted to make sure she wasn't concerned about the food. It's no secret that she doesn't like my cooking. So, I informed her that we had hired a famous chef. What's the big deal?"

"I told you that me and Janay would be attending. You knew Martina wouldn't be here."

She sighed loudly. "No, actually I didn't know. I assumed she'd show up with her husband since that's what wives normally do," she spat. "But that's not the type of woman you married. Anyway, maybe it's good she isn't here. Now you'll have a good time."

"Mom."

"That girl is so trifling," she talked over him. "After I gave her information about the brunch, she hung up on me. I just don't understand how you can put up with that—"

"Enough!" Paul roared, and his mother jumped. "I will not have you talk about *my wife* like that!"

Her eyes went wide, and she took a step back with her mouth ajar. He had never raised his voice or disrespected her in any way, but he'd had enough.

"I'm sorry, but this has to stop. I get that you don't think she's good enough for me. And you think she's not worthy to be a part of this family. But how dare you badmouth her in my face!"

"Well, I'd have to be blind not to notice that she doesn't like me either."

"But she's never treated you like you were beneath her or like she was a second-class citizen. Can you say the same?"

At least she had the decency to look contrite. Martina said her share of bad and inappropriate things about his mother. But unfortunately, it had been warranted, and Paul hated that he didn't address the situation sooner. Granted, he'd talked to his mother about her attitude towards his wife, but clearly, he needed to do more.

"From now on, if you can't show my wife the respect she deserves, I won't be coming around. I've been a fool asking her to come here with me, knowing that all you're going to do is turn up your nose to her. Well, those days are gone."

"Paul, you're overreacting."

"Am I?" he asked, moving closer and crowding her. "How'd you feel when grandpa treated you like a leper when you first started dating dad? It wasn't pleasant, was it?"

Her smug expression dropped and was replaced with one of contrite.

His father, Paul Sr. had come from old money and his parents had wanted him to marry the daughter of a friend of theirs. But his father had fallen in love with his Angelica and was willing to be kicked out of the family to be with her. It hadn't come to that, but clearly his mother had forgotten about that time in her life.

"You remember how grandfather made you feel. Yet, you're treating Martina the same way. Well, not anymore. Since you can't treat my wife with respect and make her feel welcome when she's here, neither of us will be back."

Movement in the doorway caught his attention, and he was surprised to see Martina. She was standing there looking beautiful but unsure. Dressed in a short, red halter dress that showed off her toned arms, flat stomach, and shapely legs, Paul stood speechless. He couldn't believe she was there.

Martina stepped into the room but stopped. "Hi. Sorry I'm late."

***

If you can't show my wife the respect she deserves, I won't be coming around.

Martina hadn't meant to listen in, but they were talking loud enough to be heard outside the door. It made her heart dance at hearing Paul defend her. He always defended her, but never with an ultimatum.

She swallowed hard as she stared into his eyes from across the room. The butler had let her in and told her where to find Paul, but she had no idea that his mother would be in the office too. She'd hope to have time with Paul before having to come face-to-face with his mother.

Apparently, not.

Well, here goes nothing.

Martina strolled into the room with her head held high. Her gaze stayed on Paul until she was a foot from where he and his mother stood.

She turned her attention to Angelica. "I'm sorry I'm late. I wasn't sure what to bring, but I thought that maybe your favorite bottle of wine could go with dinner." She held up The Prisoner Red Blend

2019 bottle of wine in her right hand, then lifted her left hand. "And maybe the Macallan scotch would be good for after dinner."

Angelica placed her hand on her chest, and tears bloomed in her eyes.

Okay, this is a first.

The woman actually looked grateful, or maybe that was sorrow that Martina was witnessing. She hadn't been sure what to expect upon arrival, but this wasn't it.

"Thank you," Angelica said, her words sounding heartfelt as she accepted the bottles. She set them both on the desk, and then she shocked the hell out of Martina when she embraced her.

"Martina, I am so sorry for the way I've treated you over the years," the older woman said, then pulled back slightly. "I promise you, going forward, you will know that you're always welcome in our home. I know it'll take time, but I hope you can forgive my horrible attitude."

She hugged her again, and Martina glanced at Paul and lifted an eyebrow. He gave her a slight smile and shrugged.

God, it was so good to see him.

When Angelica pulled away, she dabbed at her eyes, and Martina knew she needed to say something.

"Angelica, thank you for inviting me to brunch."

Angelica smiled. "You're welcome, dear. You're always welcome here." She grabbed the liquor and glanced between Martina and Paul before heading to the door but slowed. "Dinner will be served in fifteen minutes. I expect you both at the table and not upstairs in one of the bathrooms."

Martina gasped, and she could've sworn she heard the woman giggling on her way out the door. She swung around to Paul who was laughing.

"She knows what we did," Martina whispered.

"Sounds like it," he said and closed the distance between them.

Martina's hands started sweating. There was so much she wanted to say to Paul, but she didn't know where to start.

"I've missed you," he said.

"I've missed you more," she said, feeling a little choked up. "Paul, I'm so sorry...for everything. I know I've promised a hundred times to watch my mouth and clean up my behavior and attitude. Unfortunately, I have failed every time."

"Sweetheart."

"But going forward, I'll do better," she talked over him. She had to get this out. "You have my word that I will *never* speak ill of your mother or father again. I feel awful about the way I embarrassed you the other night. If you want, I'll apologize to the governor."

"That won't be necessary." He reached for her hand, but she threw herself into his arms and practically sent them both crashing to the floor.

"Whoa," Paul said with a laugh and righted them.

He held her close, and neither of them said a word as they stood in the middle of the office just holding each other. Suddenly, tears blurred her eyes, and she cursed under her breath.

"These damn tears."

Paul chuckled and placed a kiss against her temple but didn't let her go. "I'm sorry I left," he mumbled against her hair.

"Don't ever leave me again," Martina said, not bothering to wipe the tears that were flowing freely. "Please don't leave me."

"I won't, baby. You're mine forever. Big mouth and all."

Martina sputtered a laugh and leaned back to look at him. "Good."

He wiped her tears with the pad of his thumb and stared into her eyes. "I know I've been hard on you, but I hope you know that I love you more than anything."

"I know, and the feeling is mutual. Things are going to be better. I promise."

He nodded and gave her a quick peck on the lips.

"Now that we have that settled, let's go eat. I'm starving," Martina admitted, and her stomach growled. "Or...since we're the only two people in here, maybe we should test out your dad's desk. Do you think it'll hold us?"

Paul shook his head and laughed. "I don't know what I'd do without you."

Not giving her a chance to respond, he lowered his head and kissed her. Martina's heart melted. Paul was her everything, and she was going to do whatever it took to become the person he deserved. Even if it meant cutting out her tongue.

Chapter Thirty-Five

"Okay, so now what is this nonsense that I've heard about you acting like a normal person?" Peyton Jenkins-Cutter asked her cousin Martina.

For the last twenty minutes, they'd been discussing family reunion business. But before they hung up, Peyton wanted the scoop. She'd heard that Martina and Paul had gone through a rough patch but seemed to be back on track.

"What have you heard?" Martina asked.

"I heard that you had some type of out-of-body experience, and you've been replaced by a human."

"Ha, ha, ha. I see you have jokes," Martina said with a laugh. "My ass hasn't changed that much. As soon as I find the person who's been talking behind my back, they'll get a taste of the old MJ."

They talked for a few minutes longer, and Peyton listened as her cousin filled her in on the latest between her and Paul. Peyton had always known that the man was a saint, but the longer he put up with her cousin, the more she was sure of it. Martina was a handful, always had been, especially when they were growing up.

She and Martina weren't only cousins but also best friends. Peyton knew her better than anyone, and one thing she knew for sure—Martina was madly in love with Paul. It would've destroyed her cousin if Paul had left for good.

"Well, I'm glad you two worked everything out. I can't imagine you without him or vice versa."

"Yeah, he might not know it, but he's stuck with me. I'd follow him to the end of the earth if I had to. Okay, enough about me. What's up with you and that hunk that you're married to?"

Peyton smiled. She was sitting in the living room of their renovated brownstone, and her gaze landed on one of the photos on the mantle. It was a picture of her, Michael, their son—Michael

Jr., and her stepdaughter Michaela who felt like her own flesh and blood. The three of them were her heartbeats.

Michael might've been her second husband, but life with him was better than anything she had ever experienced. He was loving, considerate, and ridiculously protective of her. Each day with him was a new adventure, and he was everything a woman could want in a man. And that's what she told her cousin.

"Yet, you're missing Cincinnati to the point of wanting to relocate back here," Martina said in that smart-ass tone that grated on Peyton's nerves. "Have you told him yet?"

Peyton sighed. "No."

"What are you waiting for? Are you *scurred?*" she taunted, using an alternative form of scared.

"Of course not! I just want to make sure that's what I want before I talk to him about it."

"You already know that's what you want. Otherwise, you wouldn't have brought it up with me and the girls weeks ago. So, what's really holding you back?"

Martina was right. Peyton was almost positive that she was ready for a change, but not at the expense of upending her family's life.

"There's so much to consider, MJ. It's not just about me. I have to think about how this would affect Michael and the kids. So that's why I haven't said anything. I'm sure when the time is right, I'll have that talk with Michael."

That was a talk she wasn't looking forward to. Michael grew up in Brooklyn and absolutely loved the city. It was home for him. *If* she ever did share her thoughts with him about moving, it wouldn't be an easy conversation.

***

Michael Cutter didn't bother turning on the overhead light as he strolled into his small office. There was just enough sunlight slipping between the semi-opened blinds to guide his steps to his desk. Besides, the dimly lit room was just what he needed in order to take a breather.

The moment he sat in his leather office chair, he released a long, exhausted sigh. He laid his head back and closed his eyes as he enjoyed the peacefulness of the moment. He loved being a private investigator, especially now that his business had taken off. Problem was, he was barely keeping up.

No pain, no gain. The popular quote flitted through his mind.

He had wanted more clients. He got them. Now he had to figure out how to manage it all. Thankfully, his father, a retired NYPD detective, had agreed to help him out on a part-time basis. Carlton Cutter was actually his stepfather but had been more of a father than Michael's birth father had ever been.

Michael pinched the bridge of his nose trying to block out thoughts of the man who had nearly killed his mother. That was how Carlton had come into their lives. He'd been the responding police officer when Michael was a kid and barely able to pull his father off of his mother.

He shook his head, trying to shake the thoughts free. Not a day went by that he didn't thank God for Carlton. The man had saved his life more than once, and Michael would forever be in his debt.

Opening his eyes, he sat up and glanced at his smart watch. It was almost two o'clock in the afternoon. He wished he could cut out early and go home to his wife and block out the rest of the world, but daddy duty called.

Today, he had to pick up the kids from summer school and take them to their karate lessons. Throughout the year it was either that, dance classes, basketball, football, or soccer. They stayed busy, and once they all got home, he'd need to spend some quality time with his wife.

It never ends, he thought.

Michael loved Peyton and the kids more than life. Yet, there were some days when he wished he could stop and take time to breathe.

Today's not that day.

Michael booted up his computer so that he could upload pictures that he'd taken during the past week. A recent client, Bobbi Green, had hired him to get proof that her husband was cheating on her. But as of a few days ago, Paul had a feeling that the man was not only cheating but also involved in something shady.

He just needed proof.

Michael had gotten a few photos of the man leaving restaurants and hotels with women who weren't Bobbi. She would be pleased to learn that her suspicions were correct. Hector was a dog, and in the three weeks that Michael had been trailing him, he'd seen him with at least two different women.

Bobbi was planning to divorce him but wanted proof to back up her claim that Hector was unfaithful. As a wealthy woman, she'd had Hector sign a prenup. If at any time he was caught cheating, he wouldn't get a dime should they divorce.

The woman had married Hector seven years ago despite the fact that he'd been a construction worker with a shady work history and little money to his name. He was also ten years her junior. But she had made him into what she wanted him to be—a dutiful husband who helped her run her businesses and who was also eye candy. Somewhere along the line, he started to stray.

Michael uploaded the photos and other documentation. Since he still had some time before he needed to report back to Bobbi, he planned to use the time to continue surveillance on Hector. A few days ago, he'd gotten photos of him standing in the shadows outside of a bar called Charity's. What was interesting was that he'd been in a heated discussion with a man that Michael recognized. A low-level drug dealer, Curtis Barnes, who was connected to a well-known drug cartel.

Michael yawned and laid his head back against the seat as he rubbed his eyes. Man, he was tired. He was going to have to grab a coffee for a little pick me up before he picked up the kids.

"Rough day?"

Michael glanced up to see his dad's huge frame filling the doorway. Carlton was a giant of a man who Michael admired more than anyone in the world.

"More like a long day," he said. "What are you still doing here? You're usually gone by noon."

Carlton leaned on the back of one of the guest chairs positioned in front of the desk. "I had some paperwork to finish, but I'm leaving now unless you need help with something."

"Nope. I'm good. The only thing I have left to do today is officially close out the Brockman case." That required some paperwork and sending their billable hours to their accountant for her to emit a final bill to their client.

"All right, then I'll see you in the morning." His dad pushed away from the chair. "Have a good evening and give the fam a hug from me."

"Will do. See ya, dad."

It took Michael fifteen minutes to wrap up the Brockman's case and send information to the accountant. He locked up his desk and had just shut down his computer when he heard the outer office door. Normally, his dad locked that door when he left, but maybe he had forgotten.

Michael stood to check it out, but before he could round his desk, a man entered his office.

Hector Green.

He appeared a little more imposing up close. Built like a heavy-weight boxer, Hector was in his mid-fifties with a low haircut, and he was graying at the temples. Dressed in a three-piece suit that probably set him back a couple of thousands, he could've easily blended in with those on Wall Street.

"You don't look surprised to see me," the older man said.

"But I am. What do you want?" Michael asked, and stiffened when the man pulled a SIG 365 from the back of his waistband.

Shit.

Unease clawed through Michael as he tried not to make any sudden moves. It wasn't the first time someone pulled a gun on him, and in his line of work, it probably wouldn't be the last time.

Michael slowly slid his hand to the small pistol that he had velcroed beneath his desk. Like his father, he'd been an NYPD detective before leaving the force and always had a weapon nearby.

"Hector, why don't you put the gun away and we can discuss this situation like two adults," Michael tried to reason.

"No way. You and that witch I married are trying to destroy me! You don't know who you're dealing with!"

"What do you want?" Michael asked again.

"My wife accused me of cheating and told me that she'd hired you to find proof."

Dammit. What the hell was Bobbi thinking?

"I want everything you have on me. Documents, videos, photos. *Everything.* There's no way I'm going to let some two-bit private investigator ruin everything I've worked my ass off for. And since you're trying to ruin my life, maybe I'll do the same to you."

He raised the gun and Michael noted how steady the man's hands were. Clearly, he was comfortable holding the pistol.

Michael had his hand wrapped around the grip of his own gun and waited.

"I want everything now!" Hector roared. "Then I want you to call my wife and tell her that you don't have anything on me. Tell her that she's shit out of luck."

"And if you don't lower your weapon, your wife is going to be the least of your problems," Carlton's voice boomed from behind Hector, but that wasn't what made the man's fair complexion turn several shades of red. No, it was the fact that Carlton's own gun was resting against Hector's temple. "Better yet, hand the gun over now, nice and slow."

Hector lowered his weapon, and Carlton took it from him.

Michael dropped down in his office chair and released the breath he hadn't realized he'd been holding.

"I'll drop your gun off at the police station. Or better yet, I'll give—"

"You can't do that! I have a permit to carry," Hector snapped.

"Let's see it, but in the meantime, I'm going to pat you down and make sure you don't have any other weapons on you," Carlton said and did just that. "Now, where's that permit?"

"I—I don't have it on me," Hector sputtered. Suddenly he didn't look as confident as he had moments ago.

"No worries. The cops will be here shortly."

"Wh—what?" Hector said, his gaze bouncing between Michael and Carlton. "Wh—why?"

"Your ass came in here threatening my son!" Carlton roared, and even Michael sat up straighter. His father was a gentle giant until you made him mad. It was safe to say that he was livid. "I did you a favor by calling the cops. Next time you won't be so lucky."

On cue, two police officers, who were friends of Carlton's, entered the office. Holding someone at gunpoint was a class E felony, but knowing Hector's connections, he'd probably be released on bail in a few hours. That didn't mean he wouldn't eventually get jail time, especially if Michael had his way.

"What made you come back?" Michael asked his father.

"I had forgotten my phone charger, and while I was here, I received a couple of calls that I'd been waiting for. When I heard your visitor, I called the boys in blue."

Michael nodded. "Well, thanks for having my back. That could've ended badly...for Hector."

His father chuckled.

As the cops led Hector away, Michael didn't miss the anger swimming in the man's dark eyes. There was no doubt that this wouldn't be the last time he and Hector came face-to-face.

Chapter Thirty-Six

As Peyton pulled the herb-crusted turkey roast out of the oven, she thought about her conversation with Martina. Maybe it was time she told Michael about how she was feeling. She had hoped that the desire to move back to Cincinnati would pass, but it hadn't. If anything, after hanging out with her sister, Christina, in Atlanta and talking to her cousins weekly, it had gotten stronger.

She'd be the first to admit that while growing up, her sister, Martina, Toni, and Jada had gotten on her nerves more often than not. They all were close in age and had grown up more like sisters than cousins. Meaning, they spent practically every day together.

It started when their grandmother used to babysit them before they headed to grade school. As the years progressed, they grew even closer. From first dates to college, and on to when they ran the family business together, they were inseparable.

Maybe that's what she'd been missing, that closeness they once had. Now, they all had their own lives and were doing well. She was too. Teaching electrical apprentices at the community college was a dream she'd had since becoming a master electrician. But it wasn't until she left the family business and moved to New York that she had time to pursue a teaching career.

Peyton heard the front door open, and a commotion in the foyer, and knew her family was home.

"Mommy!" her baby boy yelled as he ran into the kitchen and straight to her.

He was still wearing his white keikogi, his karate uniform, and he looked so adorable. She felt the same when seeing him in his little soccer and football uniforms. With a dad like Michael, he was all boy and wanted to play every sport.

Mikey wrapped his arms around her and laid his head against her stomach. "Rex died," he said of his classroom's guinea pig.

227

"Oh, honey, I'm so sorry." Peyton ran her hand over his short curly hair and tried to sound sincere, but she wasn't a fan of rodents.

"It's okay. Daddy bought me and Kayla ice cream so I wouldn't be sad."

Peyton laughed. She didn't like it when he had sweets before dinner, but today she'd let it go.

"Dude, I thought we'd keep that to ourselves," she heard Michael say from the front foyer.

"Oh...oops," their son said, grinning. Then he grabbed his electronic tablet from the small desk in the corner and sat at the kitchen table.

"Don't even think about turning that on. Go change clothes and get cleaned up so we can eat," Peyton said, ignoring his grumbling as he took baby steps, barely moving toward the kitchen exit. At the pace he was going, he'd never get out of the kitchen.

She started to tell him to get a move on, but Michaela strolled in.

"Hey, Momma," she said and gave Peyton a quick one-arm hug.

It was yet another sign that their daughter was getting older and no longer enjoyed being lovingly smothered by Peyton. At least they still had their weekly girl's day routine. Soon, Michaela would be deep into teenage life and prefer to get her hair and nails done with her friends instead of her mother.

"Daddy said preteens aren't old enough to work, but still, I might have a job!" she blurted, vibrating with excitement.

"Oh, really." Peyton cocked an eyebrow at her handsome husband who stood in the kitchen doorway.

Her heart always pounded a little faster whenever he was near. Michael was hands down the sexiest man alive, especially dressed as he was. At over six feet tall, he was muscular with an athletic build, and his fitted black T-shirt molded over his upper body.

Though his blue jeans weren't tight, they fit snugly enough to show that he had it going on below his waist. The black biker boots covering his feet only enhanced his sexiness. If all that wasn't enough, he was staring at her with those pretty light-brown eyes that stood out against his tawny brown skin.

From day one, his good looks had stolen her breath. They'd first met on an airplane going to Jamaica for Christina and Luke's destination wedding. Since she hadn't immediately known his name, in her mind, she had named him *Gorgeous Eyes.*

It hadn't been love at first sight, but it hadn't taken him long to win her heart. Especially when he'd helped her out of a few sticky situations in Jamaica.

"Mom," Michaela said, irritation dangling on that one word.

"Oh, I'm sorry, sweetheart. I can't wait to hear the details," Peyton said, placing a kiss on Michaela's forehead. The kid's excited energy was palpable.

"Okay," her daughter said. "It all started when we were at karate, and Jimmy's mom showed up late. She was—"

"You can tell her over dinner," Michael interrupted before slipping one of his strong arms around Peyton's waist.

Her heart did somersaults in her chest. It didn't matter how long they'd been married. He still made her giddy inside.

"Daddy, it's not nice to interrupt," Michaela griped. "You should..." her voice trailed off when her cell phone buzzed.

"You're right. It's not nice to interrupt," Michael said, his gaze steady on Peyton. "But I couldn't help it. I've missed your mom today, and I want to kiss her sweet lips."

"Eww, nobody wants to see that," Michaela mumbled under her breath as she dug her phone out of her small purse.

Both kids lumbered out of the kitchen as if they didn't have a care in the world.

"You guys, hurry and get cleaned up. Dinner is ready," Peyton called out before she gave her full attention to her handsome husband. "What's this about a sweet kiss?" she said seconds before Michael's mouth covered hers.

The kiss sang through her veins and made her knees go weak. Often when he got home from work, he'd give her a lingering kiss. But this? There was so much passion and need in the deed that she gripped the front of his t-shirt and held on for dear life.

Every lap of his tongue stoked a fire inside of her, and she was going to spontaneously combust if they didn't put a halt to the lip-lock. But her husband had other ideas. His large hands slid to her butt, and he squeezed, pulling her closer. Her breasts were crushed against his chest, and she felt every inch of his hard body.

He was literally stealing her breath. He was acting as if he hadn't seen her in months versus a few hours, but she wouldn't complain. She loved when her man acted all possessive and needy.

Michael moaned against her mouth and then slowly ended the kiss. He pressed his forehead to hers. "I love coming home to you," he said, his voice huskier than it had been moments ago. "What do you say we get rid of the kids and run away for a year?"

Peyton gasped and nudged him away before laughing. "I thought you were going to say for the night or the weekend. Not a year. You know we can't live without them."

"I guess, but maybe we can try," he said, humor lacing his words as he wiggled his eyebrows. "Then I can have you all to myself. No kids. No clients. No work. The more I think about it, the more the idea is starting to take root."

He pulled her back into his arms and sighed as he held her close. Alarm blared in her mind. Call it a wife's intuition, but something was wrong.

"What happened?" she asked quietly and tilted her head back so that she could look into his eyes.

He shook his head and slowly dropped his arms from around her. "Nothing. Just...just a long day."

Peyton studied him for a few minutes, noting for the first time how tired he looked. Hopefully, he wasn't coming down with something. He rarely came home as worn out as he suddenly looked.

"Why don't you go on up to bed? We can eat without you," she said, rubbing her hand up and down his arm.

"Nah, I'll have dinner with you and the kids, but I'll probably head upstairs early tonight. Let me go wash up."

Peyton watched as he strolled out of the kitchen. He wasn't a moody person, but the way his shoulders were drooped spoke volumes. She had a feeling that something more than *just a long day* was going on. But he wouldn't talk until he was ready. So, she'd have to wait until then.

Hopefully, it's nothing too serious.

Chapter Thirty-Seven

Hours later, Michael released a long sigh of contentment as he stood under one of the shower heads in their newly renovated shower. Their master bathroom had been the last room in their brownstone to get remodeled, and he was glad they'd decided to double the size of the luxury shower. With numerous water sprays pounding his tired body, the water therapy was almost better than getting a massage.

His palms rested against the porcelain tile, and he closed his eyes. *What a day.*

Thinking about how Hector held him at gunpoint earlier had shaken Michael more than he cared to admit. He'd been playing back the moment over and over in his mind, thinking how the situation could've ended differently. If the man had pulled the trigger and shot him, Peyton and the kids would...

Michael couldn't finish the thought. When Peyton had asked him what was wrong, he'd debated on telling her about the incident. What he'd really wanted to do was hug his wife and kids and never let them go. Besides, there was no sense in him scaring her with what could've happened. Instead, he was just grateful that he'd walked away from the situation.

Even more, he wanted Hector locked up. No one threatened his life and got away with it. Especially when Michael was almost positive that the bastard was involved in something illegal. All Michael needed was proof.

"Can I join you?"

Michael lifted his head and glanced toward the opening of the shower, and the blood coursing through his veins went straight to his dick.

Damn.

After years of marriage, his body still reacted immediately at the sight of his gorgeous wife, and it had nothing to do with the fact that she was naked. Although, that helped.

"Always," he finally said.

The moment she stepped inside, he slipped his arm around her and pulled her close to his wet body. She flinched when water from one of the sprayers hit her in the face, and he turned some of them off.

"I'm glad you joined me," Michael said, peppering kisses along her jawline and working his way down her neck. "But I can't be responsible for my actions while you're in here with me."

Peyton chuckled. "Well, you have my permission to have your way with me, but..." her voice trailed off, and he lifted his head to look at her.

He gave her a quick peck on the lips. "What?"

"Are you going to tell me what's wrong?" She glided her hands up his torso, and despite her question, the heat from her touch only made him harder. "You've been distracted since you got home. What happened today?"

He smiled down at her, not surprised that she knew him so well. Still, he had no intention of giving her details. "Just another day. There's a case that has me a little stumped, but it's nothing that's worth talking about, especially when I have my super, sexy wife joining me for a shower. How about I get you a little dirty, and then we can get cleaned up together?"

A grin slid across her plump lips. "Well...I guess that would be okay," she said, the words coming out sassy as she grabbed the body wash and squirted some into her hands. She put the bottle back and gently gripped his shaft all the while maintaining eye contact.

Michael groaned and boxed her in with a hand on either side of her head as she worked up a lather as she stroked him. He moaned and squeezed his eyes shut.

"That feels amazing," he mumbled. Though it felt incredible, if he didn't stop her ministrations, he was going to come right then and there, and that's not what he wanted.

He opened his eyes and growled when he couldn't take any more.

Peyton gasped in surprise when he lifted her and pressed her against the tiled wall. He slammed his mouth over hers and slid into her sweet heat at the same time.

"Oh, yes, baby," she breathed and wrapped her legs around his waist. She showed the strength in her legs when she tightened them around him, and he almost lost it.

Desire pulsed through him, and he drove into her with an urgency he couldn't control. Sex between them had always been hot and intense, but this... Having water pummeling from overhead and feeling Peyton's interior muscles pulsing around his dick as he drove into her was almost too much to handle.

Though he wanted this to last, it was impossible. She felt too damn good. He was nearing his impending release, but he wanted her to come first. The sexy sounds she was making grew louder while she bucked against him, as if she were chasing her orgasm. And it didn't take long for her to cry out his name as she came hard and shuddered against him.

Michael couldn't stop.

He continued driving into her, determined to pull another orgasm from her, and with the way she was clawing his shoulders, she was close. It was as if the thought alone pushed her to another release that gripped her for several seconds. And as he watched her face contort with pleasure, his own release rocked him to his core and pushed him over the edge of his control.

His chest heaved as he slowly lowered her to her feet.

"Wow," she panted. "I came up here to see if you were okay and possibly comfort you if you weren't, but that..."

"You comforted me all right," he said with a laugh. "And now I don't think I can move let alone take a real shower."

She snorted a laugh. "I know, right? Good thing I insisted on us installing a bench in here." Holding his hand, they stumbled to the bench and out of the spray of water. "I was mainly thinking about it for shaving my legs, but this works too."

Michael chuckled, remembering the conversation well. "I actually can think of another use for it," he said, pulling her on top of his lap so she could straddle him. He grinned at the surprise expression on her face when she realized he was hard again.

"Dang, you're ready to go again? I've barely caught my breath."

He shrugged. "What can I say? I have a sexy-ass wife who I can't get enough of."

***

Hours later and unable to fall asleep, Michael stared down at his beautiful wife as she slept. He took in her freshly scrubbed face and cafe au lait skin tone, and his heart softened. She looked so peaceful.

He moved a few strands of her thick hair away from her forehead, giving him an even better view of her face. Seemed like yesterday when they first met that morning on the airplane bound for Jamaica.

Michael smiled at the memory. Peyton had been so tightly wound back then, and she'd had a no-nonsense vibe about her. It was as if she carried the world on her shoulders. Even her hair in a tight bun at her nape and the conservative clothing that she had worn fed into that description. He soon learned that she'd been unhappy with life at the time.

Yet, he had fallen in love with her almost immediately. Since then, Peyton had become not only his wife, but also his best friend. Her need to control every aspect of her world had fallen away. Now she was more carefree in every area of her life. Until recently.

She might've looked peaceful in sleep, but something was troubling her. Michael had first noticed it a few weeks ago, but he was just waiting for her to tell him. From day one, he vowed to make sure she was happy and wanted for nothing. He took that vow seriously, and though Peyton didn't seem unhappy, she'd definitely been distracted.

Maybe tomorrow I'll ask her what's going on. But for now, he needed to get some sleep.

Michael yawned and lifted his head slightly when Peyton stirred and turned onto her other side. She scooted back and snuggled her perfectly round ass against the front of his body.

They often slept with him spooning her or with her lying with her head on his chest. As long as they were touching in some way, he didn't much care what position they were in.

Michael closed his eyes and draped his arm around her and held her close. Damn, she felt good, and she fit perfectly against him. He nuzzled the side of her neck, closed his eyes, and breathed her in.

"Michael," Peyton mumbled in her sleep, and his eyes opened.

"Yeah, baby?" he said quietly, trying to determine if she was awake.

She didn't respond, nor did she move, and he relaxed but maintained his hold on her. He had almost drifted off when she said, "I love you."

Before he could respond, her light snores met his ears, and he smiled.

I love you too was his last thought before he drifted off to sleep.

***

Sometime later, Michael jerked awake. Lifting his head, he glanced around the dark bedroom. Something had awakened him. He was a light sleeper, and it could've been anything, but his senses were suddenly on high alert.

He gently moved his arm from around Peyton and fumbled for his cell phone that was on top of the nightstand. Glancing at the screen, he noted the time.

Two o'clock in the morning.

He had only been asleep for a few hours. Setting the phone back down, he listened for any movement outside of their bedroom. Maybe one of the kids was up. He didn't hear anything, but his gut told him that something wasn't right. And he had learned a long time ago never to ignore his gut.

On instinct, Michael slipped into the jeans that were on the bench at the foot of the bed. He zipped them but didn't bother to button them as he started for the door, but he stopped. The house was still quiet, but the unease swirling inside of him grew more intense.

Backtracking, he put on a T-shirt and stuffed his cell phone into his pocket. There was a hidden gun safe in the bottom drawer of his nightstand, and he quickly punched in the code and grabbed his gun from inside.

Leaving the bedroom, Michael let the night lights in the hallway guide his steps. He peeked into both kids' rooms and found them asleep.

Maybe it's nothing, he thought as he walked on silent feet down the stairs, but he had to make sure. Midway on the staircase, he heard a car idling outside, but that wasn't uncommon. Parking was horrible on their street, and at any given time, someone could easily be double parked.

Once he was on the first floor, Michael didn't bother turning on any lights. He strolled to the living room and eased the curtain back to peek outside. Sure enough, to the left, a car sat in front of his neighbor's house. The vehicle's windows were too dark for him to see inside, and after a few minutes, he let the curtain drop back in place.

Michael had barely taken two steps and flinched when something crashed through the family room window. Glass exploded. The house alarm shrieked. And his eyes went wide.

Fire!

"Ahh, shit!"

He stuffed his gun into his waistband and bolted into the kitchen to grab the fire extinguisher from under the sink. Before he could make it back to the family room, the smoke detectors blared, and he knew the exact moment everyone upstairs woke up.

"Michael!" Peyton yelled.

"Daddy!" the kids screamed.

"Downstairs. Fire!" he hollered, determined to try to put out the flames. "PJ, grab the kids and get out!"

He ignored her running around upstairs and aimed at the flames that licked the curtains and the sofa. If he could just keep the fire from spreading.

Several sets of feet bounded down the stairs, sounding like a herd of elephants. Adrenaline pumped through Michael, and he didn't turn to look at his family. "Get out! Now!" he roared.

Sirens could be heard in the distance but were getting closer.

"Not without you!" Peyton screamed, her hysterical voice coming from near the front hallway. "Come on!"

Smoke was filling up the first floor, but Michael was still trying to keep the fire to a minimum.

"Now, Michael!" Peyton demanded.

He glanced her way. He assumed the kids were outside. The front door stood open and the outside air flowing in wasn't helping the situation.

Admitting defeat, he dropped the extinguisher and ran from the room. He slowed in the front hallway and grabbed as many jackets and shoes as he could carry. Then he followed his wife outside.

Michael jogged down the stairs with his arms full, and once he was a safe distance from the house, he dropped everything to the ground. The kids were crying, and his wife was shaking so badly that her teeth were chattering.

He gathered them all into his arms. "It's okay," he assured them. "As long as we're all safe, everything is going to be okay."

Michael spoke the words calmly, but anger clawed through him. This was no accident. He'd find the responsible party and make them pay.

Chapter Thirty-Eight

After tucking the kids into bed, Peyton tiptoed out of the adjoining hotel room and into the room that she and Michael were using. Instead of going to his parents' home, who lived a few miles from them, Michael had insisted they go to a hotel. Now that they were there, Peyton agreed it had been a good idea.

The last couple of hours had been scary, shocking, and unbelievable as hell. Peyton adored her in-laws, but she needed time with her man so that they both could decompress.

When she walked farther into their room, Michael was pacing the length of space like a caged animal. His unrest was palpable, and she had to figure out a way to settle him down so that they could try to get a few hours of sleep.

He'd always been protective of her and the kids from day one, and tonight was no different. Thanks to him, the house didn't burn to the ground. It might've been crazy of him to try to handle the fire himself, and a firefighter said as much, but it was because of him that their home sustained minimal damage.

Peyton shook her head as flashes of the scene invaded her mind. It had been so loud with both the house alarm and the fire alarm blaring. And seeing the flames in the family room would be something she would never forget. It was still hard to wrap her brain around the fact that their house had been on fire.

One thing they knew for sure—the fire was arson. Someone had thrown a Molotov cocktail through the window.

Now that she was thinking straight, Peyton had questions, and she planned to get answers.

She sat on the edge of the bed and watched her fearless husband. She hadn't seen him this agitated since that time when her ex-husband had been stalking her. Sort of.

Peyton closed her eyes at the memory. It had been the worst time in their lives as a couple. She and Michael had been dating, and her ex, Dylan, started calling and showing up out of nowhere. But it was during one of her visits to New York that Dylan went too far.

He'd followed her there and cornered her in a store. He wanted to talk. The conversation was brief, but Dylan made the mistake of grabbing her arm. He'd been trying to keep her from walking away from a conversation, and Michael, standing at a distance, misunderstood the situation.

Peyton rubbed her eyes. Just thinking about that time had her anxiety ratcheting up. Michael attacked him in a store full of people and ended up spending a couple of hours in county lockup.

After growing up in an abusive household with his birth father, Michael had a short fuse when it came to men putting their hands on women. It was a trigger. Now, after years of therapy on how to control that trigger, he was also better able to handle his anger.

But whatever was going on now had him riled up. Sure, the fire had freaked all of them out, but Peyton had a feeling he knew who was behind the attack.

Michael stopped pacing and ran his hands down his face before he glanced at her. "It's been a long time since I've been as scared as I was tonight," he said, his voice raspy and sounding as if he was a pack-a-day smoker. "What if I hadn't been awake? I don't want to even think about what could've happened to us."

Peyton reached for his hand, glad he came to her willingly. "What were you doing up?" she asked, and he sat next to her.

Grabbing hold of her long-sleeved t-shirt, Michael tugged her backwards, and they fell back onto the mattress. Peyton laughed as she stared up at the ceiling for a second until Michael wrapped his arm around her. When he pulled her close, she rested her head on his chest and sighed.

God, she loved being in his arms.

"I thought I heard something. So, I got up to check it out," Michael said.

Peyton had seen him talking to the cops, but because she didn't want the kids to overhear whatever he was telling them, she didn't know much.

"Do you know who did this?" Peyton asked, and Michael stiffened. Seconds ticked by before he relaxed again.

"I think I do, but I need to find out for sure."

She listened as he told her about a recent case that he'd taken on. He rarely discussed his cases, and normally she was okay with that. But with there being a threat to their family, she wanted to know as much as possible.

As he spoke, she could feel the tension bouncing off of him. What she didn't understand was how a case to find out if a husband was cheating turned into what happened tonight.

"The husband stopped by the office this afternoon insisting that his wife was crazy and that we should give him everything we'd collected."

"Did he threaten to do something to you if you didn't?"

After a slight hesitation, he said, "Not in so many words, but you don't have to worry. I'm going to handle this."

Peyton started to lift up, but Michael kept her where she was, and frustration gnawed at her.

"How can I not worry when someone, who you've been tracking, might've set our house on fire?"

Michael rubbed his forehead, and she sensed there was something he was keeping from her. Granted, he couldn't tell her everything about his cases, and she didn't want to know everything, but still...

"I can't help but worry," she said instead of asking more questions. She had to trust that he'd tell her what she needed to know.

He leaned his head down slightly and kissed her lips. "I know, but I'm going to make sure you and the kids are safe."

He coughed, reminding her that he had inhaled some smoke. He'd been checked out by the paramedics but insisted that he was fine.

"Are you sure you don't need to go to the hospital to make sure your lungs are okay?" she asked.

"Positive. I didn't take in that much smoke." He ran his large hand up and down her side soothingly. "You know how we're planning to go to Cincinnati for the reunion soon?" Michael asked.

Peyton wasn't sure where this was going, but she said, "Yeah."

"I want you and the kids to leave tomorrow."

"Michael," Peyton started to lift up, but like before, he held on to her. His hold was gentle, and he added a kiss to her forehead as if to soothe her. "We're not going," she said with finality.

"Yes, you are. You've put too much work into the reunion not to attend, and I know how much you want to see your family."

"But, Michael..."

"Baby, please don't fight me on this. I'll be there by the Fourth of July. I need to finish up this case, but first, I have to know that you and the kids are safe."

She was looking forward to spending time with the Jenkins side of the family, but not like this. Not when her own life had just been turned upside down.

"We're safest when we're here with you. No one can protect us the way you can," she insisted, meaning every word.

Seconds ticked by without Michael responding. She knew he didn't want them to go any more than she wanted to leave him. They were rarely apart for more than twenty-four hours. The trip to Atlanta to be with Christina was the first and only trip Peyton had been on without him.

Some might think that meant that he kept her under his thumb. Others might think that Michael was whipped and couldn't do anything without her. In reality though, they loved being in each other's presence and doing things together.

"You do remember the last time you sent me away, don't you?" Peyton asked, knowing she was hitting below the belt with the question.

Her heart rate picked up speed just thinking about the time when he forced her to go home to Cincinnati. It had been after the Dylan incident. Michael had broken up with her while she was visiting him in New York, and then he bought her a plane ticket to Cincinnati.

Peyton hadn't wanted to leave. She had been hopelessly in love with him even though they'd only known each other a few months. Even though she knew he loved her and needed her, he had still pushed her away.

In hindsight, it had been the best decision for both of them. The breakup had crushed her heart, but she went home and tried to move on. While she did that, Michael had started therapy. It wasn't until he had completed his sessions and felt stronger mentally and emotionally that he came for her. They married shortly after, and she moved to Brooklyn to be with him.

"This is different," he said, cutting into her thoughts.

She understood why he wanted her and the kids out of town, but like before, she felt she needed to stay. Yes, she wanted to move back to Cincinnati, but not like this. Not temporarily, and not without him. Never without him. She still hadn't told him about her desire to relocate, and right now didn't seem like the right time.

"I have to know that you three are safe, and if you're not with me, there's no other place safer than with your crazy-ass family."

Peyton couldn't help but smile at that, and she recognized him trying to lighten the moment. Yeah, the Jenkins were...special, and he was right. The Jenkins estate was the second safest place for them.

"What about you? Who's going to look after you?" She lifted slightly to look at him. "I'm not leaving unless you assure me that there will be someone here to have your back."

"I've already called in some favors with buddies at a security firm and some fellas from NYPD who will have my back. If all goes the way that I'm planning, the person I believe who is responsible will be in jail in the next forty-eight hours, seventy-two max."

"If that's the case, why can't me and the kids wait for you before we head to Cincinnati?"

"Because if you're here, my focus will be on you guys and not on dealing with this situation." He shifted on the bed and now they both were on their sides facing each other. "You three are everything to me, Peyton. I won't be able to handle things quickly if I'm worried about you. Besides, I'm sure your family would love to have you home a little earlier."

Peyton sighed. Again, he was correct. She could do more to help with the reunion preparations if she was there.

"Trust me. Everything is going to be fine," he assured her, but she had her doubts.

Peyton met his tired eyes, but the love she saw in them made her heart squeeze. "I trust you, but if you're not in Cincinnati in the next ten days, I'm coming back," she said with conviction. "And I'll be the one kicking some ass and helping you close this case."

A slow grin spread across his sexy lips before he chuckled. "There's that Jenkins' fire. I love having my own warrior," he said, capturing her mouth.

The kiss was so sweet and tender; it almost made her whimper. Peyton prayed he didn't need the whole ten days because she didn't want to be apart from him for that long. But going home now would give her a chance to determine if she really wanted to relocate back to Cincinati.

Or maybe I'll realize once and for all that Brooklyn is where I'm supposed to be.

***

"If I find out he's responsible for my house being torched, there won't be any place that asshole can hide!" Michael yelled into his cell phone and leaped from his office chair.

He glanced up when his father magically appeared in the doorway not looking too pleased with him. Michael sighed and dropped back into his chair behind the desk.

"Ant, man, I'm sorry," he said to Anthony, a friend of his who was a former cop but now owned a small tech business. "Didn't mean to yell in your ear."

"Dude, you don't have to apologize to me. I get it. I'd be out for blood too. We'll figure it out. I have someone looking through street camera footage to see if we can see anyone circling the area."

Based on Michael's experience, when punks are hired to do something stupid, like set a house on fire, they cased the targeted area. Either by car or foot, they roamed around the area as they came up with a plan.

Michael didn't know every car in the neighborhood, but he wanted to see if he could see a pattern. Different camera angles would give him more information and maybe even the license plate number of the car that had been idling outside the house.

The police and detectives on the case would look into everything, but Michael knew he and his friends could get answers faster.

"It helps that your neighbors are willing to do their part," Anthony continued. "Hopefully, that partial plate you pulled from your footage will help. I already sent the info to Tank," he said of one of their friends who still worked on the force. "In the meantime, I'll keep doing my part."

Anthony was a genius with technology and was helping him go through video footage from his neighbors' outdoor cameras, including doorbell cameras. Like Michael, most of them had security inside and outside their homes.

He and Anthony wrapped up their conversation, promising to touch base later, and Michael disconnected the call. He had been in his office, working his ass off, since his family left the day before. He'd only taken a short break to go to his parents' house to shower and eat.

"You have to keep it together, son," Carlton said as he strolled farther into the office and settled into one of the guest chairs.

Michael rubbed his eyes. "I know, Dad. Sorry for the outburst. Hopefully, you weren't on the phone with anyone."

"I wasn't, but I did get an update from a patrolman friend of mine who I knew patrolled the area near Charity's Bar," Carlton said of the bar that Hector had been seen leaving days ago. "Hector was slamming a guy up against the side of the building. When they saw my buddy and his partner, they all backed off and made it seem as if they were just horsing around."

Michael growled under his breath. He had hoped to hear that Hector was put in handcuffs again. He'd been charged with a class E felony for holding Michael at gunpoint, but as expected, Hector's big shot lawyers had gotten him out on bail within a few hours. Granted, he might eventually be sentenced to a year in jail, but right now, he was walking around free.

"Anyway," Carlton continued, "one of the men who'd been with him outside of the bar got picked up because of an outstanding warrant."

Hope bloomed inside Michael, and he leaned forward in his seat. "Tell me he knows something about the fire. Or anything shady Hector is involved in."

"I don't know yet. He was just picked up a few minutes ago, but I'll keep you posted."

"Thanks. I appreciate that. I'm thinking about paying Hector a visit at work," Michael said.

Carlton shook his head. "Not by yourself you aren't. I told you the last time I had to bail you out of jail. That was the last time."

Michael didn't respond. What could he say? If he got within arm's reach of Hector, he was going to kick the man's ass and no doubt get arrested.

Carlton stood. "What do you say we get out of here and go get some dinner? I know of this great place that happens to be a few blocks from Charity's. Maybe after we eat, we can stop by there for a drink before heading home."

Michael wasn't a drinker, but a slow grin spread across his face. He hurried and shut down his computer, then grabbed his keys, and followed his father to the door. "I like the way you think."

"You just have to promise to behave yourself," Carlton warned like he used to when Michael and his brothers were kids, and there was no humor in his tone.

It was a hard thing to promise, but Michael didn't have a choice. "You have my word."

Chapter Thirty-Nine

Peyton tossed and turned before she gave up trying to sleep. She was at her parents' house, in her old bedroom, and despite how pretty the space was, she couldn't relax.

She sat up and moved her legs to the side of the bed. Glancing around what was now considered a guest room, she admired the changes her mother had made.

The walls were covered with a bluish-gray paint with white trim. Instead of the boy-band posters hanging up, there were gorgeous landscape paintings of beaches, sunrises, and there was even one with majestic mountains.

Peyton smiled when she noticed her sister's signature at the bottom right-hand corner of each painting. There was no doubt the girl was talented.

Giving up on sleep, Peyton grabbed her pink, satin robe from the foot of the bed and slipped into her house shoes. She tiptoed out of the room and debated checking on the kids who were in her brother's old bedroom. They were asleep since they hadn't crawled into bed with her. So, she headed downstairs.

Once in the kitchen, she rinsed her hands and went about making hot tea. A short while later, she was sitting at the kitchen table with her hands wrapped around the large mug, thinking about her husband. Michael was never far from her thoughts.

She sent up a silent prayer. *Please let him be okay.*

Peyton hadn't wanted to leave him the day before, but he had insisted. Even though she understood that he could work better without worrying about them. That still didn't comfort her much.

"Hey, sweetie," her mother said as she floated into the kitchen like a breath of fresh air.

Violet Jenkins was like sunshine on the cloudiest day. She moved about with as much grace as a dancer, and it looked like her feet weren't touching the ground.

Peyton always admired how there was always a peaceful and calming presence whenever her mother entered a room. No one could be around her and not immediately feel better.

Peyton smiled. Christina was just like that, while Peyton had taken after their levelheaded, no-nonsense father. She had always wanted to be cool and calm like her mother, but that gene had skipped her.

"Hey, Mom. What are you doing up?"

"I thought I heard you down here, so I came to join you."

Peyton watched her flutter around the kitchen, wearing a long, floral lounging dress that billowed around her ankles. Also, like Christina, their mother had a hippie/flower child-like vibe, and it showed in their style of dress. In addition to that, they had a natural beauty that started from the inside and glowed on the outside.

Violet set a plate of chocolate chip cookies on the table in front of Peyton. They looked delicious, but she stared at them skeptically.

"Don't worry. I didn't make them," her mother said and laughed.

Peyton laughed too and grabbed a small one. Her mother might've been the most amazing, loving, and beautiful woman Peyton had ever known, but she was a horrible cook. She often joked that God had blessed her with everything but cooking skills.

That was one thing Peyton could do that her mother couldn't, and it was all thanks to Gram. For her grandmother, cooking and feeding her family were her love language, and she made sure that her children and grandchildren knew how to whip up delicious dishes. When Peyton's father married Violet, Gram had tried to teach her to cook but gave up, saying that she was a lost cause.

"You thinking about Michael?" Her mother joined her at the table with a mug of tea.

"Yes. I can't stop thinking about him. I'm worried. I think I should go back and be with him. If I do, will you keep the kids?"

"Of course, but didn't Michael tell you that he wanted you and the kids in a safe place...away from New York?"

"Yes, but—"

"Then listen to him." Her mother reached over and covered Peyton's hand with hers and squeezed. "I know you struggle with letting others be in charge, but this sounds like one of those times when you should try. Trust your husband to handle whatever is going on at home."

Fighting back tears, Peyton dropped her gaze and stared down into her mug. Her mother was right, but that didn't mean that her opinion was easy to accept.

"He's capable, you know," her mother continued.

"I know he is, but all I keep thinking about is the time Michael beat up Dylan when he thought my life was in danger. He was arrested and thrown in jail like some criminal!" she spat the last words. "What's going to happen this time? Someone basically tried to kill us by setting our home on fire. What do you think Michael's going to do when he finds them? And I have no doubt that he will.

"Mom, he was so angry...and scared. I'm afraid he might kill whoever did this to us."

"He won't." Violet patted her hand before sitting back in her seat. "He's going to think about all that he has to lose if he goes half-cocked after someone. If you're remembering his jail time, I'm sure he's thinking about it too. Baby, trust him to handle this situation his way," she insisted. "I have faith that he won't let you down. He'll do the right thing."

Peyton bit down on her bottom lip as worry swirled inside of her. She prayed her mother was right because, if anything happened to Michael, she didn't know what she would do.

Chapter Forty

Carlton hadn't been joking when he said he knew of a place to eat near Charity's. It was an Italian restaurant that looked like something straight out of Italy. The food was probably good, but Michael hadn't had much of an appetite. His mind had been on his family and Hector.

Now they were at Charity's. They'd been there for the past hour watching a baseball game on the television hanging behind the bar. The place wasn't huge, but it was nicer than Michael expected, and business seemed to be good. Every bar stool was taken, and numerous tables that were strategically placed were all occupied.

"Can I get you two another drink?" the bartender asked, leaning in front of Michael and giving him an unwanted view down her low-cut shirt. She'd been flirting with him since they sat at the bar. Clearly, she wasn't getting the "not interested" vibe he was giving off.

"I'll have another beer," his dad, who hadn't finished the first one, said.

"I'll take a Coke," Michael said, switching it up from the club soda that he'd finished seconds ago.

"Are you sure that's all you want?" she asked him, her voice dropping an octave as she leaned in more.

Michael stared at her for a moment and all he could see in his mind's eye was his gorgeous wife who he was missing like crazy.

"I'm positive," he said with more force than intended, and he heard his dad chuckle.

The bartender shrugged and set a Coke in front of him and another beer in front of Carlton.

"I see you still attract female attention even when you don't want it," Carlton said and sipped his beer.

Michael grunted. "Yeah, I wish it would stop. I only have eyes for Peyton, and it'll be that way until the day I die." He glanced over his shoulder. The bar had thinned out some, but there were still people hanging around.

"That's how I feel about your mother. I can't even imagine being with another woman. She's the best thing that ever happened to me."

Michael smiled, glad to hear that. His mother was the sweetest, kindest, and most generous woman he knew. She'd gone through hell early in life and deserved all the happiness in the world.

"And I'm looking forward to taking her on that cruise in a couple of weeks. She hasn't stopped talking about..." Carlton's cell phone buzzed, and he dug into his pants pocket for it. "I have a text," he said while looking at the screen.

"Is everything all right?" Michael asked.

"Actually, it's news we've been waiting for. The guy who was with Hector, the one who got arrested, his name is John Howard. Supposedly, he has no problem being a snitch." Carlton smiled. "There's a warrant out for Hector's arrest."

Yes! Michael wanted to do a fist pump but restrained. "Was he responsible for the fire?" he asked.

Carlton shook his head. "Not sure. My buddy said he'd give me a call a little later, but you know I'll keep you posted." His dad stood. "I'll be right back. Going to the men's room."

As he strolled away, Michael brought his soda glass to his lips but stiffened. In the mirror behind the bar, he spotted Hector, Curtis, and one other man strolling in and looking as if they owned the place.

Shit.

Hector was laughing and shaking hands with others as if he didn't have a care in the world. Clearly, he didn't know that his ass was about to be hauled off to jail.

Michael's first thought was to call and let one of his buddies who was still a cop know where to find the bastard. But not yet. He wanted to question the guy and determine if he had something to do with the fire.

He finished off his soda, suddenly wishing it had been something stronger.

What he wouldn't give to be able to slap Hector, the smug asshole, around even if he had nothing to do with the fire. But he promised Carlton that he'd be on his best behavior, and he kept his promises. Normally.

Michael turned on his stool and leaned his back against the bar. Hector hadn't noticed him yet, but just in case he did, Michael wanted to make sure he was facing him.

As if reading his mind or feeling someone staring, Hector glanced around, and it didn't take long for the bastard to spot him. At first, surprise registered in his dark eyes, but then a smarmy smile spread across his face.

Hector approached. Tension gripped Michael with such force, he couldn't seem to shake it off.

Keep it together dude.

"So, what do we have here? You still spying on me?" Hector taunted but kept some distance between them. "Actually, it doesn't matter. My wife will never divorce me."

"Really?" Michael asked with disinterest.

"That's right. She knows a good thing when she has it, and I'll forgive her temporary lapse in judgment when it comes to hiring you."

Michael shook his head and chuckled. "It's amazing how high of an opinion a piece of shit like you has of himself. I have no doubt that your wife will soon divorce you. But don't worry, I'm sure you'll still have companionship. Once your ass is locked up, your cellmate probably won't waste any time in making you his bitch."

Hector lunged at him, but Michael predicted the move and slid to the side, causing the man to run into the bar. Off-balance for a second, Hector recovered quicker than expected and swung at Michael but missed.

"Listen, man. I don't want any trouble with you," Michael said, backing up. He didn't want to accidentally knock the crap out of the guy. "As a matter of fact, I think it would be best if I leave, and then you can hang out with your loser friends."

Hector's fair skin was a deep crimson, and he looked as if he wanted to strangle Michael.

"Everything all right over here?" Carlton's deep baritone seemed to bounce off the walls despite the noise level.

"Yep, everything's fine," Michael said and gave Hector a wide berth as he tossed a few bills on the bar to cover his and Carlton's tab.

When he glanced at Hector again, the man had a stupid grin on his face. Maybe he was high or something, but Michael wasn't going to stick around to find out. Knowing that Hector was on his way to jail was satisfying enough.

"Later, Hector," Michael said and started to walk past the man, but Hector jumped in front of him.

"What? Leaving so soon," he said loud enough for patrons in the bar to turn and look at them. "I was meaning to ask you, how was that bonfire at your house the other night? I heard that—"

Michael didn't even feel himself move. All he knew was that one minute he was getting ready to leave, and the next, he had Hector pinned to a nearby wall.

"Your ass is dead!" Michael ground out and jammed his fist into the guy's jaw and sent the man crashing to the floor. But before he could hit him again, Carlton yanked Michael back as if he weighed nothing.

"Settle your ass down!" his dad roared and shoved Michael against the bar. "What did I tell you earlier?"

Michael was shaking out his hand. Punching Hector had hurt like hell, but before he could protest, cops stormed inside.

"Police! Let me see your hands!" they yelled as they swarmed the place, moving in sync around tables and chairs. Yelling and screaming filled the building as chaos ensued.

Michael's gaze shot to Carlton. "You made the call?"

"I shot off a quick text to my buddy when I came back and saw you two facing off."

"Hector Green, you're under arrest for assault, attempted murder, arson, and..." a police officer was saying as he cuffed Hector and started reading him his rights.

"You won't get away with this," Hector said, yelling at Michael while he and his cronies were being arrested.

For the next hour, the bar was packed with law enforcement. Michael and Carlton were questioned but didn't have to go to the station. Based on what Carlton's friend told them, Hector was going away for a long time.

"Thanks for keeping us in the loop," his father said, shaking the hand of a detective who was just as tall and wide as Carlton. They talked for a few minutes longer before Carlton made it back to where Michael was standing at the end of the bar.

"Ready to go?" his father asked.

"More than ready," Michael admitted.

They were heading to the door, but Carlton slowed and slapped Michael on the back of the head.

"Ow!" Michael grumbled and moved away while rubbing his head. "What was that for?"

"You promised you'd behave yourself. I should let them haul your ass off too." There wasn't much bite in his dad's words, but it was clear he wasn't happy.

"Sorry, but when Hector made reference to the fire, I lost it. I have no doubt that he was behind it."

"I'm sure we'll find out soon enough. Come on."

His father draped his arm around Michael's shoulder and escorted him to the door.

"Thanks for everything, Dad. I don't know if I could've kept it together these last couple of days without you."

"That's what I'm here for. Now move it. The sooner you wrap up Bobbi and Hector's case, the sooner you can get to your family.

Yeah, he couldn't wait to be with them.

Chapter Forty-One

Peyton had finally arrived at her grandparents' estate, and she strolled into her grandfather's home office. It felt good to be back in Cincinnati. She and the kids had arrived three days ago and had been staying with her parents.

She smiled as she thought about the night before. Her siblings, Christina and Jerry, as well as their spouses and kids, had all met up at their parents' home. They'd sat around eating, drinking, and talking about the good ol' days. Peyton couldn't remember the last time she'd laughed so much. It had been one of the best visits they'd had in almost a year.

The only thing...or person missing was Michael. He had called late last night to tell her that he had wrapped up the case and would be joining her and the kids later today.

Giddiness bubbled inside of her. She couldn't wait to see him. It might have only been a few days that they were apart, but it felt like much longer. When she asked how he was doing, Michael claimed to be fine, but he'd sounded tired.

After she loved on him for a while, she'd make sure he got some rest. The fire at the house, being displaced, and the long-distance separation was taking its toll on her. She could only imagine what it was doing to him.

For the next few days, they would live in luxury in her grandparents' new guest house. That would give them a chance to decompress for almost a week before family started arriving for the reunion. Then she, Michael, and the kids would move to the hotel that had been booked for the family reunion.

Peyton roamed farther into her grandfather's office and warmth spread through her body. She stopped in the middle of the large space and inhaled deeply. It still smelled like him, a mixture of sandalwood and leather. And it felt like home.

Her heart swelled as she glanced around. She had spent many days as a kid hanging out in the room, and a nostalgic feeling washed over her. Good times, she thought as she took in the leather sofas, the wall of bookshelves, and a kiddie corner with Legos and fluffy pillows.

What stood out the most though was her grandfather's large desk. It was the focal point in the room.

She settled into her grandfather's desk chair and rocked back and forth. Being in his space might've felt like home, but she still wasn't sure where she belonged. Yes, she missed Cincinnati. There was nothing like hanging with her siblings and cousins, indulging during Sunday brunch, and spending quality time with Grampa and Gram. Yet, she loved the life that she and Michael had built in New York. Her extended family might not live there, but Michael's family had become her family, and she loved them dearly.

But still...she missed being in Cincinnati.

Her grandfather shuffled into the room and slowed when he saw her in his chair. "So, this is where you're hiding," he said and smiled.

Peyton watched as he set a couple of books on his desk. Her heart melted whenever she was in his presence. As the patriarch of the family, Steven Jenkins had always led by example. He showed all of them the value of hard work. More than that, he taught them the importance of family.

Family first.

In his mind, there was nothing more important or valuable than a close-knit family who stuck together. That was always his motto. It was hers too. Which was why it was so hard to be away from Michael. Not just because she hated traveling without him, but also because she feared there had been more going on with his P.I. case than he was letting on. It was hard to have his back when she was so far away.

When her grandfather moved toward the sitting area, Peyton started to get up from his chair.

He shook his head and waved his hand. "Stay there. I can sit over here." He settled himself on the sofa and stretched one of his arms across the back of it. "You looked like you were deep in thought. What's going on? Are you thinking about the fire? Do they know who's responsible for starting it?"

Peyton hadn't told anyone that Michael thought it was connected to one of his cases. All the family knew was that it had been arson.

"Michael said the person has been arrested."

"That's good," her grandfather said as he nodded, but he gave her that look. The look she'd seen often while growing up, and it was filled with wisdom and patience. It was as if he knew there was more but wouldn't pry.

"How's Michael doing?" he asked, still with *the look*.

Peyton smiled. "He's doing okay. He thought he could get here yesterday but decided to get the clean-up of our house started. Well, as much as he can do until the insurance kicks in. He said the downstairs sustained the most damage, but the upstairs will need some work because of all the smoke and some water damage."

She'd only had a couple of minutes to do a walk-through and grab a few items for her and the kids before leaving New York. Most of their clothes had smelled like smoke, and she'd had to go shopping once they arrived in Cincinnati.

"What else is bothering you?" Grampa said.

Slow to respond, Peyton stood and strolled across the room and sat next to him.

"I want to come home. I want to move back to Cincinnati because I feel like this is where we're supposed to be...I think."

His left eyebrow lifted skyward before the corners of his mouth kicked up into a smile.

"You think? What does Michael say about this?"

Peyton sighed. "He doesn't know."

She explained how she'd been feeling for the last few months and told him how she hadn't wanted to bring the idea to Michael until she knew for sure.

"I know I'm being selfish. Michael loves Brooklyn. It's home for him. He has a successful business, and all his family is there. And I feel guilty because we've built a wonderful life in New York and the kids love their schools, and..."

Peyton dropped her head back and stared up at the ceiling. Selfishness and guilt warred within her. She wanted what she wanted, but what about her family? She'd never forgive herself if she uprooted them, then realized that Cincinnati was not where they were supposed to be.

Her grandfather patted her leg, but she didn't look at him as he shifted on the sofa. All she wanted was for him to share some wisdom. Something he did extremely well.

"Not that you asked for my opinion," he started, and she smiled, "but I think you should stay in Brooklyn."

Peyton jerked up. "What?"

He loved having family all around him, and though he had wished her well when she married Michael, he'd hated to see her leave. Had something changed?

"I'm shocked you're not telling me to come home."

She wasn't sure how to feel by that revelation. Her grandfather was one of her most favorite people in the world. He'd been her mentor for as long as she could remember, especially after college. When he'd been ready to retire, and no one else in the family wanted to take over the business, she had stepped up. With his guidance, she, with the help of her cousins, had turned the organization into a multi-million-dollar company.

Now he didn't want her to return home?

He lifted his hands out in front of him. "Before that active imagination of yours goes crazy, let me explain. PJ, I have never seen you as happy as you've been since marrying Michael. You've glowed since the moment you met the young man, and I know it's because he brings you joy."

Peyton sat back and smiled. He was right. She was living her best life, and it had everything to do with being with Michael.

"Before you left Cincinnati, you were unhappy. Unhappy with your career, your personal life, and that spark of light that shone in your eyes since you were a little girl had dulled. Now..." he smiled at her, "that light in your eyes is back, and I want it to stay there."

"Grampa, I wouldn't move here unless Michael agreed."

"I know sweetheart, but maybe you should ask yourself why you want to return. Is it because you're missing your immediate family? If that's the case, visit more often or have everyone visit you...in small doses," he said with a chuckle. "You know this family can be a bit overwhelming."

"Ha! Who are you telling?" They laughed.

After they sobered, her grandfather kissed her on the cheek. "Ultimately, this is a decision that you and Michael need to make together. Talk to him."

He eased off the sofa and steadied himself, and Peyton stood too.

"Just know that we will always support you, and we'll welcome you with open arms if you do decide to move back."

They hugged, and Peyton soaked up the love that she felt deep in her heart. She couldn't imagine her life without this incredible man in it.

"I love you, Grampa."

"I love you more, sweetheart."

A knock sounded on the opened office door, and they both glanced in that direction.

Peyton screamed and took off in a run. "Oh my..."

***

Michael didn't get emotional often, but seeing Peyton rushing toward him made his heart squeeze. When she leaped into his arms, he held her so tight, he feared he'd crush her ribs.

"God, I've missed you," he mumbled as he breathed her in.

"And I've missed you," she said, tears in her voice.

They stayed like that for the longest time until she lifted her head and kissed him. It wasn't until a throat cleared did Michael remember that they weren't alone.

He set her on her feet and greeted her grandfather.

"Good seeing you, sir," he said.

"You too, son." Grampa shook his hand and pulled him in for a man hug. "I'll leave you two alone. You can stay in here as long as you need," he said and left the room, closing the door behind him.

Peyton led Michael to the sitting area. "I wasn't expecting you until tonight. Why didn't you tell me you were arriving early? I would've met you at the airport."

"I wanted to surprise you." He sat on the sofa and stretched his legs out in front of him. "I saw the kids out back. They looked like they were having a good time with their cousins."

"Yeah, they've been having a ball. It's amazing how big everyone has gotten."

Michael wrapped his arm around her and pulled her to his side. All he wanted to do was touch her. "I've missed holding you," he said into her hair. "I hate when we're apart."

Peyton snuggled closer. "Me too." She was silent for a long time before she lifted her head and looked at him, "I had something to talk to you about, but...I think I've worked it out."

"O...*kay*," Michael said slowly and waited for her to say more, but she didn't. "You sure you don't want to talk about it?" he asked. "I had a feeling something was going on with you over the last couple of months."

She told him about how she'd wanted to move back to Cincinnati, or at least how she thought she wanted to move back. He should've been concerned that she'd entertained leaving Brooklyn. But what gave him comfort was knowing that she wouldn't have left without him.

"I'm glad you've decided that Brooklyn is home, but I need you to know something."

She stared into his eyes, and his heart flipped inside his chest. God, he loved this woman.

"What?" she said.

"Wherever you are, that's where I'm going to be. So, if ever you want to move back to Cincinnati, know that I'll be right here with you."

She grinned, leaned up, and kissed him. Not just any kiss, but a kiss that he felt to the soles of his feet. There'd been a time in his life when he didn't think he deserved love. He was afraid that he was like his birth father who abused women.

But Peyton's love, devotion, and patience with him made Michael realize that not only did he deserve love, but he was capable of giving it.

"How about I show you where we'll be sleeping for the next few days," Peyton murmured, mischief in her eyes.

Michael laughed. "Like I said, wherever you are, that's where I'm going to be."

Family Reunion Banquet

As Peyton wove around groups of family members in the ballroom, she admired how beautifully decorated the room was. She thought it would be hard to create an elegant environment using the typical Fourth of July colors of red, white, and blue. Yet, Jada and her team had pulled it off.

Lights twinkled overhead, and looking up at the ceiling was like stargazing outside. Vases of red roses sat on round tables that were covered with blue, satin tablecloths.

Everyone appeared to be having a good time laughing, talking, and eating, and that pleased Peyton. They'd had a buffet dinner earlier, and now, an hour later, there were elaborate hors d'oeuvres on tables lining the perimeter of the room for those who wanted to indulge.

Peyton hurried toward the bar at the far end of the huge space. She and her cousins agreed to meet up there to have a celebratory drink. By the time she arrived, everyone was there except her sister, Christina, who'd said she'd be late.

"It's about time you got here," Jada said. "My date is waiting to dance with me. Come on. Let's have this drink so that I can get back to him."

"Like that man's going anywhere," Martina cracked. "Your husband has been following you around like a puppy dog."

Peyton shook her head. Martina was making progress, but she still had moments when she couldn't control her mouth.

"Shouldn't Christina and Luke be here by now?" Toni asked. "It's almost eight-thirty, and she said they'd be here by eight."

As the bartender filled four shot glasses, Peyton decided to call and check on CJ. When she pulled her phone from the pocket of her long dress, she realized she had a voicemail from her mother.

"All right, everyone, grab a glass," Martina said as Peyton listened to the message.

She gasped. "Oh, my goodness. CJ's water broke," she said excitedly while trying to hear the rest of the message, but her cousins were all talking at once. "Shhh." She waved them off. "My mom and dad are at the hospital. She said CJ had dilated 7 centimeters by the time Luke got her to emergency. They've been there over an hour."

"We should go too," Toni said, looking at each of them for agreement.

"We can't leave with all these people here. We're helping Gram with hosting duties," Jada said.

"She's right," Peyton agreed, though she was tempted to leave. But there were over a hundred people there, and though they'd all had dinner, there were still things to oversee. "My mom said she'll keep us posted."

"Figures CJ would wait until the last minute to go to the hospital," Jada said. "She probably didn't even realize she was in labor."

"Man, what I wouldn't give to be there to watch the Thug Lawyer lose his shit," Martina said, flashing a stupid grin. "He's been a mess for the last nine months. I can't imagine how he's going to be as he watches Christina push that baby through her—"

"Stop!"

"Be quiet!"

"Shut up, Martina!"

They all spoke at once.

"Geez, relax," Martina said, handing Peyton a shot glass. "I wasn't going to say pus—"

"*Don't* you dare finish that statement!" Toni yelled.

"Ugh, I can't with you," Jada ground out. "You haven't changed at all."

Peyton laughed and raised her glass, and so did her cousins. "To a job well done, ladies, and to family."

"Cheers," they said in unison before slamming back the tequila.

Peyton cringed, scrunched her face, and shook her head as the liquid burned down her throat. "Dang, that was strong."

After setting their empty glasses on the bar, they chatted a few minutes longer before going their separate ways. But Peyton stopped when her cousin, Ben Jr, who they called BJ sidled up to her.

"I have to say, Cuz, I'm impressed," BJ said as he glanced out over the crowd. People were heading to the dance floor when the Cupid Shuffle song boomed through the speakers. "You guys did a good job with the reunion."

"Thanks, did you have a favorite part?"

"Hmm." He nibbled on his bottom lip as he thought about the question. "I'd have to say the off-roading we did yesterday morning. That was fun. We're going to have to do that again."

That had been Michael's favorite activity too. Well, that and poker last night where he'd won two hundred dollars. Peyton had no idea they'd been playing for real money until he strolled into their hotel room with his spoils.

"Is Michael still in the basement with some of the guys?" she asked her cousin.

When BJ didn't respond, she glanced at him. He was staring at a pretty lady who was looking down at a fancy camera. Peyton realized that she was one of the photographers hired to take pictures during the reunion.

"*Sooo*, do you think she's cute?" she asked her cousin who was still staring at the woman.

As if sensing him watching her, the woman glanced in their direction. A slow smile spread across her lips, and after a slight hesitation, she lifted her camera to her eye. Turning a few knobs, it looked like she was trying to focus it or zoom in or something. Then she snapped a couple of pictures.

Peyton looked at BJ who was grinning, and she nudged him with her elbow. "She's going to mess around and break her camera if she keeps snapping shots of you."

He chuckled. "Shut up," he said and finished off the drink he'd been holding. "Here." He handed Peyton the empty glass. "I'm going over to introduce myself. Who knows, maybe she'll let me snap a few pictures of her. Or better yet, maybe I'll get her digits. She might just be the next Mrs. Jenkins. Wish me luck. Oh, wait, I don't need luck."

Peyton burst out laughing. "Yeah, keep telling yourself that," she called after him.

When he made it to the photographer, the woman looked at him shyly, but her smile said that BJ might actually get her telephone number.

"What are you looking at?" Michael asked and slipped his arm around her waist.

"Ben Jr. is over there trying out his rap game on our photographer," Peyton said, nodding in their direction. Now the two were shaking hands and laughing at something BJ said.

"As interesting as it is watching your cousin flirt with a woman, we should probably..." his words trailed off when the DJ lowered the music.

Peyton and everyone else in attendance looked toward the stage where Grampa was standing with Gram.

"Sorry to interrupt your good time." Grampa's deep voice boomed through the speakers before he pulled the microphone back a little from his mouth. "We just wanted to say a few words. First, thank you for attending the family reunion. I don't know about you, but I've had a blast."

Cheers went up around the room, and Peyton's heart sang. Pulling a family reunion together at the last minute was no easy feat, but seeing how much people were enjoying the Fourth of July weekend made it worth the effort.

"One of my granddaughters asked me which activity was my favorite," Grampa continued. "I'd have to say the picnic this morning. It's always great getting family together, but to have four generations of Jenkins in the park today warmed my heart."

Peyton listened as he talked about the importance of family sticking together and how most of his choices in life were based on the needs of his immediate family. When he started Jenkins & Sons Construction, it had been to support his wife and kids financially. But he'd also wanted to leave a legacy for them and generations to come. Everything he did, and the sacrifices he made, were for them.

Peyton smiled at his words. He was doing more than leaving a legacy. He'd been the perfect example of a man leading while also loving his family.

Family first had always been Steven Jenkins's motto. He had taught the concept to his kids, and they taught it to Peyton and her cousins. Now she and the others were doing the same thing—instilling *family first* into their own children.

If you can't count on anyone else, you can always count on your family, her grandmother once told her. She'd been right. There'd been plenty of times when the comfort of knowing that someone always had her back was all Peyton needed to keep moving forward.

"My favorite part of the picnic?" her grandfather was saying when she tuned back in. "I'd have to say—the games. I kicked butt in cornhole and horseshoes. It's all in the wrist, baby," he joked, and everyone laughed.

"What about that three-legged race?" someone yelled from the crowd and people fell into a fit of laughter, including Gram and Grampa.

"Okay, I'll admit, I might be getting too old for some of the picnic games. I nearly broke my hip with that one," Grampa said, still chuckling.

Christina had done a great job coming up with games and other activities for the reunion. Peyton had to admit, the three-legged race for people over sixty had been hilarious to watch. She'd been surprised to see her parents and grandparents out there.

It seemed everyone started talking at once, debating what activities were their favorite. Peyton heard a few say that they enjoyed the scavenger hunt. While others insisted that the kite flying activity the day before had been amazing.

"It sounds like we all had a ball," her grandmother said when she took over the microphone, "but I can't let this night end without thanking some very important people—my granddaughters. Where are you, girls?"

"Here," they all said and lifted their hands wherever they were in the room.

"Everyone, before you leave, please thank them. This reunion couldn't have happened without all of them. When the idea came to mind, I enlisted their help, and they made all this happen. The event has exceeded my expectations, and I personally want to say to them—thank you, girls. I love you all!"

"We love you, too," Peyton and her cousins said in unison.

"Now, let's head outside." Gram pointed to the patio doors. "Toni said the fireworks will be starting soon."

"That's what I came over to tell you," Michael said and pulled Peyton against his side before kissing her.

Peyton glanced at her watch. Sure enough, it was almost nine-thirty. It was Christina's idea to have fireworks as an ending to the reunion. Too bad she wouldn't be there to enjoy it.

Peyton had turned the volume up on her phone, hoping to hear back from her mother. So far, nothing. She filled Michael in on the news that Luke was going to be a father soon, and he said that he'd heard. Apparently, Martina and their grandmother had started spreading the word.

When they neared the patio doors, almost everyone was already outside.

"Did you talk to the kids?" Peyton asked.

"Yep, Michaela said they were having fun at the center."

"Good to hear."

Peyton slipped her hand into Michael's and felt so blessed to be surrounded by family. The last couple of weeks had been a little stressful, but at this moment, her life seemed perfect.

"I'm glad Gram insisted on the reunion. It's been..." her voice trailed off when her cell phone rang. She hurried and answered when she saw that it was her mother. "Hey, Mom. Am I an auntie again?"

Michael looked at her expectantly as she listened to her mother on the phone.

"Okay, I'll let everyone know," Peyton said and grinned as she disconnected the call. "Baby, I need you to do that whistle thing you do so that we can get everyone's attention." Considering how loud everyone was outside, she wasn't sure if it would work.

Michael put two fingers in his mouth and let out a loud, piercing whistle that got mostly everyone's attention.

"I have some news!" Peyton shouted. "CJ and Luke had their baby. It's a girl!"

Cheers went up all around, and then the fireworks started, and bursts of colors lit up the sky.

"This has been an amazing day!" Peyton squealed and threw her arms around her husband.

"Every day is amazing when I get to spend it with you," Michael said and kissed her with such passion that she melted into him.

With a love as strong as theirs, it didn't matter where they lived. Her life was perfect as long as they were together.

SHARON C COOPER

***

*If you enjoyed this book by Sharon C. Cooper,
consider leaving a review on any online book site, review site or social
media outlet.*

Join Sharon's Mailing List

To get sneak peeks of upcoming stories and to hear about giveaways that Sharon is sponsoring, go to https://sharoncooper.net/newsletter to join her mailing list.

Other Books by Sharon C. Cooper

Atlanta's Finest Series
Vindicated (book 1)
Indebted (book 2)
Accused (book 3)
Betrayed (book 4)
Hunted (book 5)
Tempted (book 6)
Committed (book 7)

Jenkins & Sons Construction Series (Contemporary Romance)
Love Under Contract (book 1)
Proposal for Love (book 2)
A Lesson on Love (book 3)
Unplanned Love (book 4)

Jenkins Family Series (Contemporary Romance)
Best Woman for the Job (Short Story Prequel)
Still the Best Woman for the Job (book 1)
All You'll Ever Need (book 2)
Tempting the Artist (book 3)
Negotiating for Love (book 4)
Seducing the Boss Lady (book 5)
A Love So Strong: A Jenkins Family Reunion (book 6)
Love at Last (Holiday Novella)
When Love Calls (Novella)
More Than Love (Novella)

Reunited Series (Romantic Suspense)
Blue Roses (book 1)
Secret Rendezvous (Prequel to Rendezvous with Danger)
Rendezvous with Danger (book 2)
Truth or Consequences (book 3)
Operation Midnight (book 4)

A LOVE SO STRONG: A JENKINS FAMILY REUNION

Casino Heat (book 5)
Stand Alones
Something New ("Edgy" Sweet Romance)
Legal Seduction (Harlequin Kimani – Contemporary Romance)
Sin City Temptation (Harlequin Kimani – Contemporary Romance)
A Dose of Passion (Harlequin Kimani – Contemporary Romance)
Model Attraction (Harlequin Kimani – Contemporary Romance)
A Passionate Kiss (Contemporary Romance)
Soul's Desire (Unparalleled Love series)
Show Me (Irresistible Husband series)
His to Protect (Harlequin Romantic Suspense)
His to Defend (Harlequin Romantic Suspense)
Business Not As Usual (Romantic Comedy)
In It to Win It (Romantic Comedy)
Kiss Me (Irresistible Husband – Contemporary Romance)

About the Author

USA Today bestselling author Sharon C. Cooper loves anything involving romance with a happily-ever-after, whether in books, movies, or real life. She writes contemporary romance, as well as romantic suspense and enjoys rainy days, carpet picnics, and peanut butter and jelly sandwiches. Her stories have won numerous awards over the years, and when Sharon isn't writing, she's hanging out with her amazing husband, doing volunteer work, or reading a good book (a romance of course). To read more about Sharon and her novels, visit www.sharoncooper.net[1]

Website: https://sharoncooper.net [2]

Join Sharon's mailing list: https://bit.ly/31Xsm36

Facebook fan page: http://www.facebook.com/AuthorSharonCCooper21?ref=hl

Twitter: https://twitter.com/#!/Sharon_Cooper1

Subscribe to her blog: http://sharonccooper.wordpress.com/

Goodreads: http://www.goodreads.com/author/show/5823574.Sharon_C_Cooper

Pinterest: https://www.pinterest.com/sharonccooper/

Instagram: https://www.instagram.com/authorsharonccooper/

Bookbub: bookbub.com/profile/sharon-c-cooper

---

1. http://www.sharoncooper.net/

2.   https://sharoncooper.net

13.99

CPSIA information can be obtained
at www.ICGtesting.com
Printed in the USA
BVHW041915110623
665764BV00004B/63